The Alien Nation

MV ATLANTIC HERO
28 NOVEMBER, 2013

"TO GOD BE THE GLORY, IN HIM WE TRUST"

the ALIEN NATION
(The Quest for Earth)

"A PRODUCT OF MY TWISTED IMAGINATION"

CAPT. MARLON G. CANO

PARTRIDGE
A Penguin Random House Company

ISBN:	Softcover	978-1-4828-2915-0
	eBook	978-1-4828-2916-7

To order additional copies of this book, contact
Toll Free 800 101 2657 (Singapore)
Toll Free 1 800 81 7340 (Malaysia)
orders.singapore@partridgepublishing.com

www.partridgepublishing.com/singapore

* * * E.T. CLOSE - ENCOUNTER * * *

I, Marlon G. Cano, witnessed and testify my close-encounter and actual sighting of an E.T. Flying Saucer, was on 09th December, 2013 about 0515Hours in the morning, in the boundary and vicinity of KAMCHATKA, RUSSIA and WEST ALEUTIAN ISLANDS near ALASKA, while I was on the BRIDGE, the marine term for conning position of the ship, on-duty as Navigating Officer of a cargo ship named MV ATLANTIC HERO, a bulk carrier ship of seven cargo holds, usually called Panamax Ship in Marine Terminology, of 80,000 Metric Tons Gross Tonnage navigating NORTH PACIFIC OCEAN coming from TACOMA, WASHINGTON, USA going to INCHEON, SOUTH KOREA. On that fateful day, we are encountering heavy bad weather, BF 9, sea-waves of 6 meter high, sea-swell of 5 meters, mostly cloudy skies, and on that early morning and crack of dawn, suddenly a distant faint light above the horizon I thought to be a star rapidly moved towards my ship in a circling and spiral movement of fascinating super-speed, then moved left defying gravity, go backwards abruptly as if just playing back and forth like a firefly, then moved again towards my vessel as if observing us and stopped suspended in the space in-front just above the vessel's forward mast about 20 meters high, and flashed a radiating white light, the source of light about the size larger than a fist, radiating for about five minutes. I was in awe, flabbergasted and couldn't believe what was happening in-front, I told my duty seaman and helms-man that what's happening was not a natural phenomenon, but an ALIEN doings, an Extra-Terrestrial activity. I hurriedly went to my cabin and grab my camera then went back to the conning position and took a snap-shot but the ship's bridge window bounce back the camera light after taking a picture producing a black picture, and just as I about to take a video of the bright circle of light larger than a fist radiating, suddenly moved away to the horizon vanished, I waited for it to re-appear but the bright light was gone no more to be seen. What happened was truly remarkable and worthy of pondering, for once in my colorful life, it proves that there is really other much more intelligent life and entity other than us humans, it adds excitement and delight to myself knowing how vast the Universe is, and it's secrets and mysteries embedded within. There should be an Alien Nation out there, perhaps, a parallel life somewhere in the Galaxy. The event that I had seen was also witnessed by my Duty Helms-man, Able-Bodied Seaman Marlon Morato.

* * * APOLOGIES * * *

All that was been written in this futuristic science fiction were a product of my complex imagination, profound observations and out of this world thinking, whatever scenario that reflects actual reality and stories should be disregarded and not to be concerned with by all readers, or whoever feels deem affected.

The author's intention is good and not to misled the readers, neither to cause any defamation or harm among those entity characterized, nor to tarnish any individual character of its disposition, if we should have to compare this fiction story in relation to what is fact, and what is going on in reality.

And if ever, you, the reader happens to read your name and character in this fiction story, the author nevertheless apologize for un-intentionally including you in the story to put life and breathe, that this science fiction story may live-up to reality.

PLEASE ACCEPT MY DEEPEST AND SINCERE APOLOGIES.

"THE TRUTH WILL SET US FREE; THERE IS MORE TO LIFE THAT WE SHOULD KNOW, ALL FORBIDDEN THINGS WE OUGHT TO KNOW!"

THANK YOU.

CAPT. MARLON G. CANO
THE AUTHOR

* * * ACKNOWLEDGEMENT * * *

First of all, glory to God Almighty, the great and loving Universal God.

To my loving wife, MARIA ELEONORA, for her undying support and the one who holds the DELIGHTS OF MY HEART.

To my children, Shawn Troy, Sean Levon, Shane Nicole and Sheen Ezriel, who serves as my inspiration and joy of my life, the fruits and DELIGHT OF MY HEART.

To my kind and loving parents, GENARO and AMPARO, for their understanding and full support all through-out my life, being their first borne fruit and DELIGHTS OF THEIR HEART.

To my siblings, DINNIS, HAZEL at KIMVERLY, for their outstanding encouragement to continue my work and respect being their ELDER sibling.

To all my Dear Friends and Foe alike, whom I had meet, mingle with, and played important roles in my life, for with-out them, I would not become of who I am today.

To all Entities in whatever way I meet and came across along my passage of time, for with-out them, my life, this Circus Drama of Life I am unfolding won't be complete.

To all People with Godly deeds and mind, who, in whatever way help me published this profound story, there is so many of you to name names, but I do know in my heart that YOU do know in your heart you are part of this GREAT STORY.

Thank you to you, GOD ALMIGHTY, THE GOD OF LIFE.

"Hopefully all of you, readers will find Truth in your heart, and by God's grace you'll be bless."

"TO GOD BE THE GLORY, IN HIM WE TRUST"

Capt. Marlon G. Cano
March 20. 19XX
Piscean . . . a Rat.

HE BELIEVES IN MIRACLES. HE'S LIVING FOR THE IMPOSSIBLE DREAM. HE WANTS TO KNOW YOUR SECRET FEARS, HE WANTS TO REVEAL HIS. HE MAY BE CONVINCED HE'S LED A PAST LIFE IN MEDIEVAL EUROPE, SHIVERING IN A COLD CASTLE OR STACKING MASONRY ON A GREAT CATHEDRAL, TO SAY THAT HE IS MERELY ROMANTIC BELITTLES HIS GREAT GIFT OF LOVE. AS THE FINAL SIGN OF THE ZODIAC, THE SENSUAL PISCES IS TOO WISE TO LIVE AND LOVE WITH ANYTHING OTHER THAN THE DEEP, EMOTIONAL, SENSUAL CORE OF HIS BEING. HIS POWERS OF OBSERVATION ARE ASTOUNDING, MUCH OF THE TIME HE IS OPERATING ON A PURELY PSYCHIC LEVEL, HIS FAVORITE WOMAN IS A PRACTICAL YET SIMPLY BEAUTIFUL VIRGO, WHO PROVIDES BALANCE IN HIS SOMETIMES CHAOTIC LIFE. SCORPIO BRINGS HIM LUCK, SHE IS EQUALLY EMOTIONAL, BUT PRAGMATIC WHEN IT COMES TO SOLVING PROBLEMS. HE MAY WRITE POETRY ABOUT LEO, WHO TRULY MYSTIFIES HIM. A FELLOW PISCES WOMAN COULD BE HIS DEAREST FRIEND. HIS PERFECT SEXUAL MATCH IS THE MOONCHILD, CANCER. SHE TREASURES AND PROTECTS HIS VULNERABLE FEELINGS BECAUSE SHE KNOWS WHAT IT'S LIKE TO BE STUNG. HE TRUSTS HER WITH HIS DREAMS AND TOGETHER THEY CAN HAVE SOME REALLY WILD NIGHTS. IF YOU WANT HIM TO NOTICE YOU, WEAR HIS COLOR, BLUE. HE ALSO LIKES A BIT OF LACE, OR ANYTHING DIAPHANOUS. HE IS SHY, SO YOUR INITIAL APPROACH SHOULD BE ON THE COY SIDE. SHOW SOME IMAGINATION, WRITE HIM A LOVE POEM OR DRAW A LITTLE

STICK FIGURE SKETCH, IT'S THE THOUGHT THAT COUNTS. HE IS SENSITIVE, EMOTIONAL, SUNNY, IMPRESSIONABLE, DREAMY, CREATIVE, PSYCHIC AND MYSTICAL. PISCEANS MAKE GOOD LISTENERS, CAN SEE DIFFERENT SIDES OF ISSUES, HAVE GREAT SYMPATHY FOR THE SUFFERING OF OTHERS. THEY ARE CAPABLE OF GREAT STRENGTH AND HAVE THE ABILITY TO TAKE LIFE AS IT COMES. HE BELIEVES THAT IN NOTHING THERE IS SOMETHING. HE BELIEVES IN THE BALANCE OF REALITY.

PROLOGUE

THE REBELLION THOUSAND YEARS BEFORE: THE 1ST GALACTIC WAR...

SUPREME COMMANDER LUCIFER, who was then assigned as IN-CHARGE OF GALACTIC SPECIAL FORCES EXPEDITION TO BLUE PLANET EARTH did every-thing in his utmost capacity and leadership all necessary measures to contained the savage species roaming Blue Planet Earth, and along with his loyal Commanders and Legionnaires protected the ADVANCE RESEARCH SCIENTIST PARTY OF THEIR PLANET NIBIRU, experimenting on making new species for their civilizations advancement.

After the great scientific research and experimentation of various creatures on Blue Planet Earth and perfecting a new breed of SPECIES, under the jurisdiction of Planet Nibirus UNIFIED HIGH COMMAND OF UNIVERSAL GALACTIC DEFENSE ADVANCE SCIENTIFIC RESEARCH PROJECT, which later on they called this new breed of Species as HUMANOIDS, for the sole purpose of enslaving to excavate the Earth minerals needed to power the energy of their Planet called Nibiru, Supreme Commander Lucifer began to contemplate his fate as a GOD, a God subject to much higher GOD, for he knows in his heart that He will never become a GOD of GODS, which He has been dreaming of ever since he became Supreme Commander of Galactic Special Forces Expedition to Blue Planet Earth. Yet at some point in time, He began to realize in his longing lonely mind that his dream of becoming GOD OF GODS is plausible and possible, and that all he needs to do is to make a perfect plan and take actions to put it into perspective and reality, the only problem is that, He can be that GOD OF GODS he have been dreaming of, but not in their Planet of Nibiru, but in this Blue Planet called Earth.

In his ambitious calculating mind, the Blue Planet Earth is just so perfect for his grand plan of becoming a God of Gods, for he saw the great opportunity he had been waiting for. At that time when he began to plan the realization of his ambition, Supreme Commander Lucifer was re-assigned as BLUE PLANET EARTH MINING OPERATION OVER-ALL IN-CHARGE TASK COMMANDER, the one in-charge in supervising the great mining of Blue Planet Earth VAST MINERALS from its entire domain, including different sub-mining places on Blue Planet Earth, each under Sub-Commanders under his Wing Band and Commandant-ship. Supreme Commander Lucifer was tasked overseeing all operations and output of all mined minerals, and sees to it that all minerals needed by their Planet Nibiru were supplied without delay.

As years gone by, He began to despise the GODS OF NIBIRU, for he feels that all his efforts and dedication mining the Blue Planet Earths minerals for their Planet Nibiru has gone un-noticed by the Gods, and that as per his expectations, He, Supreme Commander Lucifer, being the overseer of the great mining operations for their planet Nibirus much needed energy deserves a Galactic Royal Palatial Recognition, yet as fate dictates, it seems that the GODS OF NIBIRU, in their GODLY DOMAIN AND ABODE OF HAPPINESS, forgot about him and his GALACTIC SPECIAL FORCES EXPEDITIONARY COMMAND, worse, as he feels in his heart, never care about them, and that excruciating thoughts dwelling in his mind annoyed him so much, driving his egoistic vanity mad.

Because of this notion that He began to hate the Nibiru Gods and plot in his mind the imprints and details of his Grand Master Plan of Rebellion against the God of Gods of Planet Nibiru. He began to inculcate in his mind that He is the GOD OF GODS OF BLUE PLANET EARTH, and instilled in the heart and mind of all his GALACTIC SPECIAL FORCES EXPEDITIONARY LEGIONNAIRES that BLUE PLANET EARTH will be their new KINGDOM, and that by his self-proclaimed power as GOD OF GODS of Blue Planet Earth, they will unite to fight the GOD OF GODS of Planet Nibiru by all means available and to defend the Blue Planet Earth from any GALACTIC AGGRESSORS that will want its vast minerals of ENERGY, including their own Planet of Nibiru if it needs so, and to achieve that Grand Master Plan, they will need the help of the HUMANOIDS they had created through their scientific experimentation of mixing their DNA BY COPULATION to different species until they mastered to perfection what is now they called SPECIES OF HUMAN SLAVES, THE HUMANOIDS.

In that era of time mining Blue Planet Earths precious minerals, Supreme Commander Lucifer started building defense infrastructure disguised as Temples for his great ambition plan of Rebellion against Planet Nibirus God of Gods. Supreme Commander Lucifer use humanoids and dinosaurs to make PYRAMIDS in strategic places and remote areas of Blue Planet Earth. Supreme Commander Lucifer erected various pyramids in the jungles of Central and South America, in the desserts of Africa, and in the mountains of Europa, where He and his Commanders, employed the Cyclops humanoids controlling the dinosaurs to haul and put the massive stone blocks piece by piece until the Pyramids Defense Initiative he devised and invented were erected.

One day Lord God Adanis, the Ruling God of Planet Nibiru decided to wander and roam Blue Planet Earth, and planned to visit as well Supreme Commander Lucifer to observe and find out himself the operation of Blue Planet Earths minerals mining activities for their Planet Nibirus much needed minerals and use as their fuel and energy.

After the welcome Parade of Honors and Salute and extravagant accolade for the visiting Ruling God, Lord God Adanis and his Royal Escort Legionnaires experienced and enjoyed the hospitality of Supreme Commander Lucifer. Legends and myths says that what happened next was indescribable, there was a misunderstanding and altercation during the official meeting of Lord God Adanis and Supreme Commander Lucifer discussing the future of Blue Planet Earth.

There was a hearsay that Supreme Commander Lucifer didn't agree of Lord God Adanis plan to put to Intelligence Test the humanoids, and to integrate the Humanoids into Planet Nibiru society if they shall so pass this SECRET TEST, but Supreme Commander Lucifer for whatever REASON in his mind and heart didn't agree and argued angrily with Lord God Adanis, and after a lengthy and heated debate, finally Supreme Commander Lucifer lose his temper, and claimed He is the only God of these new species called Humanoids, and goes to proclaim his REBELLION against Lord God Adanis, and to all the Gods and Goddesses Of Planet Nibiru.

The Book of Time somewhat have a hidden pages that don't divulge as to what really happened during that time, although at present under Goddess Nakki's reign, there are select few who knows and have knowledge of these hidden pages. The only witnesses who could give accounts as to what really happened were two Royal Guard Escort Legionnaires survivors that was escorting Lord God Adanis in that tragic and fateful day, whom Supreme Commander Lucifer spared their life to navigate the Royal Space Shuttle Vimana back to Planet Nibiru, but the two Royal Guard Escort Legionnaires were terribly shocked of what they have witnessed and seen that sometimes they couldn't speak intelligently as if they have lost their sanity, yet all evidence of what befalls them was found inside the Royal Galactic Space Shuttle which was splattered all over by the bloods of the Royal Guard Escort Legionnaires, and of Lord God Adanis.

They were monstrously killed and massacred cruelly. Supreme Commander Michael was beheaded but his body was full of traces of cuts and wounds that suggest they never give up and fight THE ENEMY up to their last breath, Commander Gabriel body was terrorized that one can't recognized, the other ten Royal Guard Escort Legionnaires body were never recovered and nowhere to be found, their Heads severed and found pierced to their laser sword, around Lord God Adanis body which was crucified upside down as if mocking the whole Planet of Nibiru.

It was a grotesque sight and shocking moment for all Nibirunians that ignites and started the 1st Galactic War, The war of Blue Planet Earth and The Nibirunians.

Legends in the Book of Time recorded that when the 1ST GALACTIC WAR broke out and passed, almost all living creatures that walk on Blue Planet Earth land died and perished including all the Cyclops and Dinosaurs, because of a big flaming meteorite that hit the Blue Planet Earth believed to be fired by the Nibirunians in retaliation to Blue Planet Earths Pyramid Defense Initiative.

After a time when Blue Planet Earth is recuperating from its massive destruction, Supreme Commander Lucifer with his surviving Commanders and Loyal Legionnaires who survived the 1ST GALACTIC WAR began re-structuring their Blue Planet Earth Galactic Defense Initiative and employed NEPHILIMS, giant humans to do the job of hauling massive stones to built pyramid temples again, as strategic defense initiative for future Galactic War, because all the giant creatures including the dinosaurs and humanoid Cyclops which they had employed and used before have died and wiped out, extinct and buried in the ashes and dust of Blue Planet Earth realm.

After the First Galactic War, the Nibirunians were never heard of again, vanished in the abyss of Galaxy and Universe. Supreme Commander Lucifer and the surviving Commanders and Legionnaires became the God and demigods of Blue Planet Earth, enjoying for thousand years the lustful abundance of Blue Planet Earth's riches and the intoxicating PLEASURE of POWER.

But there was no PEACE at all in the mind and heart of Supreme Commander Lucifer, for He absolutely knows there will be a time the Nibirunians will come back for REVENGE and avenge their forefathers humiliating lost. In his thoughts always dwells "ITS JUST A MATTER OF TIME, SURELY, THE GODS AND GODDESSES OF PLANET NIBIRU NEVER FORGETS."

SERPENTUM, SYMBOL OF NIBIRU PLANET THRONE SOVEREIGN CROWN

"THE FEAR OF GOD,
IS THE BEGINNING OF WISDOM"

PROVERBS 1: 7

"FEAR NOT,
WHEN CONSCIENCE IS CLEAR"

MonaC

CONTENTS

BOOK - 1

"THE SECOND COMING"

* * *

"... FOR SUCH CRUELTY OF FATE
JUST GO ALONG ENDLESSLY
THIS SPACE IS FULL OF PROMISE
ALONG THE WAY ARE SURPRISES
OF HAPPINESS AND LONELINESS ..."

* * *

* * * THE SECOND COMING * * *

*** CHAPTER – 1 ***

THE FATE

In a distant planet wandering in the abyss of universe, orbiting a known passage in its eon years of existence, there, in its computerize and mechanically built cities of towering and gigantic titanium steel embedded in a rocky mountain terrain, a colonies of advance civilization, it's lights glittering like fireflies amidst canyons of rocks, camouflaging like a chameleon of starlight's, there above the horizon of mountain gorge, while the night is young and evening invites frivolity, two lovers bask in the radiance of the twinkling stars, silhouetting by the starlight's on rocky hills of their realm cajoling and murmuring sweet nothings, talking deep feelings and future concerns, caressing each other as if there is no tomorrow, the sultry ambience inviting of what yet to come, watching in their gigantic computerized wall monitor of their room that mysterious far-flung yet enticing blue planet, of its' wild and beautiful living creatures roaming and inhabiting what their ancestor called species, exchanging opinions and ideas of the results of their spy-legions advance scientific research, that they both know will affect their future life as couple, and as the next ruler, the Goddess and God of their ailing planet called Nibiru, a wandering ember, for in its thousand years of existence and piloting the vast universe, they had exhausted their energy, their planet so advance in technology came to a point of awakening of in-coming self-destruction, and they both understand the complexity of future to come, for they know in their hearts and mind, the key solution to avert their civilizations obliteration would be to go back in their past, the annals of their ancestral history, recorded in what they called Book of Time, all their civilizations secrets encoded within, and yet, to summarize the solution for their planet and civilizations survival is to go back in that space of time where a dark chapter of their recorded ancestral history took place, to go back in that enticing blue planet called Earth, befriend the beautiful yet hostile living creatures inhabiting that planet, to seek its Goddesses and Gods, it's rulers to make an alliance and accord of inter-planetary co-existence, exchanging their knowledge of advance scientific technologies in-return of the Earthling's precious minerals in-which their dying planet needs. All this plans and ideas they both shared and discussed while they lay in their crystal clear bedroom soothing each other, under the skyline above them as seen from their electro-magnetic crystal bedroom shield, both optimistic and full of hope for the day ahead seems so perfect, when that day of tomorrow comes of their grand union, their sacred day of wedding, in that festivities where they both know the future looks dim, they agreed unto each other, by their union will come a new beginning, and there in the middle of laughter's and merriment, they will reveal and announce to their Elders, Legions and Subjects, it's TIME, time for them all to know the TRUTH, the realization of their dreams and plans for the future of their planet, there will be no WAR but PEACE, an inter-planetary and galactic CO-EXISTENCE with other Planets in the Universe, especially that Blue Planet called Earth in the Galaxy of Milky Way.

And while they both lay out there transfix to that blue planet and their future plans, the vast stars shines and glitter above them, penetrating the crystal shield of their bedroom, lighting all energy that is around them, like rainbow sparkling, all the radiant colors glowing, making them enamor, embracing each other, wanting each other, as if tomorrow couldn't wait much longer, hearts desires dictating FATE, mind and heart entwine as one, longing and yearning, panting for that salacious natural urge, they look unto each other longingly, then kiss passionately as if there's no tomorrow, and make love to each other ardently.

"THE LOVE MAKING OF THE GODS"
BY MONAC
(POETIC BREEZE, POETIC FROTH PART 1 – POEM NO. 173)

LOVER – GOD ANUK:
. . . Oh my beloved, you're so beautiful
Adoring in every way
You're my flower in the universe
Lily, Dandelion, Orchid, Poppy, Marigold
Geranium, Tulip, Jasmine, Lavender
A fragrance all together
A perfume of my desire
You're my goddess of beauty
Isis, Cybele, Ishtar, Aphrodite and Venus
Rolled into alluring one
Oh my beloved are you ready
I will love you
The way a GOD does
The way a poet does . . .

BELOVED – GODDESS NAKKI:
. . . Oh you're so sweet and romantic
My ever dearest lover
Your words are fire in my loins
Igniting passionate whim deep within
I am here reeling and waiting
Take and love me
Ravage me as you please . . .

LOVER – GOD ANUK:
. . . Oh beloved, hear my words
Stay, don't move where you are
I'm going to make love to you now
I will make this moment
A glorious one to cherish
Hold on, I'll make love to you soon
Make love to you like a poet does

BELOVED – GODDESS NAKKI:
. . . Oh my lover, my naked body is all yours
I am yearning inside
I need to feel you
Touch your hardened manhood
Make me feel am not alone
My Goddess-hood is arouse
My stomach is churning
Oh please, soothe and quench
This burning desire now . . .

LOVER – GOD ANUK:
. . . Patience is a virtue my dear Goddess
Delight in my naked body
I won't delay no more
Whispers of breath-taking romance
May my words brings excitement
Of erotic bliss in your heart
Sensation in-between our being
Ever realm of utmost ecstasy . . .

BELOVED – GODDESS NAKKI:
. . . Oh stop this tormenting pleasure
Sweetest words stirring my desires
Oh my lover read my lips
My heart is longing
My womb is stirring
My royal vagina is aching
I can't wait no more
Come on now my lover
Fill me with your Godly desire . . .

LOVER – GOD ANUK:
. . . All the pleasures of love will be yours
Just obey what I say
My dear sweet Goddess
I will love you
Like a God of Love
Like a poet does

But, please
Don't you ever
Lay your hands on me . . .
Oh dearest sweet, sweet Goddess
Fire is crouching in
Your ears I will lick
Your neck smells so sweet
My tongue will flicker
Into your breast and nipples
It will feast
Darting its way down
Open your heaven my darling
I will lick tenderly
Then suck hungrily
The sweetness of your royal vagina
Tickling your clitoris
With my loving tongue
And drink the wetness within . . .

BELOVED – GODDESS NAKKI:
. . . Oh my Godly lover,
My dearest pleasure
Make love to me now
Please I am begging
Make love to me
Or I'm going to come now
Make love to me my Lover
I want to feel you inside my womb
Make love to my heart
Make love inside my longing soul . . .

LOVER – GOD ANUK:
. . . A million pleasures
A tickle of ecstasy
I'm going to make love to your heart
We will be united as one
Hold on, stand firm, don't move
Remain your hands upward
Reach your joyous joy

Satisfy your Goddess-hood desires
Reach-out your hand sky-high
Clench your fist to infinite bliss
Fly with your erotic dreams
I will love you
The way a God does
The way a poet does
But, please, don't you ever
Lay hands on me . . .

BELOVED – GODDESS NAKKI:
. . . Whatever you say dearest
I will obey you wholeheartedly
Just make love to me now
The way you want
The way you do
The way a poet does
Oh hurry my lover
I am waiting and reeling
My stomach is churning
My vulva's on fire
Aching with desire
Come now and fill me with your Royal Penis
My Royal Vagina is dripping wet
Fill me now please
My lover, my one, my heart . . . my God...

LOVER – GOD ANUK:
. . . You're my Venus, my Aphrodite, oh my Goddess
You're my Goddess of Love
All pleasures will be yours
I'm going to love you
The way a poet does . . .

BELOVED – GODDESS NAKKI:
. . . Oh speak no more
You're words are tormenting me
Sweet temptation in-between
Come now my dearest

Point your hardened royal manhood
Shove it hard inside of me
Let your words come to play . . .

LOVER – GOD ANUK:
. . . Oh dear sweet, sweet Goddess
Daughter of Universe
Come fly with me
We'll be lovers alright
Unite with me my love
So wet and so sweet
I'll bring you happiness way beyond
I'll bring you satisfaction
Until eternity we'll explode as one

BELOVED – GODDESS NAKKI:
Oh… I am on fire
Speak no more
My Royal Vagina is gaping wet
Million ecstasy and energy
In my womb awaiting
Make love to me now my Godly lover
Or I will explode all alone

LOVER – GOD ANUK:
Open your legs now
Get ready my beloved
Royal Manhood so hard
Open it wide apart
Like a piercing sword
Penetrating its scabbard
I'll make love to you now
Strong, yet patiently thrusting
Pleasure and ecstasy is all yours
It's all in my warmth breath
All in my caring touch
All in my loving heart
It's all in my burning soul
It's all in my hardened desire . . .

BELOVED – GODDESS NAKKI:
. . . Oh please, I can't wait no more
I need you inside now
Fill me now my lover
My minds screaming
My hearts reeling
My wombs yearning
My vulvas tingling
My royal vaginas waiting
Shove it hard now
Nice and slow
Fill me now my lover
All the way in
All the way out
Make love to me my poet
Make love to me
My dear better half
My dearest one
Make love to me like a poet does . . .

LOVER – GOD ANUK:
. . . Unite my Godly penis and your holy vagina
Oh flesh to flesh, sliding gently
Standing, shoving by the back
Our passion, inside and out
Savoring love
Quenching our desires
I'll bring you to heaven
We'll entwine as one
I'll be your eternal bliss
I will love you until the end
We will be sweethearts
And lovers for all seasons
We'll be husband and wife forever
We will be one soul until eternity . . .

BELOVED – GODDESS NAKKI:
. . . Ah my lover, it feels so good
Ravage me the way you want

Slide your manhood hard
In and out my sweet and wet royal vagina
Oh my lover, my sweet, sweet lover
So warmth your royal penis, so full
Make love to me so sweet
We will make love the whole night
I will be your beloved alright
The delight in your words
Flesh to flesh
Soul to soul
Savoring love as one
Sweet as honey in our lips
Unquenchable fire in our belly
Come let us scorch the night
Consume more that love in our heart
Ah my lover, oh so good
So long, so full, so warmth
Oh love me, love me forever, my lover . . .

LOVER – GOD ANUK:
. . . Ah my beloved, so tight and so wet
Ride my piercing manhood
Hungry and fierce
Sliding rhythmically
Receive my sweetest love
We will be lovers alright
All night long
Oh beloved, desire is so ardent
Feel my wanton thrust
Lovingly, the way I do
The way a poet does
I promise we'll be as one forever
Night will rejoice with us
The sweetness as one
Body to body
Reach that utmost bliss
EUPHORIA
One sweet explosion
Fire consume that love of ours

Let us drown in ecstasy of our love
Let our love live and dwell
The very depths of our beauteous soul . . .

BELOVED – GODDESS NAKKI:
Oh my lover, I am coming
. . . Oh, Ohh, Ohhhh, AHH, AHHHHHH
One glorious moment
One cry, one sigh
One ecstasy entwine
Ahh, ah, ah, aooooohhhhhh
Fill me with your holy royal seeds
Ahh, ohhh, ahhh, ahhh, ohhh
Oh Great God, my Godly poet lover
Come now together
Our cosmic energy rumbling
Ahhhh……we'll explode as ONE

LOVER – GOD ANUK:
. . . AHHHHHHHHH. . .
ALL COSMIC ENERGY BELONGS TO YOU
OH SWEET SWEET GODDESS
I am all yours
I love you sweet beloved
My Universal Goddess
My one and only
My eternity . . .

BELOVED – GODDESS NAKKI:
Thank you my sweet, sweet God lover
Thank you for loving me
My dearest, my one, my Poet
Our love is now eternal
Joyous joy beyond
Euphoria, rapture
ONE SWEET EXPLOSION
Oh my lover, with you as one
In my womb
ONE COSMIC EXPLOSION

Union of our mind
Union of our heart
Union of our soul
Cometh the breathe of life
My Great, Great sweet lover
Your love, the sweetest of them all . . .

It was a glorious feeling of copulation and gratification between God Anuk, Son of the Star Sirius, Blood of the Constellation Orion, and Goddess Nakki, Daughter of Planet Nibiru, Blood of Milky Way, entwined as ONE, oblivious of their nakedness and of what is unfolding in their Kingdom, and almost forgot their in-coming Grand Galactic Sacred Wedding.

Indeed their coming union as Wife and Husband, the Universal Galactic Crown Royal Couple, as reigning Goddess and God of Planet Nibiru that will possess and protect the Crown Scepter of Planet Nibiru's Throne, the symbolic jewel of Utmost Power for Planet Nibirus ruling God and Goddesses, is a Grand Event all good Nibirunian Unigalitizines have been waiting for a long time, but the Grand Galactic Sacred Wedding was also marred with controversy and jealousy for those other entity HUNGRY FOR POWER.

After a while, the two lovers came back to their senses, tired and exhausted of their love-making, they both know how important they are for each other, and that LOVE in their heart will be their pillar of strength whatever happens, comes better or worse, their LOVE for each other is ETERNAL.

God Anuk, Son of the Star Sirius, Blood of the Constellation Orion

Goddess Nakki, Daughter of Planet Nibiru, Blood of Milky Way

"...that was so exhilarating of you making love to me, my God Anuk, I felt every universal cosmic energy, so intense pleasure and ecstasy in my womb, this seed you had planted will be the bond and new breathe of our future generations and of our Kingdom to come...a hope of our blissful union when our twilight comes" whispered Goddess Nakki

"...oh my Goddess Nakki, may my Royal seed I planted blossom in thy womb, the covenant of our life and love to each other, for I will be yours forever, until eternity, I will be at your side, I will be your better half and pillar of strength, I will defend you and our fruits of union from any aggressors, and foe alike that will try to destroy your honor and Kingdom, I will be of service to you until my last breathe if it needs so, that's my pledge my beloved..." replied God Anuk, doubtful of future to come, for deep in his mind and heart, are disturbing and gruesome thoughts of what might unfold during their grand union and wedding, his gloomy gazed betray his thoughts

"...what is it my God Anuk that bothers your heart, you speak eloquently of your love and affection to me, and yet judging by the look in your eyes, I sense of chaotic mind, as if there is something I am missing, please enlighten me oh my God Anuk, tell me the secrets of your mind, tell me honestly what is bothering you..." replied impatiently by Goddess Nakki, her big eagle-shape blue-green eyes radiating yet piercing

"...there is nothing to unfurl my Goddess Nakki, be still, calm your mind, there is tomorrow to look up to, our Universal Galactic Grand Union, our sacred wedding, alas, by then you will be the Grand Ruler of our Planet, oh Goddess Nakki, think not of anything but the delights tomorrow will bring, don't stress yourself of anything worrisome, there is nothing to doubt even fear, my Goddess, sleep now my Goddess, tomorrow is FULL OF SURPRISES... sleep a Godly sleep my Goddess, you will need your energy tomorrow more than ever...I love you...oh my Goddess Nakki...until eternity..."

Goddess Nakki on hearing God Anuk's assuring words, felt so secure and safe, slowly close her eyes, and like a melodious song, the words of God Anuk flow into her being and she slowly fell asleep, and as she totally slouch in stillness of slumber, she manage to whisper "...I love you...too...my God Anuk... forever..."

And while Goddess Nakki fall asleep, God Anuk quickly get up from their bed-capsule and walk to the other end of the room, upon reaching the wall, touch it with his right hand, and instantly, the wall become a giant luminous computer, of several windows showing different sites of their palace, like a webcam, others beaming what's happening in their cities, or other planet he chooses to, yet, it's not what interest him most, after checking and making sure that his computer correspondence is secured with password and not recorded, he touch again the wall screen, and there in front of him, are numbers and coordinates of distant position, he quickly programmed that coordinates into another window, put a launch timing of 10 seconds, as if he is anticipating of an emergency evacuation operation, then when he's sure all are in order and ready, he then upload again every data and vital information he could program including automatic control landing mode initiative into the time-capsule deep space shuttle he has been working on the last couple of weeks, upon sensing of what danger lies ahead for the Kingdom and the throne.

"…there should be no room for error, it must be precise otherwise it will be a tragedy…" God Anuk murmuring to himself

"…I can't afford to lose you oh dearest…I will do everything to save you from any wrongdoing and harmful elements…I won't let them trample upon you my beloved, you are just too good for them, so righteous…" he keeps talking to himself as his hands continuously typing and programming what he had already prepared the day before into the electronic memory of his time-capsule deep space shuttle.

Two weeks ago, he came to know of a TOP SECRET vital information received back from their Planet's advance contingency of SPY-LEGIONS in Milky Way Galaxy, who were sent by the Unified High Command of Universal Galactic Defense Inter-Galaxy Intelligence Office headed by Supreme Commander Caezarous, and were sent through the portals of Black Holes well in advanced for espionage of Blue Planet Earth, to gather and store information of the Humanoids War Defense System and capabilities, to await that Special Order, and prepare for possible attack, led by COMMANDER MACHIAVELLI, who along with his elite Legionnaires are already encircling the Blue Planet Earth aboard Nibiru's thousand years spy satellite BLACK KNIGHT, under the Commandant-ship of COMMANDER MARLONUS, awaiting that TOP SECRET SPECIAL ORDER from the UNIFIED HIGH COMMAND OF UNIVERSAL GALACTIC DEFENSE INTER-GALAXY

INTELLIGENCE OFFICE under the WING BAND of SUPREME COMMANDER CAEZAROUS, with full knowledge and authorization from one of the UNIFIED HIGH COMMAND OF UNIVERSAL GALACTIC DEFENSE CENTRAL COMMAND HIGHEST SENIOR RANKING OFFICER, SUPREME GENERAL BHUDASIAN.

The Top Secret message, unknown to Goddess Nakki, was disclosed to him by a childhood dear friend, SUPREME GENERAL JHESUSAN, serving as Supreme Universal General and the SUPREME HEAD of the UNIFIED HIGH COMMAND OF UNIVERSAL GALACTIC DEFENSE TACTICAL ARMADA CENTRAL COMMAND, who told him about a rumor of CONSPIRACY amongst the hierarchy of Nibirus Higher Ranking Officers against a "Compromise Peace-Accord" with Blue Planet Earth, in-which THE ELDERS kept the message received fron the advance contingency of SPY-LEGIONS in Milky Way Galaxy totally TOP SECRET to Goddess Nakki, for fear of reprisal, and abandonment of their eons of planning masquerading as Energy Research Program, CODENAME: "ENGLUEBOLDERGY2015", for which God Anuk is so frustrated himself that he can not divulge the content of the message to his beloved, for if Goddess Nakki will know the Top Secret message, she will undeniably act decisively as to what she believes is morally right in her righteous capacity in-which will create confusions and chaos amongst the Planet Nibiru's structure of high command, to which some of the Elders and Legionnaires are awaiting as cue for their ambitious and rogue plans of annihilate and control, which Goddess Nakki ever since strongly contravene. He just could not expose the Top Secret message received because of its complicated content and for fear that if it gets out of hand, it might cause his Galactic Grand Sacred Marriage to Goddess Nakki a set-back and might eventually wouldn't push through, worse will result to Coup D'etat from the Power Hungry ELDERS, and the complete transition of absolute power and Kingdom-ship to Goddess Nakki will abruptly end.

As for now, time is cautiously ticking, and all what he could do is prepare, and await the right time, upon completing uploading all vital information including the Book of Time Data's into that time-capsule deep space shuttle memory, he then auto-programmed the space shuttle with Automatic Self-Defense Initiative (ASDI) encompassing Anti-Enemy Radar Detection and Auto-Launch Firing Program of any threat detected, with various sort of advance energy weaponry such as laser beams, sound-cannons, electro-magnetic rays, highly charge energy pulse-wave, and so on, for he knows that in-order to survive and arrive in that programmed coordinates of destination, the space shuttle must defend itself automatically precise without any intervention from its controller and passenger. And lastly, he install and program the last defense initiative, the time-capsule deep space shuttle's AUTOMATIC ELECTRO-MAGNETIC DEFENSE SHIELD in-case the space shuttle run-out of ammunition or of its energy weaponry, it is the last resort of defense initiative that will protect the Deep Space Shuttle and its passenger to arrive safely to that coordinates of destination He programmed, if ever the Deep Space Shuttle survive passing the Passage of Wormholes and Black-holes.

And while he's waiting to complete the program, He throw a backward glance to his beloved, Goddess Nakki, peacefully sleeping in their bed-capsule, her curly long shiny golden-white hair glowing like a radiating supernova, her heart shape perfect diaphanous face radiating with universal tranquility and her silky smooth exotic fair skin naked body resting like a galaxy of stars glistening, not suspecting of anything treacherous but only peace, not knowing in her virtuous mind of impending Inter-Galactic War that is brewing.

God Anuk wants to cry, yet, subjugate his tears and emotions, "I must be strong", he exhaled, for He knows that time is slowly diminishing every seconds of their time together and that He must act fast in order to save his beloved, even if it will cause them to separate for eon of years, he wouldn't care if it's THE FATE, as long as Goddess Nakki is safe from evil-minds of the ELDERS who are hiding in their saintly mask, masquerading their evil-plans with Godly-deeds, yet at the back of their mind and agenda, in their HEART, a power-hungry and tyrannically ruler-ship.

He then pauses and asked himself "Who am I?"

God Anuk looked in the vastness of Universe and pondered to himself what future lies ahead.

"WHO AM I" (THE GREAT MYSTERY)
BY MONAC
(POETIC BREEZE, POETIC FROTH PART 2 – POEM NO. 231)

Spawned from ancient seduction
Condemned heir of blissful union
Cast to play in a game of freewill
A masterpiece of a great mystery

Against the author of all this
Betrayal of existence a case to plead
As such, what is known is known
Only a mere play of right and wrong

So, naked I opened my eyes
Saw the sweetest light of sin
Heard the laughter's of the sinners
And cried my first taste of pain

Threading the journey of my being
Saw enticing vipers scattered around
Gradually instinct makes me realize
The path is full of sweeten snares

Heard the voices that whispers
Colourful world of alluring follies
Wreaking havoc in my daily thoughts
Condemning my will of curiosity

A dust wandering carried by the wind
A sand expose on a shoreline nakedness
Perhaps, a salt that may lost its saltiness
Temptation ever seducing my sinless sane

WHO AM I then in this quizzical chasm
Nothing but a mere subject am sure
A pawn in a great act of play
Where deception is a sweet corruption

So oddly strange, scarred enough
Came to breath for the great act
Adversaries waiting for the final cut
I will die beautifully, perhaps, live miserably!

"Who are the NIBIRUNIANS?"

He asked himself again, and search answers in his reasoning mind, delve into his deepest thoughts of balance reasoning and logical answers, while waiting to complete the uploading of his programming… "ahh the NIBIRUNIANS"…. he muses to himself…

Nibirunians are Time-Space Travelers Unigalitizens (Universal Galactic Citizens), a radiant highly developed living forms from all over the universe planets of different DNA and appearance, they are the HIGH-BREED who pioneered the NANO-TECHNOLOGY and SINGULARITY; great thinkers, planners, builders with brilliant minds, great philosophers and astrologers, highly intelligent creatures, yet in their façade of super advance civilization and different appearances is a distinctiveness, internally their mind conform in unison and confluent to UNIVERSAL DEGREE OF BALANCE REALITY, for if one entity cross that logic and DEGREE OF BALANCE REASONING and put into actions his/her HEART'S desires and plans of an evil deeds, will surely and automatically reveal his/her grotesque and monstrous exterior appearance, a horrible and dreadful forms, ugly living creatures of highly demonic and diabolical breed, all that is good and intelligent reasoning within will vanish, and in one's hearts and mind will rule THE KNOWLEDGE OF GOOD AND EVIL, GREED AND LUST in all forms of thoughts, so that within the planet's subjects, the UNIVERSAL DECREE COMMAND for all of its Unigalitizens, for all to follow and uphold, inculcated in their inter-galactic mind is that, "GODLY DEEDS, LIVE BEAUTIFULLY OR DIE MISERABLY", a decree enforced to all Planet Nibiru's Unigalitizines to follow universally for all of them to live and exist, and not to cross that boundaries of Universal Degree of Balance Reasoning, for if they do so, they would not want themselves transform into a horrible, ungodly and ugly monsters, for which the UNIFIED HIGH COMMAND OF UNIVERSAL GALACTIC DEFENSE AERO-POLICE AND SPACE-FORCE under the WING BAND of SUPREME COMMANDER NAPOLEONIOUS, would distinctively identify, arrest, condemn, punish, exile and freeze to the eternity of galactic deep space, forever lost in the vast universal time, their Id, frozen to eternal death in the abyss of Galactic Universe.

PLANET NIBIRU FEMALE NIBIRUNIAN'S

"BALANCE OF REALITY"
BY MONAC
(POETIC BREEZE, POETIC FROTH PART 2 – POEM NO. 297)

Wisdom and Folly
Indeed, Beautiful End
Death in Itself
A Life Reborn
A new Breath
A pulse of Time

The Beauty bestowed
Began ever since Birth
One Glorious Moment
Of Womb spitting Life

Prowling Air of Peccadillo
Aroma of Death begins
Enticing colors of life
Avoid the pit-trap of shame

Counting Years
Deeds will Account
Colorful Tears and Laughter's
The Shades of Being

There and Then
Live miserably, perhaps
Die beautifully

Wisdom and Folly
Death Springs Life
The BALANCE OF REALITY!

While God Anuk was lost in his thoughts and pondering, just as his programming completed, a beeping sound rings out in another window of his wall screen… "beep, beep, beep, beep…in-coming call…..alert, alert, alert… in-coming call…." was the sound warning registered in his wall screen, and the identification of the in-coming call was from one of the ELDERS, Lord Cainos….he felt a sudden surge of uneasiness, perhaps fear within his mind and heart, yet he gathers himself and calm down, and just as he accepts the call in his wall screen, he sees to it that Goddess Nakki is still asleep in her deep slumber, he then push a command button in his wall screen and suddenly a luminous shield appears forming from one side of the bed-capsule to other side that transform their bed into a machine-like capsule, the appearance slowly diminishing from crystal clear to metallic black covering the flawless naked body and sleeping beauty of Goddess Nakki's view from the wall screen.

"This is strange, had the Elders found out what I am planning?"
He asked himself, in doubt of Lord Cainos purpose of visitation.

"No, it can't be, for if they already knew what I am intending to do, they could have arrested me already, and condemn me to eternal frozen death in the abyss of galaxy, yet, I am still here, my intention is reasonable and true, I will not transform into that horrible monster, I am a God in my own right, my hearts delight is pure and truth, fair and just" he re-assured himself.

He then touch the luminous wall screen monitor, and there in-front of him in his electronic wall screen monitor appeared Lord Cainos, who is one of the pioneers and elders of Planet Nibiru. Lord Cainos is well verse and adept to Planet Nibiru's past history encoded in the Book of Time, he is one of the most respected and trusted ELDERS. He also noticed that Lord Cainos was not in THE ELDERS CHAMBER OF TRUTH, but was contacting him from his own private abode.

He then stand straight in military manner, clench his right hand fist and raise to his chest, then held high above his head like saluting.

"Gracious High, Lord Cainos, it is a pleasure seeing you on this wonderful moment, it's been a while since I last saw you, What can I do for you?" he greeted and asked, then put his right hand down, his eyes caught a glimpse of the upper right side of the wall screen that their electronic correspondence is officially on-record and automatically encoded.

After customary saluting each other, Lord Cainos replied "Most Gracious High, my God Anuk, indeed, a wonderful moment seeing you again, truly it's been a while since our last, and I am much delighted seeing you again, but I am afraid I have something for you, a bit of a query so to speak, my Gracious High. I am concerned because of its importance especially for you and Goddess Nakki, it concerns you both about the safety of your life, and I am greatly disturbed about it, in-fact it is causing me so much stress and anxiety.

"…as per intelligence data recorded and was brought to my attention by the UNIFIED HIGH COMMAND OF UNIVERSAL GALACTIC DEFENSE INTERNAL INTELLIGENCE under the WING BAND of SUPREME COMMANDER ALEXANDROUS, it seems that you are working on a project of your own without the full knowledge of the ELDERS, and that it is not also officially encoded in the Book of Time. The Universal Galactic Unified High Command don't like to suspect you of anything, for as you know yourself, you are a God, you do what is right, fair and just, but the disturbing questions brought to me by the Head of Intelligence Command and asked me to ask you, and find out the truth, is that, What special project you are working on that it is totally secret, encrypted and couldn't access by the Unified High Command of Universal Galactic Defense Internal Intelligence Office? And also the confirmation and records of your activities are not encoded in the Book of Time? What is it that you are doing and brewing in your mind, my Most Gracious God Anuk?" replied by Lord Cainos, speaking in a polite manner yet questioning with authoritarian grace, demanding and expecting for answers from God Anuk.

He then added "I don't like to suspect you of anything, my Most Gracious God Anuk, you are well-respected, and very dear to me like my own son, hours from now will be your Galactic Grand Sacred Union, your sacred wedding to Goddess Nakki, and right now I feel immense happiness in my heart knowing that you, my Most Gracious God Anuk, Son of Star Sirius, Blood of Constellation Orion, will wed Goddess Nakki, the Royal Daughter of Planet Nibiru, the Blood of Milky Way, a grand union of Universal Galactic civilization, a grand galactic wedding every entity on this planet of ours have been waiting for a long time, you and Goddess Nakki by your union will be the SAVIOUR of our dying planet, your Godship with Goddess Nakki is our new breathe of hope in order for our civilization and our planet to survive this in-coming dilemma of our planet's self-destruction. Now, tell me then my Most Gracious God Anuk, what's on your mind, your plan, and your project? Your self-secret I suppose? And that I could protect you and Goddess Nakki of any untoward surprises and circumstances this dilemma might eventually brings"

Lord Cainos firmly asking, hungry for answers, his eyes blazing like a tormenting sword, which seems like He's expecting him to tell everything, and yet, in his thoughts are reservations and uncertainties, after all, Lord Cainos belongs to the ELDERS, in his logical reason, what he has learned and known about the Top Secret message from Supreme General Jhesusan is already dangerous enough to cause his arrest and condemnation to eternal frozen death in the abyss of universe, what more of his secret project the last weeks he's been attentively doing without the ELDERS knowledge, for he knew in his heart, if they learn what he is up to, there will be no Universal Galactic Sacred Union, there will be no INTER-GALACTIC WEDDING, and the last HOPE of their dying planet will come to an end, and worse of all, his greatest fear, the annihilation and destruction of the BLUE PLANET EARTH.

No, he can not divulge to Lord Cainos what he is been doing the past two weeks, or everything will be compromise, in his mind silently resonates this logical reason, that if He tells Lord Cainos He's real project and what he is building, surely the whole ELDERS will come to know instantaneously for He knows that their conversation is on record and being monitored live, any slightest chance He will give-in for them to suspect him, and they will immediately convene in THE ELDERS CHAMBER OF TRUTH to debate his fate, will be judge by the Galactic High Tribunal Court as per THE ELDERS advise and guilty verdict, and had him arrested, condemned to eternal frozen death in the abyss of Galaxy, as well as his dear beloved, Goddess Nakki will also be strip of her power, and she will become a diplomatically motivated galactic prisoner, exile in the realm of UNIFIED HIGH COMMAND OF UNIVERSAL GALACTIC DEFENSE INTER-GALAXY PRISONER-GARRISON under the WING BAND of SUPREME COMMANDER HITLEOROUS, A CUNNING AND AMBITIOUS GALACTIC OFFICER, WHO HAS A HABIT OF PUTTING TO TEST INTO THE EDGE OF BOUNDARIES THE DEGREE OF BALANCE REASONING as part of his own palatial self-amusement.

"No, I could not afford that to happen" he told himself, and he look straight into the eye of Lord Cainos, put his both hands at his back above his buttocks, as if concealing something and preparing for a confrontation of powers, ready to unleash a lightning strike, but it's not what He wants to do, after all, He is a GOD, and must act such one. He then pose a GODLY stand, his glaring deep blue-sea colored eyes penetrating the core of Lord Cainos, and authoritively throw back a question that make Lord Cainos mumbling.

"Lord Cainos, Why is it that you question with suspicion your own GOD, I am GOD ANUK, MOST GRACIOUS, if I like to conceal what I am intending to do, wouldn't it be fair not to judge and question it, worse suspect of it for any reason, after all, I AM A GOD, your GOD Lord Cainos, if I am doing something wrong and not confluence to THE DEGREE OF BALANCE REASONING, if I, GOD ANUK, have cross that boundary line, wouldn't it be obvious by now that I have already transformed into a DIABOLICAL and HORRIBLE MONSTER, and that as per our Kingdom's Decree, I will be arrested and condemned to eternal frozen death in the abyss of the galactic universe, and yet here I am, Lord Cainos, radiating as one GOD can be, for in my heart are pure truth, my mind is just and fair, I am here standing in front of you Lord Cainos as your beloved GOD, the MOST GRACIOUS, GOD ANUK, SON OF STAR SIRIUS, THE COSMIC BLOOD OF CONSTELLATION ORION" God Anuk replied in Godly manner.

Lord Cainos was taken aback and speechless of what he had heard from God Anuk, surely He is right, he told to himself, if God Anuk has cross that boundary, he could have transform already into a horrible monster, yet there he is, in all his glory and splendor standing in front of him, GOD ANUK, THE MOST GRACIOUS, HANDSOME AS EVER, RADIATING LIKE A THOUSAND SUN…TRULY THE SON OF STAR SIRIUS…

Lord Cainos then spoke to God Anuk again, yet in Lord Cainos humbling mind, would be to appease God Anuk, though inside his heart and mind, he is not satisfied with the answers God Anuk replied to him, yet it's better for him to leave God Anuk in peace, that he may take a GODLY REST, for the clock is ticking short, that hours from now will be GOD ANUK AND GODDESS NAKKI'S grand union, the great sacred wedding everyone in Nibiru has been waiting for, THE SACRED UNION OF THE DAUGHTER OF PLANET NIBIRU AND THE SON OF STAR SIRIUS, THE GREAT UNIVERSAL-GALACTIC WEDDING.

"My sincere apology, oh MOST GRACIOUS, GOD ANUK, I come in peace, I only seek the truth for us ELDERS to know, yet in your greatness, oh MOST GRACIOUS, you have enlighten my mind, and now, for I know you must take a GODLY rest, I will leave you in peace, accept my deepest and sincere apology oh MOST GRACIOUS if I had doubted your greatness, surely you are just and fair, and the truth lies within you, oh MOST GRACIOUS, forgive my arrogance and candor, I only acted in good faith" and as he close his monitor screen, Lord Cainos clench his right fist, gesture to his breast and raise above his forehead, signaling God Anuk that their correspondence is over and finish, and the window screen of Lord Cainos went off.

God Anuk sees to it that the on-line recording of their correspondence has also cease as he confirm it from his wall screen monitor, he then walk to other end of the luminous room towards the veranda, his Godly strong muscular built naked body glowing as if an electric blue-current is flowing around from head to toe, as he approached the luminous electronic shield, instantly a door open, he walk pass through and there by the terrace overlooking the grandeur of the Planet Nibiru's colonies structures and buildings, and the dark space buzzing and whizzing with aerospace aircraft coming from everywhere like flying saucers, the lights in each window of their subjects edifice and homes are glittering with different incandescent colors like clinging fireflies amidst blackest darkness, a million sight of starlight's that twinkles in the vast rocky mountain terrain of their Kingdom, there in the serenity of the universal galactic night, he pause and ponder, amuse of what had just happen, and in his Godly heart is satisfaction, he smile knowing in his heart he is on the right track, that whatever He is doing for the safety of his beloved Goddess Nakki, and for the goodness of the GALACTIC UNIVERSE is indeed, a Godly deeds and wise decision, a wisdom of a God, and that he must accept all the consequences no matter what THE FATE dictates.

God Anuk look down beneath the terrace, and couldn't help himself bewilder by the sight he is seeing, the view is alluring and breathtaking, but beneath its luster is a dying planet, the flickering lights in the darkness like fireflies clinging to chasm of rocky mountains and rugged terrain betrays the grandeur of the colonies it use to be, God Anuk couldn't help himself ponder what had gone happen to their civilization that they arrive at this situation, on the brink of Planet self-destruction due to diminishing energy, how could they, so advance in civilization and technologies didn't foresee that one day their magnificent planet will run out of energy, he asked himself, "Where are the great planners and thinkers of our planet?", as if not satisfied with his question, he asked himself again, "Why did the ELDERS let this thing happen, and didn't do any planning and preparation, or any future emergency contingency?", and yet again, another question pop out in his Godly mind, but this time, the question seems so very ironic and inconceivable, for it questions the integrity of the ELDERS, he search his thoughts, seek his deepest subconscious mind, as if the question that hangs on his mind needs an answer at once, perhaps a link to what has been happening to their ailing Planet and Great Civilization of Nibirunians…

Then He murmur so softly to himself, "Is it possible that the ELDERS deliberately did not plan nor undertaken future emergency contingency so that their planet energy will be exhausted during their eon years of voyaging the universe so that when that day comes, when that day their energy will run out, they, the ELDERS will have an excuse and agenda to go back to Blue Planet Earth to mine their needed energy, an alibi that's surely acceptable to all Nibirunian Unigalitizines.

"Yes, it's possible for the minerals, EARTH is so rich with minerals like gold, silver, copper, bronze, zinc, mercury, hydrogen, titanium, DEUTERIUM and so on…" he answered himself, and yet for the sake of satisfying his curiosity and quest for truthful answers, he entertain in his thoughts again of one un-Godly question, a theory inconceivable in a normal thoughts and thinking of a Nibirunians, but reasonable and credible, for in his GODLY MIND MANIFEST THE THOUGHTS OF THEORY OF CONSPIRACY, THE ELDERS DELIBERATELY PLAN TO HAVE THEIR PLANET NIBIRU EXHAUST IT'S ENERGY SOURCE SO THAT THEY COULD MAKE AN ALIBI AND PLANS TO GO BACK TO BLUE PLANET EARTH, JUST LIKE WHAT IS HAPPENING NOW, BUT NOT FOR THE NATURAL RESOURCES AND MINERALS OF BLUE PLANET EARTH…." at that precise moment, he was aghast, he had seen in his thoughts what the ELDERS had been trying to maneuver eon of times, in his Godly reasoning, he now understand what is this all about, it's not only the EARTH'S MINERALS that the ELDERS yearns and wants for Eons of Time, it's all clear now he thought so, "IT'S ALL ABOUT VENGEANCE, THE REVENGE OF PLANET NIBIRU TO BLUE PLANET EARTH".

“VENGEANCE”
By MonaC
(POETIC BREEZE, POETIC FROTH PART 2 – POEM NO. 412)

Oh sweet vengeance
I’ll pay my revenge
My pleasure your pain
I’ll drink your failing
Grief comes within
Crying moments in-vain
My laughter’s your misery
In your eye begs mercy
There and then
Peace I’ll contend
Cheer’s to your fate
The sweetness of your end!

SUPREME COMMANDER JHESUSAN, SUPREME HEAD OF THE UNIFIED HIGH COMMAND OF UNIVERSAL GALACTIC DEFENSE TACTICAL ARMADA CENTRAL COMMAND

He was totally shocked of what he had just contemplated, considering over and over again in his thoughts the possibilities of such perception and theory, then he muttered to himself, "If this is true, then the ancient legends of 1st Galactic War written in the Book of Time is TRUE and not just primordial MYTH", and for the first time in his existence, even in his stature as a GOD, he fears more than ever, for now he knows with clarity that dark chapter mentioned in Planet Nibirus ancient history of Galactic War with Blue Planet Earth will not be the first and last, and then again, he felt tremble and dread in his heart, for as he was standing there gazing in the blackness of universe with its million stars glimmering, he saw a million bolts of energy exploded in his thoughts, "THE FATE - A SECOND GALACTIC WAR, THE REVENGE OF THE ELDERS AGAINST THE BLUE PLANET EARTH, AGAINST THE HUMANOIDS, and the DEMIGODS who help the humanoids defeat the Nibirunians with an advance weapon of that time, constructed by the humans bare hands but with advance knowhow and technological intervention of the Demigods, so powerful with its electromagnetic laser energy, that sent the Planet Nibiru and its RULERS AND GODS during that era of time fleeing into universal galactic space like a vagabond cowering in fear", and with that he concluded in his thoughts of pondering "CONSPIRACY AND VENGEANCE, I MUST ACT FAST" he utter bewildered

And calculating time in his mind, as per DEEP-SPACE NAVIGATIONAL INFORMATION DATA he daily receives from the UNIFIED HIGH COMMAND OF UNIVERSAL GALACTIC DEFENSE AND DEEP SPACE NAVIGATIONAL CONTROL under the WING BAND of SUPREME COMMANDER SHAWNTROY, they are now nearing the Blue Planet Earth Galaxy of Milky Way, a million light years away from the constellation they are currently navigating, only a matter of time The Nibiru Planet will reach the Passage of Space and Time, the whirling WORM-HOLES of universal galactic space, THAT GATEWAY OF UNIVERSAL GALACTIC INTER-CONSTELLATION ROUTE THAT WILL TAKE THEM TO THE GALAXY OF MILKY WAY, THE HOME-GALAXY OF BLUE PLANET EARTH, along with its eight other neighboring planet and its satellite moons, MERCURY, VENUS THE RED PLANET, MARS, JUPITER THE RING PLANET, SATURN, NEPTUNE, URANUS AND PLUTO, INCLUDING ITS UNFORGIVING GALACTIC STAR, THE SUN.

God Anuk was so engrossed pondering and discerning the future to come he came to know and understand moments ago, by this time his heart is so filled with grief and anguish, for he knows and realize in his heart what devastating and catastrophic effect this 2nd Galactic war will bring to the Blue Planet Earth and it's unsuspecting inhabitants if they attack, knowing Two Battalions of their Legionnaires under COMMANDER MACHEAVELLI, COMMANDER OF SPY-LEGIONS and COMMANDER MARLONUS, COMMANDER OF SPY SATTELITE BLACK KNIGHT were already in the vicinity of Blue Planet Earth aboard in that deep space spy-craft BLACK NIGHT, who had set a garrison camp (FORT MOON) in the satellite moon of the Blue Planet Earth just waiting for that TOP SECRET SPECIAL ORDER from the UNIVERSAL GALACTIC DEFENSE CENTRAL COMMAND to attack.

God Anuk fixed his gazed into the eternity and vastness of space, there is uncertainty in his thoughts, for again questions run havoc in his mind. "WHAT IF?"...he ponders and re-think... "WHAT IF THE BLUE PLANET EARTH STILL HAS THAT ADVANCE WEAPONRY THEY HAD USED EON OF YEARS AGO TO DEFEAT THEIR NIBIRUNIAN ANCESTORS WHO FIRST CAME AND VISITED EARTH, WHAT IF THAT WEAPON WAS UPGRADED AND MUCH MORE ADVANCE THAN THEIR HIGHLY ADVANCE TECHNOLOGICAL WEAPONRY, WHAT WILL BE THE CONSEQUENCES FOR BOTH PLANETS, WHAT IF...?" He left the questions un-answered, for he knows deep in his reasoning heart and mind, THE FUTURE LOOKS UNCERTAIN.

Yet in his mind, there is one thing he is so certain with, whatever THE FATE will bring during THE WEDDING with her beloved Goddess Nakki, he will push his plan, if THE ENEMY will reveal their identity during their sacred grand union, worse come to worse, he knows in his heart he must have to help Goddess Nakki ESCAPE, and in his reasoning heart and mind, Goddess Nakki will have a greater chance surviving the Nibiru Kingdom's enemy onslaught by escaping into the realm of that BLUE PLANET called EARTH.

* * *

"... NOW I AM HERE
PURSUING WHAT IS RIGHT
SEARCHING FOR WAYS
THAT WOULD HOLD ME SO TIGHT
TO FACE THE FUTURE
I WILL ALWAYS BELONG
AND TO EMBRACE THE MOMENTS
I DEARLY LONG ..."

* * *

*** CHAPTER – 2 ***

THE GALACTIC DILEMMA

God Anuk was so occupied contemplating that he didn't notice Goddess Nakki was already awake sitting by the bed side, watching him from his deep pondering and thinking. Goddess Nakki felt strangeness in her heart, kind of incongruity, because in their existence as couple, she never saw his beloved God Anuk so emotionally drain the way he was acting the past days, as if there is something she can't explain, perhaps known that is consuming the sanity of his beloved God Anuk, and in her mind are compelling questions longing for answers.

"If we are going to be married, as husband and wife, sacredly bind together for eternity, then I must know his deepest and secret fears, He must have to tell me everything whatever He is holding on and hiding from me" she murmured to herself

"He should TRUST me the way I will trust him all my life forever, for in trust, there-in, true love will be built upon, for TRUST compliments LOVE, then RESPECT, for in love, there should be TRUST to one another, and if we trust each other, then we RESPECT each other, and if we have TRUST and RESPECT, then for ETERNITY, LOVE WILL BLOSSOM IT'S WAY, for us to succeed as husband and wife until eternity, TRUST, RESPECT AND LOVE should be our guiding decorum, not because we will be bind by sacred matrimony, but because we are OPEN AND HONEST to each other, and there is joy in every meaningful day of being together, sharing day to day life conforming to the cosmic glory of the universe, nothing to fear and ashamed of, for hand in hand we will cross the bridge across forever, we will weather our way through ups and downs, helping each other when someone is down and broken, cheering and encouraging one another to lighten up life, yes, that is the DELIGHTS OF OUR HEART, that is all our relationship is all about" Goddess Nakki whispering to herself

Goddess Nakki then stand up, and in all her curvaceous Goddess nakedness, their room soon radiates and became like a nebulae absorbing all the cosmic colors, Goddess Nakki effortless stride to where God Anuk is in the terrace overlooking the Nibiru's enormous colonies. "I must soothe his heart" she told herself

Just as about Goddess Nakki will pass the door to veranda, God Anuk turned around upon noticing the radiating lights coming from their room, and when he turned around, alas and behold, in his eyes the most beautiful creature in all universe, standing just by the door, in all her scintillating naked glory, ravishing and so alluring, the GODDESS OF ALL BEAUTY, there in her Goddess nakedness standing and both arms stretching, inviting him to embrace and cuddle her, all smiles with glee, as if heaven had open it's door, God Anuk in all the delights of what he is seeing of Goddess Nakki, abruptly forget all his worries and anxiety, and his loins instantly was filled with desire.

"Oh beloved Goddess Nakki, I didn't know you are already awake, I am lost in my pondering, forgive me oh beloved that I leave you alone sleeping, while am here in veranda contemplating" said God Anuk to Goddess Nakki while he walk towards her extending his both arms as well, his Godly muscular built naked body striding with so much arousal and energy.

"Oh my God Anuk, the delights of my heart, I've been watching you for the last minutes, and your deep pondering concerns me" replied Goddess Nakki who's eye longingly transfixed to God Anuk's naked body and manhood, and she stride fast to meet the warmth embrace of God Anuk in the veranda.

God Anuk cuddle gently Goddess Nakki in his Godly arms, the head of Goddess Nakki resting at the muscular chest of God Anuk while she as well embrace so tight her beloved "Oh my God Anuk, my dearest, my love, please tell me what is it that bothering you so much, your actions betrays your thoughts, please my dearest, please enlighten me" Goddess Nakki lovingly pleading to God Anuk.

God Anuk moved his right hand to caress the back-head of Goddess Nakki and run his fingers to the long smooth golden-white hair of his beloved, while his left hand wrap-around Goddess Nakki's curvaceous naked body just above her buttocks, implanting sweet caresses sending shocks of waves after waves of million sensation inside Goddess Nakki's emotions, as if delaying himself to answer what her beloved yearns to know, He thinks lightning fast and searched his functioning mind what to tell Goddess Nakki.

And while they are both lost in their own world of thinking, a sudden surge of sensation was felt by Goddess Nakki in the warmth embrace of God Anuk, she felt the Godly manhood of God Anuk was totally arouse and hardened, as if it's alive and searching deep beneath in-between her legs, she can't withstand this sweet temptation from her beloved, she must have him inside or she will be scorched with desire.

God Anuk found enchantment in his heart and mind, for right in-there in the palace terrace of their room atop the rugged hills overlooking the awesome view of their colonies and dominion, he's desire for his beloved came to life and felt so intense heat and immense sensation just embracing Goddess Nakki, all their worries soon forgotten as he began to kiss fervently Goddess Nakki with all love's desire he could empower, and Goddess Nakki response with such delight and pleasure in her heart, they kissed tongue-tied with million bolts, caressing each other, touching their intimate parts, yearning and panting for more pleasure their love could offer and bring, murmuring sweet words of loving, and when Goddess Nakki couldn't stand any longer the heat and passion inside her, she runs to the edge of the veranda and bend her oozing rear majestically for God Anuk to see all her inviting and gaping glory, God Anuk strides fast to catch his beloved, like a Knight in a Shining Armor charging, his Godly manhood so aroused like a spear of steel, poised and ready to enter the scabbard of love, the depths of innermost passion and ecstasy, and when they finally convene as one, a gasp of cosmic sigh escape Goddess Nakki's breath, joy, bliss, rapture, heavenly lust explodes in harmony of ecstasy, God Anuk trembles in sheer delight of passionate love-making with his one and only beloved Goddess Nakki who is also panting in cosmic rapture, for they both know, SEX with LOVE is the sweetest of them all.

No words came out of their mouth as they rest standing in the edge of the terrace, still entwine as one, savoring the sweetness of their love-making, as if their mind in unison talking silently in the stillness of the galactic night, understanding each other's thoughts, not spoiling the romantic ambience they both created, their naked Godliness interlace as one cosmic powerful energy of radiating lights of different galactic and universal colors, that can be seen miles and miles away, lighting with intense radiance their balcony.

After a while, their passion subsides and the colorful lights emitting from their entwine bodies begins to faint and dim, God Anuk standing at the back of Goddess Nakki, lovingly whispered "I LOVE YOU" in Goddess Nakki's ears, as he gently pull-out his godly manhood from Goddess Nakki's rear vagina entry.

"THANK YOU FOR LOVING ME" Goddess Nakki whispered back to God Anuk, and as she turned around to face her beloved, God Anuk noticed there's a TEARS OF JOY streaming down on Goddess Nakki's cheeks, He licked the tears and embraced so tightly his beloved Goddess Nakki, "I WILL BE YOURS FOREVER, UNTIL ETERNITY" he whispered back

Goddess Nakki remove herself from God Anuk's embrace and walk towards the center of the veranda, her eyes glaring at God Anuk eyes as if questioning, and then speak firmly with-out kindness.

"Now tell me God Anuk, what is it that you are hiding from me, enough of these enchanting words and sweet endearing you're showing me, I want you to be honest with me, your actions betrays your emotions, tell me the truth, don't lie, or I will never be the Goddess Nakki you want me to be, or this dying Planet Nibiru wants to be" Goddess Nakki suddenly voiced out to God Anuk

God Anuk was astounded of what he had just heard from Goddess Nakki, all the sweetness was gone, but a Goddess ruler asserting her power of dominion. He must have to conceal everything and yet, now his beloved is asking truthful answers. God Anuk gazed back at Goddess Nakki with intense feelings, he is now ready to spill out everything, "This the right time", he muttered to himself, for he knows time is ticking fast and that their grand sacred wedding moment is just hours away.

"My Goddess Nakki, my ever fairest, accept my deepest apology if I have cause you such dilemma up to this point, as you know, I will never lie to you nor be dishonest with you, but the past weeks brought so much tense and stress in my heart and mind, not that because of our in-coming grand sacred union, but because of disturbing thoughts and information I came to know concerning the future of our Planet Nibiru, and of that Blue Planet Earth, which directly affects us, especially you oh my dearest Goddess, being the sole ruler of our planet after our grand sacred wedding. I tried to contain such information's and contemplated in my reasoning mind what actions I must do, for I fear of your safety more than ever, after I have solve in my mind this great puzzle of information I came to know and understand" God Anuk amicably spoken to Goddess Nakki

Goddess Nakki on hearing what God Anuk had just spoken tone herself down; search her heart of what fine words to utter back to God Anuk.

"Oh my God Anuk, tell me then the secrets of your heart, your fears, that I may come to know and understand what is on your mind, there and then perhaps I could help, and, together we will battle our way out of this dilemma, and we will find solutions to appease our hearts and mind, to feed answers to my curiosity, and stop this doubts in my heart, please enlighten me then" She answered back

"I had came to know of a vital information through my childhood best friend, Supreme General Jhesusan, the Grand Supreme General of Tactical Armada Central Command of impending attack to Blue Planet Earth by our Legionnaires, in-fact, two Battalions of Legionnaires under Commander Machiavelli and Commander Marlonus were already sent well in advance and establish an advance contingency command operation and spying activity on Blue Planet Earth, and established a fortress called FORT MOON in the Southern Hemisphere of the Blue Planet Earth's moon awaiting that TOP SECRET SPECIAL ORDER for them to commence their mission of attack." God Anuk began explaining to Goddess Nakki, and continued narrating.

"They were sent in MILKY WAY GALAXY, the home galaxy of Blue Planet Earth, aboard the thousand years old spy-satellite of our own Planet called BLACK KNIGHT through the galactic worm holes, under the full authorization of SUPREME GENERAL KRISHNAN, HEAD OF UNIFIED HIGH COMMAND OF UNIVERSAL GALACTIC DEFENSE SCIENTIFIC ENERGY SUPPLY CENTRAL COMMAND and SUPREME GENERAL BHUDASIAN, HEAD OF UNIFIED HIGH COMMAND OF UNIVERSAL GALACTIC DEFENSE ADVANCE SCIENTIFIC RESEARCH CENTRAL COMMAND, with the full knowledge and backing of some of THE ELDERS."

God Anuk paused for a second, making sure that Goddess Nakki is attentive and following all what he is narrating because he don't want to repeat all over again what He is explaining for fear that the Intelligence Command will pick up their conversation, and will endanger them, especially his beloved, Goddess Nakki.

Goddess Nakki, petrified of what she is hearing from God Anuk, couldn't say a word, her eyes gazing God Anuk's eyes with tearful look, she's lost for words, in her heart and mind are thousand words she could ask to God Anuk, but she remain composed, and calmly gesture to God Anuk to continue narrating.

"Apparently until now, no one knows who is the MASTER MIND of this entire plot among the ELDERS, and ultimately who will give the full authorization and final order of the attack, even the UNIFIED HIGH COMMAND OF UNIVERSAL GALACTIC DEFENSE CENTRAL COMMAND organization leaders are at lost, as if there is a GALACTIC CONSPIRANCY going on and that nobody wants to talk about, as if the SUPREME GENERALS are just passing time waiting for that day to happen, and when it does come, there, they will cross the bridge and decide which way they choose to fight, perhaps become ally, but for now, they are playing the cards with utmost caution, secrecy and plasticity so as not to determine which enemy is which." God Anuk continued explaining.

"This is all absurdity" Goddess Nakki shouted back, her anger brewing because of what she's hearing from God Anuk, why was she kept out and not informed of this Galactic Conspiracy Theory.

"I could not understand perfectly well that in my stature as a Goddess and in-coming ruler of this Planet Nibiru was not well-inform, worse keep at bay by THE ELDERS" Goddess Nakki continued whining and questioning God Anuk

"Now tell me my God Anuk, what is it that you came to know and understand out of all this information that I may fully understand the scope and severity of this conspiracy, that I may punish those entity who dare to create trouble in my dominion" Goddess Nakki added

God Anuk perplexed of Goddess Nakki's questions and statements replied back "Oh my Goddess Nakki, don't be so naïve, all they are waiting is your anger to explode, that will be the enemies cue to reveal them-selves, and I reckon they will make public of their diabolical plans during our grand union."

Upon hearing of what God Anuk had just said, Goddess Nakki wants to explode all her anger and confront THE ELDERS at once, and settle once and for all this dilemma before the grand sacred wedding, she doesn't want lies and being fooled by the ELDERS, she is fuming mad that her body power energy is slowly building up, as can be seen like her body is on fire, luminous smoke coming out of her body, as if readying herself for a confrontation with the ELDERS.

God Anuk upon sensing of what is happening and of Goddess Nakki transforming, dash to where Goddess Nakki standing in and embrace her again, comforting and pacifying her anger, "My Goddess Nakki, calm down, don't rush and be a fool, listen to me first before we take actions, or we will end up losers, and prisoners of our own mistakes, I had a counter-plan, please hear me first oh my Goddess, before anything else, that we may become totally as one by our grand union and sacred wedding, that we may fight them both with advantage, there is a right time, a proper time to let all out our anger, don't waste your energy my Goddess, you will need it more during our sacred wedding, there, is the battle my dearest, for now keep calm, gather your composure and tranquility, please TRUST me oh my Goddess, my love, my eternity " God Anuk calmly spoken to Goddess Nakki

Goddess Nakki upon hearing God Anuk's words of wisdom, and feeling the sincerity of her beloved, calm herself down, embrace back God Anuk, look into his eyes deeply and asked "What should we do then my love, my God Anuk?" then proceeded to convinced God Anuk

"Here I am ready to confront them, and unleash my anger and power, yet you speak of wisdom my Most Gracious, my God Anuk, truly you are the ONE for me, I will heed to your advice but enlighten me more before our grand sacred wedding come so that I may fully prepare myself of this impending confrontation with THE ELDERS, I don't like to go there a fool, and not knowing everything, that I could not defend every words I will throw at them, I need everything, I need every information you know and understand, that I may speak with lucidity infront of our LEGIONNAIRES AND OUR SUBJECTS, and of THE ELDERS, so that I will know WHEN and WHERE I will unleash this great energy of anger building inside my body, there and then they will see who I am and what I AM capable of, I AM GODDESS NAKKI, DAUGHTER OF PLANET NIBIRU, ROYAL BLOOD AND DESCENDANT OF LORD GOD ADANIS" Goddess Nakki retorted back to God Anuk as if taunting and warning him.

"Oh Goddess Nakki, surely your time will come, and I will be at your side as ever, supporting whatever decisions you will make, I will be at your disposal, and your wish my sole command" God Anuk consoling Goddess Nakki

"…so listen to me very carefully, chew in your mind what will I have to say this very moment because I don't want to repeat it again, I know there are eyes watching us now, perhaps, trying to comprehend what we are arguing with, one thing I know for sure, our room is not bug with their advance technologies and spy-gadgets, we are safe from their eaves-dropping, but whatever I will divulge to you now, I will say it only once, so please my dearest, pay attention very closely, understand every words I will have to say, for in here comes your decision making, THE GREAT WISDOM of your great entity to save yourself, and fight back with all your might and power, for in your sanctity beholds the SALVATION OF OUR PLANET NIBIRU, AND THE SALVATION OF THAT BLUE PLANET EARTH" Goddess Anuk speaking as if THE END is coming, and that whatever the future holds back will make them apart, and with so much uncertainty.

"Please God Anuk, speak no more but come to the point, enlighten me now, please tell me everything, I am calm and ready to absorb everything you will say, please don't delay no more, my heart and mind is open, I am wide awake" Goddess Nakki assuring God Anuk that she is paying attention, yet in her heart is restlessness for she knows as well how God Anuk spoke, as if there is so much danger going on that put her beloved edgy and secretive, as if there is uncertain tomorrow yet to come, and that they will be separated for a long time, and in her heart she spoke, "I WILL FIGHT BACK WITH ALL MY MIGHT AND POWER FOR US, FOR OUR LOVE, AND FOR OUR PLANET NIBIRU, I WILL NEVER GIVE-IN TO OUR ENEMIES PLAN."

God Anuk continued his unfolding, "Please forgive me oh my Goddess Nakki for withholding from you these vital and sensitive issues and information, I was so concerned with your safety, you know very well how much I love you, and I will do everything in my own power to protect you from these scrupulous entity, with their self-driving lust for power and own agenda, until now they are masquerading with their godly deeds, concealing their true heart's purpose…" God Anuk paused again for a while as if searching for the right words to utter.

"Oh my Goddess, it's not only Blue Planet Earth's minerals and energy supply THE ELDERS wants, there is much more complex reasons and hidden agenda they had been planning-on eon of times, our dying Planet's problem of energy shortage was indirectly connected to this well planned agenda of the ELDERS, it's one of their alibi so that we will go back to Earth, and mine again for the Earth's wealth of energy, THE ELDERS had deliberately cause not to plan for the future's energy consumption, because they are awaiting for the Planet Nibiru to consume all its energy source, and then voted and conform to go back to Blue Planet Earth, yes for the energy source on lighter side, but, at the back of their mind is another or second agenda which they keep secret." God Anuk continued explaining.

Goddess Nakki was at lost for words, she couldn't believe what was she hearing from God Anuk, her mind is spinning round with anger, revolt, compassion, fear and justice, but she let God Anuk continued with his stories and narration, "Tell me more, WHAT IS IT THE ELDERS WANT?" she mumbled as she removed herself from God Anuk's embraced and walk towards inside the bedroom hand in hand with God Anuk tugging him along with her.

"Oh Goddess Nakki, some of THE ELDERS are direct descendants of the first Nibirunians who came and visited Blue Planet Earth eon of times ago, legends and according to the Book of Time, our ancestors were defeated in the 1st Galactic War and were driven out into galactic universe like a cowering vagabond by the HUMANOIDS, the intelligent living creatures of the Blue Planet Earth, with the help and assistance of the DEMIGODS, under the influence and leadership of Supreme Commander Lucifer and what happen during that era of time, I couldn't comprehend well for now, but one thing I do know and understand right now is that, THE ELDERS wants to go back to Blue Planet Earth to exact REVENGE upon the Blue Planet Earths inhabitants and hunt down to kill the DEMIGODS who helped the Humanoids during that time, for as per INTELLIGENCE INFORMATION gathered by our advance forces, under Commander Marlonus, Commander of the Spy-space-craft Black Knight, the DEMIGODS are still alive and hiding from Blue Planet Earth's vast oceans, mountain caves and caverns, lakes, and

PLANET NIBIRU'S SUPREME COMMANDER LUCIFER

even inside the volcanoes, the DEMIGODS are roaming Blue Planet Earth like Gods of their own, and had built advance cities underwater to hide from the HUMANOIDS who turns out to be much more intelligent than expected, and with advancing knowledge of human's civilization after eon of years, it seems that they had perfected well the ART OF WAR as per Intelligence Report of our spies occupying Fort Moon…" God Anuk then go on narrating while Goddess Nakki positioned herself sitting by the bedside, while God Anuk lay down on the other side of the bed-capsule, looking at the galactic skies through the luminous electronic shield

"My Goddess Nakki, some of THE ELDERS wants REVENGE, and avenge our Planet's loss to the humanoids, THEY WANT VENGEANCE and the ultimate destruction of HUMAN CIVILIZATION, for they could not forget that dark era of time recorded in our history which they, THE ELDERS, tried to conceal from the young generations of Nibirunians, such as YOU, my dearest... They couldn't forget how the humans defeated our ancestors, with so little wisdom and knowledge, and they couldn't forget what SUPREME COMMANDER LUCIFER DID, the DEMIGOD LEADER who disrupt and destroy the peace and harmony of that eon of time when that Blue Planet Earth is under the hand and control of our ancestors, under the Leadership of the FATHER OF YOUR FATHER ABRAHAMUS, THE LATE GREAT LORD GOD ADANIS."

Goddess Nakki was so mystified of what she was learning from God Anuk, she felt so naive and depraved of all these secret information's, she knows now how burdensome all this DILEMMA that was unfolding on the heart and mind of her beloved God Anuk, she now understand why her beloved kept her away of all these troubles, so as not to keep her under stress and anxieties, in her heart was grief, yet a sense of pride for her beloved God Anuk for his actions only shows how much He really love her, he really wanted to protect her from all these dreadful DILEMMA.

"What shall we do then?" asked Goddess Nakki and proceeded to add "… if we're going to announce our grand ultimate plan of GALACTIC PEACE AND INTER-PLANETARY CO-EXISTENCE during our grand sacred wedding which based from what you had said my God Anuk, that some of THE ELDERS wouldn't want and agreed upon, then they are just waiting for their right time as well to reveal who really they are, who really the enemies are, and they are waiting for that final hour of our grand wedding merriment when every SUBJECTS are active in the state of enjoyment and celebration, making love to one another in state of cosmic bliss, there they will unleash their grand plan of taking over our Kingdom, a COUP D'ETAT will take place, a perfect timing for their great plan…" Goddess Nakki analyzing the situation at the same time giving God Anuk time to think and consider what will be their next actions and decision to make.

Goddess Nakki continued speaking with her excruciating gazed fixed at God Anuk's eyes "…and yet here we are my God Anuk, discussing all these possibilities, we have the ACE OF FATE in our hands, we know what they up to, it's up for us how we will counter-attack them, let us make a plan that will trap these fools to their condemnation and be damned eternally frozen in the abyss of the universe…"

God Anuk felt a chilling fear in his Godly being, for here is her Goddess Nakki, speaking of unreasonable plans against the SUPER-GODS of their planet, THE ELDERS, and lucky her for which he knows, Goddess Nakki was only thinking and planning, and not yet of actual deliberation of her heart's desire, for if it is so, she must have transform herself into ugly and demonic monster, and as per Nibiru's UNIVERSAL DECREE COMMAND and DEGREE OF BALANCE REASONING, she had condemned herself to frozen eternal death, and yet he felt relieve because he knows, Goddess Nakki will not be that stupid to do so, and He is there to prevent it from happening, in his heart, yes, they will devise such plans but with his own scheme and planning so as to avert disaster and catastrophic confrontations, that may endanger the life of his beloved Goddess Nakki, and the life of their SUBJECTS, the Nibirunians.

"Oh Goddess Nakki, my ever dearest, be rational and logical enough, we know what they up to, but we know not who they really are, so let us not make hasty decisions that may endanger our life, much more our Subjects, it is of our prerogative to seek peaceful resolution as always, we should consider all the possibilities, the pros and cons of our actions" God Anuk said back to Goddess Nakki, and continued speaking "…and yet the question that hangs on my mind is, WHO ARE THE ENEMIES OF ENEMIES?..." and look to Goddess Nakki as if waiting for her to suggest names, or perhaps name names she knows are antagonistic to their plans of UNIVERSAL PEACE AND INTER-PLANETARY CO-EXISTENCE.

Goddess Nakki think very carefully of this important question for she knows this is where the battle should begin, to know their allies and who their enemies are. She then one by one mention to God Anuk the possibilities of which is which and who's on their side and their enemy, while she lay down on the bed and positioned herself beside God Anuk, her head resting on God's Anuk's muscular chest.

"...among the five Supreme Generals..." Goddess Nakki started "...for sure, Supreme General Jhesusan, Head of Tactical Armada Central Command and Supreme General Sun Rah, Head of Planet Nibiru Palace Security Central Command will be on our side, then, Supreme General Bhudasian, Head of Advance Scientific Research Central Command and Supreme General Krishnan, Head of Scientific Energy Supply Central Command would be on our enemies side because of obvious reasons that they are direct descendants of the first Nibirunians who visited Blue Planet Earth..."

Goddess Nakki pause for a while, she then continued with a question to God Anuk "...How about Supreme General Ahllakdan, Head of Advance Energy Weaponry Central Command, do you have any idea which side he will go to and defend, He is of such important stature for He commands the supply of weaponry..."

God Anuk replied "...yes, Supreme General Ahllakdan is of important persona, He is a vital entity because He has the power and the supply of our advance weaponry, yet, I am lost to which side He should defend with, all I know is that, He is an official of good standing and records, no bias in his judgmental reasoning as I observed, but then again the question is, "WHICH SIDE HE IS?..."

Goddess Nakki added "...then if we don't know which side he is, then we are at stalemate, and for that we should summon him at once and talk to him, get his inner feelings and assess his judgment, from there we could decide THE FATE and our cards..."

"...it's too late for that my dearest, my Goddess Nakki, it's noon-night now, another quarter of day and it's the beginning of the celebration of our grand sacred wedding, of our grand union, there is no time anymore my dearest but to prepare ourselves, especially YOURSELF my DEAR GOD, for tomorrow brings so much excitement and joy, and yet, along with it are surprises of sorrow and loneliness..." Goddess Anuk spoke as if He already knows what is going to happen, and emphasize in his speaking of Goddess Nakki's importance to prepare herself.

"…oh my God Anuk, my body wants to rest, and yet, my mind is restless with all these happenings, and of tomorrow that will come during our grand sacred wedding, there are a lot of things I am thinking about, of all the prejudice that might happen, if FATE will allow it so, if FATE will allow THE ELDERS of their evil plans…" Goddess Nakki answered back

"…take a rest now my beloved, sleep now, gather and charge your energy for tomorrow is another day to tackle with, whatever future would brought and offer, in joy and happiness, even in worse to come, always remember in your heart and mind, I AM YOURS FOREVER, UNTIL ETERNITY…YOU WILL ALWAYS BE MY ONE AND ONLY GODDESS, MY GOD…" God Anuk whispered and assuring Goddess Nakki, betraying his emotions with his tearful eyes

Goddess Nakki raise her head and look straight into the eyes of God Anuk, she felt his heartbeat beating fast as if all the worries, fears and uncertainties finally came to merge waiting to explode.

"…oh my love, my dearest, don't speak like that as if it's THE END, don't make my heart cry or I will shed tears now and then, be strong for me my God Anuk, I know you will do, if tomorrow comes with surprise, then I promise you my God Anuk, whatever will happen, whatever FATE will dictate, I WILL FIGHT THEM WITH ALL MY POWER AND MIGHT, and it will NOT BE THE END OF THE BEGINNING…I PROMISE YOU…MY LOVE, MY GOD ANUK…" Goddess Nakki spoke back to God Anuk, her eyes swelling with tears as well "…if it's tomorrows THE END then IT'S ONLY THE BEGINNING…I promise you my dearest…" and she rested her head again in God Anuk's muscular chest hiding the building up of tears in her eyes which she knows will soon stream down her goddess face, but this time wrapping around tightly her arms to God Anuk's torso as if it will be their last together.

God Anuk was speechless, for he himself can't contain his emotions, if he ever utter a single word that precise moment he knows Goddess Nakki is in anguish, for sure they will both cry out their emotions, he knows they are both in anguish, and only their hearts for that moment are talking silently, consoling each other, tomorrow is not the end, he has his plans, he assured himself. And they both fall asleep embracing each other, their hearts filled with ambiguity.

"YESTERNIGHT GOODBYE"

By MonaC

(POETIC BREEZE, POETIC FROTH PART 1 – POEM NO. 169)

Twilight exploding its glory
greeting YESTERNIGHT GOODBYE
colourful years of existence
doesn't know what's happening

In the edge of the night
everything's choke up enough
eye's blinking and tired
mind's abused and confused

Thoughtless thoughts needs answers
all around wearily worn out
time has eaten time slowly
colours vanishing away in tears

Shattering what dreams to come
what's this all about
somebody enlighten someone
speak enough, loosen up

Today lives because of yesterday
arise, continue the journey
awake from that slumber
don't wait to come

When time swallow's time
until then forget everything
sleep not, until your end
chew all this in mind
Greet yester-night goodbye then!

* * *

"READ THE VOIDS THAT FILLS THE ROOM
EACH CRAVING FOR THE TRUTH
FAR AHEAD IT FLIES TOGETHER
FILL EACH GAP AND DON'T SURRENDER"

* * *

* * * THE 2ND COMING * * *

*** CHAPTER – 3 ***

THE WEDDING

God Anuk was so exhausted when he lay down his body in the bed-capsule, his teary eyes after a lengthy discussion with his beloved Goddess Nakki wants to explode with tears for He knows time is ticking fast and fate surely will bring surprises of happiness and loneliness, yet again He suppress his feelings, He wants to show Goddess Nakki how to be strong and not be broken down, he wants that both of them should be steadfast and would stand firm strong for each other, for He knows in his heart it will come to pass that Goddess Nakki and him will be apart for a long time because he sees and understand what fate is dictating to unfold during THE WEDDING, and whatever that will happen, He must have to abide by his plans whatever the consequences, even if it will cause their parting, in his heart and mind, there is a divine purpose of why all these troubles are coming, and that Goddess Nakki and him are a part of this Universal Galactic qualms for which He knows they will play an important roles for the Salvation of their Planet Nibiru, perhaps even the Salvation of Blue Planet Earth. EVERYTHING HAPPENS FOR A REASON, He muse.

In his solitude, He heard a faint voice speaking as if uttering a question. He opens his eyes and search where the faint voice was coming from. He saw a door slightly open with radiant lights coming out from inside. He walk down the door and slowly open it, there again he heard the voice speaking as if asking a question, for him, the voice sounds familiar, that he had already heard that voice in his lifetime, he knows for sure that the voice is coming from the Royal Palace SHAMAN.

Again, the SHAMAN voice speak asking a question, yet this time he can hear loudly what the question is, and he was terrified of what question he had heard, for how it can be a SHAMAN would ask such question. He open the door widely and entered the room, and he was amazed of what he sees, an oceans of Nibirunians shouting and cheering, as if celebrating, yet he can't hear any sounds of happiness, as if the air is muted and the only sound he can hear was coming from the SHAMAN. He explore the room with his vision, trying to locate where the Shaman is, and then again he was shocked by what he sees, there at the end of the hallway coming from the door he entered are groom and bride kneeling in-front of the Shaman being bless like in a sacred wedding. He looks around to really comprehend what's happening, yet it seems like everybody is in oblivion, not caring of who is around, all their eyes transfixed to the couple being married.

He wanted to shout, but no voice is coming out from his mouth, as if he's voice dried out because of what he is witnessing, He had recognized that the Bride was no other than his beloved, Goddess Nakki but couldn't distinguished the Groom, He wanted to shout and call the name of his beloved Goddess Nakki, but nothing is coming out of his voice, and then again, He heard the SHAMAN voice, speaking in question, but this time is so loud in a thundering voice asking, "IS THERE ANYONE OF YOU AGAINST IN THIS GALACTIC SACRED MATRIMONY?"

He told himself "…such a stupid question?... for why will a Shaman ask such insane question in the middle of a wedding ceremony when the couple being married knows in their heart they loved each other, otherwise they will not be in that moment, it's already been decided and planned that these two couple loved each other and that's why they are being married, to forge allegiance to each other and become one in unison with their future, and as customary law in their Planet Nibiru, the ultimate submission of man's dominion and power to his bride to be, and that the groom after the wedding had pledge his life for his beloved, and that he will become the protector of his wife, and he no longer can love any other being, for which he knows wholeheartedly the consequences, as what happened to Goddess Nakki's father, who was condemned to die frozen in the abyss of the galactic universe. He will be loyal to his wife for eternity, and that's the essence of a Nibirunian wedding he thoughtfully knows in his heart.

Then again, he heard the Shaman's thundering voice asking same the question, "...IS THERE ANYONE OF YOU AGAINST IN THIS GALACTIC SACRED MATRIMONY?"

He can feel his heart beating rapidly for how could this be, he told himself, how could this thing happening, "...AM I THE GROOM?..." he muttered to himself, and yet he asked himself, "...WHO IS THE GROOM BESIDE MY EVERDEAREST GODDESS NAKKI..." he wanted to shout, there is anger boiling in all his nerves, in his mind are words of treachery and betrayal, how could Goddess Nakki done this, he shouted to himself.

He run fast to the front altar where the groom and bride is, and when he reach the middle of the aisle, he stopped, and all who were there witnessing the wedding suddenly turned their head and glare at him as if questioning him "WHERE HAVE YOU BEEN?", he was so stunned of what's happening, he tried to shout again, calling the name of her beloved, but no sound was coming out of his voice, he was so frustrated he wanted to run havoc and disrupt the wedding, he continued approaching the altar yet this time slowly walking, carefully looking around, trying to sense out what is really going on, and then in one moment of time he was greatly puzzled for he noticed that all the scattered different flower petals that lingers the path are colored BLACK, the blackest black he could ever imagined. He paused again, and question him-self, "...How can it be that a joyful day of wedding will have a shower of flowers petals with such colors of GRIEF and SORROW?" Again, the Shaman voice echoed in the hall with the same thundering question, "...IS THERE ANYONE OF YOU AGAINST IN THIS GALACTIC SACRED MATRIMONY?"

And that's when he understand why he was there, why such question are being ask again and again before proclaiming a couple fully wed and sanctified with sacred ceremony, in his heart the wedding taking place is not meant to be, for he reckon there is anguish and grief because of the black flowers petals he saw scattered, he deeply feels that the bride must be in anguish, and that the wedding taking place is against her will for he knows that the bride who is Goddess Nakki will love no other Nibirunians but only him,...and that's when he grasp in his reasoning mind why a Shaman would ask such terrible question if there is somebody who is against the on-going sacred wedding ceremony, it is to make sure that both couples being married are not in a bondage of forbidden love, that there is no other third party who will wreck the marriage in the future, that there will be no alibis and excuses for such marriage to fail and end up in a mess of separation, it is to protect and uphold the sanctity of matrimony, and with those reasons, now he has fully comprehend that he was there to stop the wedding, he's fate leads him there to fight for his undying love to his one and only beloved Goddess Nakki, for in love, there is no greater fight than to fight for your love one, whatever the consequences it will bring, even if it will cause his life, he must have to prove his worthiness, in his heart and mind, TO LOVE IS THE BEDROCK OF ONE'S EXISTENCE, to fight for the one he love the most, to prove his love and affection to Goddess Nakki until his last breath, even if He has to die, even his DEATH WILL HONOR HIS LOVE TO GODDESS NAKKI FOR ETERNITY.

He continued walking the aisle towards the altar where the couple being wed is, and when the Shaman again repeat for the last time his question in a thundering voice, he shouted back on top of his lungs "…I AM AGAINST OF THIS WEDDING…I AM GOD ANUK, AND I AM AGAINST OF THIS WEDDING…I AM HERE TO FIGHT AND CLAIM MY ETERNAL LOVE AND AFFECTION TO MY ONE AND ONLY, MY EVER DEAREST, GODDESS NAKKI…" his voice reverberated in every corner of the chamber

And all of a sudden there was cheers in the hall, as if all the Nibirunians came to life, as if they have waited for a Knight in Shining Armor to rescue their Goddess Nakki from the anguish and sorrow of Galactic Matrimony, there was applause everywhere and such jubilation, and in his heart he felt immense pleasure and satisfaction when he saw Goddess Nakki turned around, tears streaming down her face, not of anguish and grief, but TEARS OF JOY, he stretched his both arms towards Goddess Nakki at the same time dashing towards her, he had come to rescue his beloved, and he couldn't avoid any longer, he too felt his tears streaming down his face, HIS LOVE FOR ALL INFINITY BATTLED IT'S WAY INTO THE HEART OF HIS BELOVED.

And when they embraced and held each other in their loving arms, they were carried away by their emotions that they couldn't stop crying, as if there is a universal rain of glittering colors, pouring out from above, and when the rain subsides, he took Goddess Nakki holding tightly but gently her hand going to the door where he entered, and as they walked together hand in hand in the aisle, he saw that the Nibirunians are cheering wildly and all the scattered petals of different flowers came to life of their own colors, all the flowers he could think of, Lily, Dandelion, Orchid, Poppy, Marigold, Geranium, Tulip, Jasmine, Lavender, a fragrance all together as ONE FLOWER OF UNIVERSE, a perfume of his Godly desire, he walked a Godly walk with head held high as if he had conquered the universe, in his arms the most beautiful and beguiling Goddess of the Universe, Goddess Nakki.

In that state of the moment, he thought, he would take a look one last glance of who was the GROOM in the altar, for it's very important for him to know his nemesis in the heart of his one and only beloved Goddess Nakki, for him to know who is worthy of his adversary, and when he turn his head to take a glimpse of the face of the groom, he saw a radiating light and felt an extreme energy of acid heat burning his face coming from the face of the groom, like a roaring Dragon spewing un-imaginable acid fire, consuming him, and he shouted in pain, and his heart was filled with terror and fear not for his safety, but for his beloved, Goddess Nakki. He shouted in pain, and shouted again and again, "…run my Goddess, run, save yourself, run my love, run…" and he shouted one last cry "…RUN, MY EVERDEAREST, RUNNNNNN…."

It was the last cry he could remember, he felt so exhausted, and he opened his eyes, so strange he mumbled, then again closed his eyes as if he's not believing, it's all pitch blackness, and then again, he opened his eyes, this time he's sure, he felt so happy within, he reach out and felt Goddess Nakki sleeping lovingly beside him, HE WAS JUST DREAMING.

* * *

"… FOR IT WAS A DREAM YOU CAME
BEWITCHING IN A GLOOMY NIGHT
FULL OF FRAGRANCE AND PULCHRITUDE
AN ALLURING GODDESS OF INFINITY …"

* * *

PLANET NIBIRU'S THRONE SCEPTER

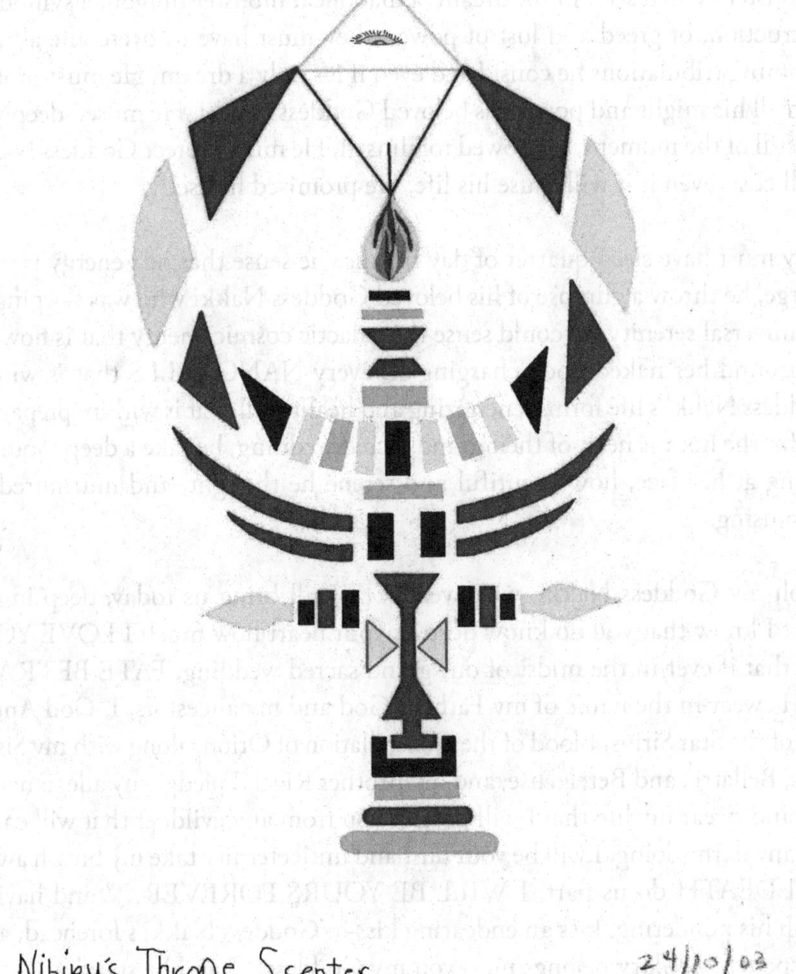

God Anuk put a smile on his face, a delight in his heart, he felt so relieve knowing he was only dreaming, yet again, in his mind are worries, could it be THE DREAM a premonition of what yet to come during their wedding, what a monster he had seen in his dream, a diabolical monster dragon, a symbol of destruction, of greed and lust of power, they must have to overcome all this incoming tribulations he considered even if it's only a dream, He must protect with all his might and power his beloved Goddess Nakki. He mused deeply in the still of the moment, He vowed to himself, He must protect Goddess Nakki at all cost, even if it will cause his life, He promised himself!

They must have sleep quarter of day because he sense that he's energy is fully charge, he throw a glimpse of his beloved Goddess Nakki who was sleeping in all universal serenity, he could sense the galactic cosmic energy that is flowing on around her naked body charging all every NANOCELLS that is within Goddess Nakki's life forms, energizing and healing all that is within, preparing her for the hour is near, of their grand sacred wedding, he take a deep moment gazing at her face, how beautiful and serene he thought, and murmured in his musing.

"...oh my Goddess Nakki, whatever FATE will bring us today, deep in my heart I know that you do know deep in your heart how much I LOVE YOU, and that if ever in the midst of our grand sacred wedding, FATE BETRAYS US, I swear in the name of my Father's God and my ancestors, I, God Anuk, Son of the Star Sirius, Blood of the Constellation of Orion, along with my Sister stars, Bellatrix and Betelgeuse, and my Brother Rigel, I pledge my allegiance to you and swear my life that I will protect you from any evildoer that will cause you any harm-doing, I will be your husband until eternity take my breath away, until DEATH do us part, I WILL BE YOURS FOREVER..." and having finish his pondering, kiss an endearing kiss in Goddess Nakki's forehead, and whispered "...Glory belongs unto you my Goddess..." and he stand up.

Goddess Nakki in her deep slumber felt the warmth kiss and breathe of God Anuk, that awaken her being, she too felt the energizing galactic cosmic energy flowing around her body charging her NANOCELLS, and in her sleepy mind, she's happy because she needs all the cosmic energy she could charge her body, for this is the day she thought, this is the day she will commit herself to God Anuk, her LOVE OF A LIFETIME, and whatever will happen, she knows deep inside her Goddess being, she must have to be strong not only for her beloved, God Anuk, but also for the love of her Subjects, The Nibirunians

Unigalitizines, this is the day she will become THE GODDESS OF ALL UNIVERSE, THE SOLE RULER OF PLANET NIBIRU, and she will not disappoint them, The Nibirunians, especially her beloved, God Anuk, she must have to prove she's worthy of the Galactic Kingdom, she must have to prove on her Father's name, the late Lord God Abrahamus, and reclaim their lost dignity, and to redeem her ancestors glory. She will show to THE ELDERS she's worthy of the The Nibiru's Universal Galactic Throne, and in her awakening, she told her-self "…I WILL ABIDE BY OUR ANCESTORS CODE AND LEGACY, I WILL RULE FAIR AND JUST, WITH IRON HAND BUT OF GRACE AND MERCY, THERE WILL BE UNIVERSAL PEACE IN ALL GALAXIES, LOVE OF LIFE IN ALL UNIVERSE WILL PREVAIL…"

Goddess Nakki then slowly opened her eyes and she was greeted by CHERUBS and SERAPHIMS flying around their room, playing music of celestial melodious melancholy as if signifying the long day of merriment, the coming of her grand sacred wedding to God Anuk, they were playing with their harps, trumpets, tambourines, and various kinds of musical instruments that brought Goddess Nakki fully awake. She's enjoying THE SOUND OF MUSIC she's hearing from the cherubs and seraphs playing, echoing outside their room blending with the galactic cosmic air, the wind carrying the melodious and melancholic sound across the Nibiru's colonies signaling the beginning of the day, signaling The Nibirunians of the beginning of the much awaited affair, THE GALACTIC UNION, THE GRAND SACRED WEDDING OF GODDESS NAKKI AND GOD ANUK.

"ALLURING STAR"
By MonaC
(POETIC BREEZE, POETIC FROTH PART 1 – POEM NO. 80)

Beyond the horizon of love
A twinkling star shines above
The endless light of romance
The intoxicating perfume of love
Alas, a bewitching beauty in heavens
Beneath the galactic-light skies
There it sways around with glee
Dancing with the radiant stars
Sparkling eyes of charm, behold
So naive of its aura and grace

Perhaps it is so interestingly intriguing
Can't deny the sweetness of innocence
The serenity of thy exuberant beauty
Hard to betray the exquisite feelings
Lovers will dance with persistence

Perhaps destiny will gamble its way
For what will be the reward, oh heavenly star
To bestow thy benign soul of pulchritude
Love and romance, perhaps an infatuation
Goddess of love show the path of affection

Hearts melts with thy lustrous light
Heaven and Universe, rejoice at once
In eternity love will dwell its glory
Comets will dash a shining knight
In every night ALLURING STAR shines!

Goddess Nakki having fully recovered from her slumber tried to find where God Anuk is, and gestured to the Cherubs and Seraphs to disperse, to which one by one they get out of the room into the veranda still playing with their music, and into the outside space each going everywhere. Goddess Nakki stand up, make a round of stretching for her body to energize the flow of energy rhythmically and energetically, then walk to the end of the room and touch the wall, instantly it become giant computer wall screen monitor, and there, in-front of her in different windows of the computer wall screen monitor are various locations and places showing every preparation being made for the in-coming affair. She could see in one window the Palace Royal Hall being decorated with different kinds of flowers and decors lavishly, and nearby, the Galactic Symphonic Orchestra practicing under Maestro WOLFGANG A. MOSSARTO's piece of The Marriage of Figaro, which the Maestro knows it's her favorite musical piece, she could see the aero-streets of their cities being deck with garlands and being prepared marvelously with colors and lights for the Grand Parade, in one window screen are the Palace Universal Galactic Royal Guards under SUPREME COMMANDER HANNIBALKAN, in their colorful Red and Blue Gala Uniforms practicing their Parade of Honors for the day's event in-front of the Palace Royal Parade Ground, and even the Palace Kitchen area and Galley staff are so busy preparing sumptuously for the foods and beverages they are going to serve for the wedding as she can see from one of the window monitor, she felt excitement in her heart, truly it's one great day, and she was delighted of what she was observing, for she thought everybody's busy preparing, all the Elite of Elites will be there, and that the whole colonies of The Nibirunians are very eager awaiting for that final hour of their Grand Union.

Goddess Nakki's heart feels overjoyed, and before she touch again the wall screen to push one command, she paused for a moment and tried to locate where God Anuk is from the small window monitor in the upper screen of the computerize wall, she look at the windows one by one, and then finally located God Anuk in the adjacent Room of Universal Stillness, she could see that God Anuk is suspended in mid-air of the center of the room in Yoga Position meditating, his arms stretch outwards right angle to his side with his hands and fingers in close-fist position making round movements, head tilted slightly upwards and his eyes closed, his face is serene and radiating of luminous rays and rainbows of colorful lights, the room is space dark and configured with heavenly stars of different constellations and spiraling nebulae and various galaxies as if floating in a Space of Time, gleaming and glittering with different cosmic colors, God Anuk's body and mind in unanimity to

UNIVERSAL HARMONY, all his cosmic energy flowing freely all around his body encircling him as if he's on cosmic purification.

She was humbled and felt deep respect for her in-coming husband, and profound admiration for she knows whole-heartedly he is THE ONE, the only one who can love her the way he does, TRUTHFUL AND KIND, FULL OF PERSEVERANCE She muse, and there He is, getting ready and meditating all his vigor, funneling all cosmic force He could get into his body for that energy He will need for the sacred occasion, He is readying himself for the Grand Wedding.

"...I will not disturb him...I must get ready myself, I must summon at once the Kingdom's Royal Beauteous Artisan, VICE GANDAHEH, she must have to prepare me grandiosely, she's a beauty herself, she knows the Art of Universal Galactic Beautification" she murmured to herself, and when she is satisfied looking and admiring her beloved, God Anuk, she touch the command button she wanted to touch before hand, and at once a door was opened near their bed-capsule head-wall of luminous electronic shield, and she walked passed right into it, into another dimension, into the world of Galactic Gorgeousness, the beauteous realm of Vice Gandaheh.

"Welcome to my abode of Beauteous Perfection, your Royal Goddess, our Goddess Nakki" exclaimed Vice Gandaheh upon seeing Goddess Nakki entered her domain and added.

"...what can be your modest and loyal subject be of service to you oh Royal Highness..." her arms stretching upward in graceful manner with her head bowing down as gesture of respect to Goddess Nakki

Goddess Nakki smiled, walking slowly admiring the beauty and loveliness all around the room, and commanded, "Vice Gandaheh, beautiful as ever, Beauteous Pride of Planet Nibiru, at ease and be confident yourself"

"Thank You, your Royal Goddess, your compliment shows your inner beauty of kindness, for there is no one in our Planet Nibiru as lovely and beautiful as you are, you are the only one that commands and possess the words PERFECTION OF BEAUTY, you yourself defines the Essence of Beauty, a UNIVERSAL GODDESS, BEAUTIFUL IN ALL PERFECTION, TRULY YOU ARE THE QUEEN OF UNIVERSE" replied Vice Gandaheh trying to at ease herself, for once in her lifetime, a Goddess come into her abode and appraise her value, such delight and elation She feels in her heart.

"I come here not to exude all the beauties of our Planet Nibiru, and certainly not to ascertain my right as the most beautiful one in the Universe" Goddess Nakki replied with innate charm, and continued speaking.

"TRULY, CHARM IS DECEPTIVE, AND BEAUTY IS FLEETING, BUT TRUE BEAUTY COMES FROM THE HEART, IT IS KIND AND UNDERSTANDING, HUMBLE AND RESPECTFUL, COMPASSIONATE AND ADORING, IT IS EVERLASTING TRAIT, FOR WHAT IS THE ESSENCE OF BEAUTY WITHOUT CHARACTER, BUT A ROTTEN AND DECAYING SHELL OF SUPERFICIAL BEAUTY, THERE WILL BE NO REMEMBRANCE IN TIME, VANISHED IN SPACE AS COSMIC DUST. TRUE BEAUTY LAYS WITHIN, UNFATHOMABLE AND PROFOUND ELEMENT CONFORMING TO UNIVERSAL HARMONY OF PEACE, IT IS THE HEART OF GOLD, BEAUTEOUS AND PRICELESS, BEAUTY IN THE EYE OF THE BEHOLDER, BEAUTY IN THE HEART OF THE BEHOLDER, BEAUTY AS TIME ALLOWS, BEAUTY AS SPACE SANCTIFY, IT IS BEAUTY AND IMMORTALITY" Goddess Nakki wholeheartedly explained

"Oh Royal Goddess, what a divine enlightenment you had just uttered, truly a Words of Wisdom, a food in my thoughts I will dwell and chew upon, so profound in meaning yet so true and comprehensible, you truly are a Goddess, not only a Beauty of Aura and Grace, but of Beauty of Wisdom and Character, I am so much delighted and blessed of your presence, thank you Oh Royal Goddess" Vice Gandaheh meekly answered back and then proceeded to asked. "What is it then that you require of your humble servant, Royal Goddess?"

Goddess Nakki began speaking, with her eyes wandering around the room, walking around trying to admire the beauty of numerous hanging portraits of Nibirunians, some of them she knows so well, the Elite of the Elites, wife and daughters of prominent Nibirunians who came and seek Vice Gandaheh's expertise of Galactic Beautification, but for Goddess Nakki, it's not what she wants, it's not what she came for, she knows well herself, confident of what she possess, she don't need BEAUTIFICATION no more, "I am a Goddess" she whispered herself.

"You know well in your heart that I am going to get married today, I will tie the knot with God Anuk, Son of the Star Sirius, Blood of the Constellation Orion, a God in his own right, I come here, Vice Gandaheh, to seek your help, not of additional superficial beautification, but to make me a grandiose Wedding Gown I could be proud of for eternity, I am here commissioning you, to use your universal gift including all your scientific beautification tools and servants, to use your talent and knowledge of Art of Universal Galactic Beautification into something new, to sew and embroider me with a beautiful wedding gown, not only me I can be proud of, but all of my Subjects, a Wedding Gown all Nibirunians will remember and be proud of for generations to come, sparkling and dazzling of all the Precious Stones and Jewels our Planet have, you must adorn and garnish THE WEDDING GOWN with Diamonds, Emeralds, Sapphires, Rubies, Tortoise, Crystal Stones, Gold, Silver, Bronze, Titanium, Aluminum, and all that you can use, like glistening STARS that twinkles in colorful radiant, beaming with pride and splendor when I wear it during my Grand Sacred Wedding, my Universal Galactic Union with God Anuk, and my annunciation to the Universal Galactic Throne of our Planet Nibiru, it will be the symbol of my SOLE RULERSHIP AND ASCENSION TO THE KINGDOMSHIP." Goddess Nakki commanded Vice Gandaheh

"…I will require it very soon, there is no shortage of time, I know in my heart you can and will do what I require and ask of you…am I clear to you..." Goddess Nakki asked Vice Gandaheh with kindness but commanding voice.

"…Oh Goddess Nakki, there is nothing to say but, YES, in all splendor I will embroider you a BEAUTEOUS WEDDING GOWN for all eternity to last and be proud of by all Nibirunians, the symbol of your Power and Rulership, IT WILL BE YOUR GALACTIC WEDDING GOWN BEAMING WITH PRIDE AND GLORY…" Vice Gandaheh answered back with smiles all over her face, and happiness within, there is immense pleasure in her heart for this Royal task, a galactic challenge to her expertise of universal beautification.

"…very well then, I shall summon you when I am ready to wear the wedding gown, there's no need for me to see first and judge, my instinct and wisdom trust you, get to work and start doing what you do best, I shall see you very soon…" Goddess Nakki implied to Vice Gandahae and walked away to the door in graceful exit, Vice Gandaheh bowing her head again, and rush to her tools and instrument, signaling her servants to enter her room upon Goddess Nakki's exit to start her arduous task, The Creation of Grandiose Galactic Wedding Gown.

"BEYOND NOTHING"
BY MONAC

To create from nothing
Is as awesome as Universe
To draw out of thoughts
Is a gift beyond

To express in different ways
Is a talent few can
To sketch ideas into life
Is showing One's belief

Dissecting what is beyond nothing
Profound way of understanding
Where an open mind never SEEK
It only comes out and flow

Just go along mindlessly
Create what's inside dictating
Behold it is a cosmic gift
The imprints of your being

As infinite as it is
Everything is possible
It's all in the mind
Beyond nothing there is something!

Goddess Nakki upon leaving Vice Gandaheh's domicile, went straight to the Royal Palace Security and Intelligence Office room and summon the Commander of the Palace Royal Guards, COMMANDER LEVONNE, and asked if everything is alright and according to plans, she checked and scrutinized the SECURITY PLANS AND LAY-OUT, and had her Royal Palace Security Briefing by Commander Levonne, then specifically ordered him to put all members of the Palace Royal Guards on Galactic High Alert status, keeping eye on any suspicious activities, or any creature and individuals that will try to destruct the wedding ceremony, she asked that the very best among the very best of Palace Royal Guards be place and station near the ceremonial altar, to guard and protect them, especially God Anuk, from any attack or act of betrayal. She told Commander Levonne that it is a confidential Security Order directly coming from her, and she expect them to do and fulfill with utmost diligence even if it will cause their life, for which the Commander pledge and swear in his Family's name and honor to abide unquestionably along with his comrades in arms, The Galactic Palace Royal Guards. And before Goddess Nakki leave Commander Levonne, she asked and commanded him "...Commander Levonne, please be so kind to look after my beloved God Anuk, guard and protect him from any harm of anyone...today's ceremony might bring a lot of surprises, be alert and open your eyes, I don't want any harm befalls my beloved".

Commander Levonne bowed down his head and put his right arm in his chest with his fist close and said "...Oh Goddess, your wish is our command, we will guard and protect you, and God Anuk, until our last breath, we will defend and live to our creed, The Creed of being a member of the elite Galactic Palace Royal Guards, "Honor and Glory even in Death, Defender of Kingdom's Throne, Defender of Nibiru's Royalties." And Commander Levonne raised his arm saluting Goddess Nakki.

Goddess Nakki satisfied with Commander Levonne's allegiance, left the Palace Security and Intelligence Office room, and She wanders more, walk pass the Ceremonial Altar Assembly Hall, observing the preparation that's going on, and all the life forms that She meets along the way bow down their head in respect to her Highness, all smiles in their faces, their eyes filled with admiration for their Goddess Nakki's aura of beauty and grace, and in their hearts, She is the HOPE of the future to come.

Goddess Nakki waving and smiling back to the workers doing the preparation, acknowledging their respect to her, yet her mind is working on another dimension, instilling in her thoughts the positions and lay-outs of every tables and chairs, every decors that adorn the hall, the position of the Symphonic Orchestra under Maestro WOLFGANG A. MOSSARTO, the position of the ELDERS, the position of the Supreme Generals, Supreme Commanders and the Commanders, the position of distinguished guest, the Elite of the Elites, the position of the Nibirunians amongst the invited list, the position of the Galactic Palace Royal Guards, the position of the ceremonial altar to which she and God Anuk will stand along with the Shaman for their blessing and confirmation as galactic couple, and lastly, the most important she reckon, the position of the Nibiru's Throne Royal Chair where God Anuk will walk her to sit and rightfully claim the sole rulership of Planet Nibiru. "I must have to be ready in all aspect" she told and convinced herself.

After finding satisfaction in all what she is observing, she then proceeded to the Palace Galactic Royal Sauna called The Garden of Edenna, where the River-Falls of Life, the Tree of Life, and the Tree of Knowledge of Good and Evil are located, there she will prepare herself, she will take a bath in the River-Falls of Life where her trusted servants will sponge-soothe and wash her smooth Goddess body, then she will feast and eat the fruits of the Tree of Life to purify herself from her self-desires, and will seek the Forbidden Fruit of the Tree of Knowledge of Good and Evil, where only Gods and Goddesses are allowed to eat, because the Forbidden Fruit of the Tree of Knowledge of Good and Evil possess immense Power of Enlightenment, that if it will be eaten by a normal creature, it could empower an entity or any persona of so much wisdom that if it could not be controlled, will set lust and greed in one's heart and desire, that is why, it is a law and forbidden to all their Subjects to eat this fruit, that there is a great prize of punishment for whosoever disobey the law will be punish to condemnation of eternal frozen death in the abyss of galactic universe. It is only they, the God and Goddesses of Planet Nibiru are allowed to eat the Fruit of The Tree of Knowledge of Good and Evil, for they had perfected their being, unblemished of any sinful thoughts of greed and lust, no malice in any sanely form.

The Garden of Edenna is a paradise sanctum of alluring fragrance of different kinds of flowers and exotic trees, with different species of Butterflies flying and flapping wings from flower to flower, collected from different planets and galaxies during the Planet Nibiru's wandering and exploration of the Universe, it is the ultimate collections of flowers because of their scents producing a divine aroma that soothes the Gods and Goddesses smell, that transforms the River-Falls of Life into a lagoon and river of aromatic perfume of universal delight, that anyone who will bathe in it will have the body scent and aroma of a GOD or a GODDESS that can be smelled miles away and can pollute the air with so much perfume and fragrance that can bring one's senses into a heavenly feeling, that is why THE GARDEN OF EDENNA is a PARADISE SANCTUM exclusively only for the Gods and Goddesses.

After Goddess Nakki's indulgence in the Garden of Edenna, she then goes back to their abode and dwelling, her Goddess body odor and scent perfuming all the passage way of the Royal Palace with divine aroma, which the palace air duct carried across their colonies, as if that beautiful day, the whole Nibirunians were blessed with delightful heavenly air.

Goddess Nakki look for her Groom to be, God Anuk, where she had left him meditating in the Room of Universal Stillness, and found God Anuk was not already there, she then retired to their room and saw that their computer wall screen monitor was open that caught her attention, she walk up front closely to see what are the scenes on the different window screen above the wall screen monitor. She touch the screen of one window that fills her interest and curiosity, and the window screen become much more larger occupying half the wall screen monitor enough for her to see clearly what's transpiring.

She feels amaze of what she is seeing in the monitor screen, the airspace entrance of Nibiru's Royal Galactic Palace was lined up with so many different sleek spacecraft hovering above the mountain gorge queuing for their turn to be receive by the Royal Palace Usherettes, "…my invited and distinguished Guest are already started coming…" she exclaimed.

She touched another window screen and this time the screen monitor shows the Royal Palace lobby to see who already arrived, she could see the building-up of their wedding guest, Dignitaries of different colonies, Nibiru's Elite of Elites, and some High Ranking Officials. She recognizes also some of the guests lining up to enter Royal Palace Grand Chamber and Ceremonial Altar Assembly Hall, and her heart was filled with pride and honor, and joy for she saw that the Lord God of the Forward Northern Part Colony of Nibiru, Lord God Alexus along with his Royal Family members came to grace her wedding, she felt immense pleasure in her heart and so thankful because her family owe them a great favor, she also saw the well-respected and feared Lord God Allankz of Southern Part Colony of Nibiru attending, and the different faces of guest she was seeing in the screen monitor brings so much delight in her well-being because today, in her Grand Sacred Wedding, despite of all the worries and reservations she and God Anuk had discussed before they sleep, she could sense there is UNITY amongst all Nibirunians, "…This is for you Father, my Lord God Abrahamus, our Family's Code and Legacy will live on forever…" she whispered to herself and amuse herself looking at the other window sub-screen monitor showing different video feeds scenery of what's going-on inside and outside the palace.

"…I must get ready myself now…" speaking to herself but her eyes subconsciously and distinctly caught a glimpse of one screen monitor that was blurry and not showing any videos but blankness, it's the room Security Video webcam of THE ELDERS CHAMBER OF TRUTH.

Goddess Nakki pause for a while and find time to think why is it that the Security Video feedcam of THE ELDERS CHAMBER OF TRUTH room is OFF, she was trying to rationalize her reasons when suddenly God Anuk called her from behind.

She turned around carefully, in her heart tickles threshold of excitement, and to her amazement, exclaimed, "OHH DIVINE GALACTIC GOD…HOW SPLENDID AND MAGNIFICENT"

Goddess Nakki felt LOVE-STRUCK upon seeing God Anuk in his GODLY WEDDING SUIT, inside her heart are million TICKLES OF LOVE flowing like a burning current bringing sheer sensation all over her body. God Anuk in his majestic muscular built body was standing in-front of Goddess Nakki wearing his Wedding Suit in all his grandeur.

God Anuk's body was covered like a star-dust glittering, his upper torso was covered with a Legionnaires armor breastplate fashioned like his upper body, all the details of his breast muscles elaborately detailed, made of Pure Gold, and the nipples in his breastplate like upper body are Diamond stones, glittering and sparkling of intrinsic variant reddish color like his twin star Sisters, Bellatrix and Betelgeuse shining in the heavenly skies. The neckline and all edges of the breastplate are adorned with different kind of jewels in fashionable arrangements making it more lustrous, his chiseled muscular abdomen presents an imposing vigorous appearance like a belly of a serpent Cobra with his navel pierced and covered with another Diamond, glistening of intense bluish color like his Brother star, Rigel.

God Anuk's lower body was covered only from hips with skirt made of a fabric so smooth they called Golden Silk, where pure gold and the finest silk fabric are mixed and blend together to produce such quality of textile, and his belt securing the Golden Silk skirt are adorned by Emeralds and Sapphires all around, with three distinguished Diamonds align in the center above his manhood area like the Stars of Orion's Belt embedded in his belt's buckle of SWASTIKA made of pure Gold. He has lower and upper arm bands made of gold that shows his muscular arms powerful and strong, his sandals are made of the finest leather and laced up to his knees fully adorned with sparkling precious gems.

It was a sight Goddess Nakki so proud of in her entire life and being, God Anuk in his splendor standing in-front of her is truly a magnificent display of a NIBIRU GOD, his head adorned with a winged shape crown full of shining jewels.

"...Oh my God Anuk, your aura possess all the splendor of a GOD, you are my Adonis for all Eternity, my ONE and ONLY STARLOVE..." Goddess Nakki uttered with so much amazement

God Anuk smiling and beaming with pride, turned around showing Goddess Nakki his cloak which again mesmerized Goddess Nakki, for the design of the cloak God Anuk wearing hanging and flowing smoothly on his back down to his knees, reminds of her past, it was the Symbolic Flag of her Family and Ancestors, a long rectangle soft flowing fabric of silk with colored white triangle of equal sides pointing downward, and serve as boundary of two colors of blue and red comprising of the rectangle shape, depicting Peace and War respectively, and in the triangle's center embroidered a circle made of shining gold depicting their Planet Nibiru, with eight embroidered sunrays adorned with diamonds depicting the Eight Colonies of Planet Nibiru who joined together in the 1st Galactic War. The triangle also have embroidered Star made of jewels such as ruby, emerald and sapphire in each corner respectively representing the Three Great Places in the Universe Planet Nibiru traveled and visited in the Abyss of Universe which are The Milky Way Galaxy (Home Galaxy of Blue Planet Earth), The Andromeda Galaxy (Spiraling Galaxy, the

Twin Galaxy of Milky Way Galaxy) and The Orion Constellation (Home of the Star People, home of God Anuk).

Goddess Nakki was so speechless of what she was admiring in-front of her, she could only gasp and sigh, she wanted to embrace God Anuk but then as she walks toward him, God Anuk walks to the door, and said "…Oh my Goddess, time is so excruciatingly preciously ticking like an eternal yearning, I am agonizingly waiting for our Grand Sacred Union…I will leave you now for you to prepare and attend yourself, I will wait for you in the Ceremonial Hall, even for ETERNITY, I will wait for you…" God Anuk intensely told Goddess Nakki with his eyes full of longing, full of expressions as if trying to convey something; it was a weird feeling for him.

When God Anuk was completely out of sight, Goddess Nakki wanted to cry in delight but quickly subdued and returned hurriedly to the computer wall screen monitor, she touched one window and appeared on the screen her Palace Royal Personal Servant, Amparose. She asked her about the list of the day, then commanded her to tell the Palace Royal Wedding Planner, Raychelle, that she will arrive in the Ceremonial Hall as per scheduled time and as planned, and to summon Vice Gandaheh to bring her Royal Wedding Gown she had commissioned her to make, in her mind flashes excitements and elation.

Goddess Nakki then touch another window screen and appeared Commander Levonne, in-charge of Palace Royal Guard Security. Goddess Nakki ordered him to prepare themselves, The Palace Royal Guard Escorts, in thirty minutes time, for her Grand Entrance, and asked him if the Palace Royal Space Craft which will take her to the Royal Palace Grand Chamber and Ceremonial Altar Assembly Hall is ready and inspected thoroughly, to which Commander Levonne affirmatively confirmed.

And lastly, she contacted SUPREME COMMANDER NAPOLEONIOUS, HEAD OF UNIFIED HIGH COMMAND OF UNIVERSAL GALACTIC DEFENSE AERO-POLICE AND SPACE-FORCE if the route to Royal Palace Grand Chamber and Ceremonial Altar Assembly Hall where her Grand Sacred Wedding and Union to God Anuk will be held is safe and secured, and free of any undesirable traffic or any disturbances, to which Supreme Commander Napoleonious also affirmatively confirmed all in order and as planned.

She was about to switch off the wall screen monitor when again she remembered the screen video webcam of THE ELDERS CHAMBER OF TRUTH, she then scrolled the video webcams windows to find the room and when she finally does, she was confused and startled, because it's now functioning and showing Security Video webcams feedbacks, but the room is empty.

"…Maybe I am wrong, and I am just thinking so much and anxious, I guess…" she told herself

"…this is my grandest day, I must not worry myself too much, what I am thinking are just figments of my imagination…" she convinced herself that everything is fine and her Grand Sacred Wedding will start and finish according to the Palace Royal Wedding Planner's plan, "…NOBODY'S FOOL to disrupt my wedding, I am their LAST HOPE, The Planet Nibiru Unigalitizens needs me, I have their trust and blessing, I know, no one will spoil MY GRANDEST DAY…" she murmured to herself.

Suddenly an incoming Security Video call alert alarms in one of the window screen monitor, it was Amparose, her personal servant, she touched the window screen, and she can see from monitor that she is asking permission to enter her room, and along with Amparose is Vice Gandaheh, who was glistening and glowing like a Galaxy of Stars, for a moment she was fooled but then come to her senses that Vice Gandaheh is radiating not because of her beauteous presence, but of a material she was holding on, it was her Wedding Gown that was fabulously glowing.

Goddess Nakki exhaled with such delight and exclaimed "…WOW what a wonderful surprise, this is truly an art of work, a fine craftsmanship…" and she told them to go inside at once.

Upon seeing her personal servant, Amparose, and Vice Gandaheh walking towards her inside the room, she joyfully uttered "…LET'S DO IT…"

And looked straight in the eyes of Vice Gandaheh in compelling fashion and told her, "THANK YOU, MAGNIFICENT AND FABULOUS WORK INDEED"

***

"... LOVE, FULL OF PROMISES AND HOPES
SO SWEET AND ENCHANTING DREAMS
AS IF TOMORROW HAS GONE AHEAD OF TIME
ONLY TO BE SHATTERED BY DREADFUL FATE ..."

* * *

Everybody in the audience and guest-alike awaiting for the grand arrival of Goddess Nakki were excited and very eager to see their Goddess, especially the wives and daughters of the Elite of Elites because there was a hearsay that circulated amongst the gossipers of the Elites that Goddess Nakki employed and commissioned Vice Gandaheh, a known expert in Art of Universal Galactic Beautification across Planet Nibiru. They were quite intrigue of what kind of beautification will Vice Gandaheh will do and add more to their Goddess appeal who's already a beauty herself, they were there attending as well to showcase their kind of beauty amongst the Higher Society of Nibirunians and competing themselves as to "WHO'S IN AND WHO'S NOT" in the list, for the Grand Sacred Wedding of Goddess Nakki and God Anuk is simply one of the grandiose occasion the Planet Nibiru had in eon years of its existence, amongst the Elites, it is what they called, "WHO'S WHO AND WHICH IS WHICH", they want to see and compare each other's gala's and gowns with their luscious cleavages wantonly wants to burst out, they were there to see who's make-up is more fashionable and trending, and they were there to witness Goddess Nakki's Galactic Universal Wedding Appearance.

Earlier, the guests and the audiences were already mesmerized and awed by God Anuk's arrival, especially the Feminine audiences, they keep giggling of God Anuk's masculinity, it was oozing with raw sex appeal and power, and lustered more with his Wedding Costume and Tunic, truly a GOD MAGNIFICENTLY SHINING IN THE MIDST OF THE NIBIRUNIANS.

At first The Galactic Symphonic Orchestra under Maestro Wolfgang A. Mossarto were playing soft and low pitch tone of music echoing the wedding hall as if one is in heaven, then slowly building up becoming louder, as if going to a grand finale, everybody paid attention and caught up with their emotions the sound of music is stirring within each and everyone listening, the music is going faster and louder with melodious tones and rhythms, as if hearing one's ecstasy in music, and with one forceful yet graceful stroke of the Maestro, the music echoing the Ceremonial Hall came to stop, and there was silence.

And then suddenly Trumpets played a distinctive sound, the sound of announcement that one important persona or event have arrived, it played its tunes and beats until again, it stop abruptly.

Then came the announcement everybody in the Ceremonial Hall have been waiting for, everybody's filled with excitement, except for God Anuk who was been very anxious and tense ever-since He arrived in the Ceremonial Hall because of one significant message he learned from his childhood and dear friend SUPREME GENERAL JHESUSAN, HEAD OF THE UNIFIED HIGH COMMAND OF UNIVERSAL GALACTIC DEFENSE TACTICAL ARMADA CENTRAL COMMAND, who approached and disclosed to him an event that happened just before he arrived in the Ceremonial Hall.

Supreme General Jhesusan told him that THE ELDERS, prior to coming in the Ceremonial Hall, along with some GENERALS AND COMMADERS, made an un-announced and urgent meeting in THE ELDERS CHAMBER OF TRUTH, that Supreme General Jhesusan was not invited to attend said meeting and was kept out of the loop. Supreme General Jhesusan warned him to keep his eyes open and be extra careful, he said that, THE ELDERS are cooking something fishy and dangerously brewing a COUP D'ETAT. He doesn't know when but reminded him that THE ELDERS had been Eon of Time planning of such event. God Anuk readied himself; he feels in his heart something strange is going to happen amidst their Sacred Wedding.

"...ALL RISE, Hail Thee, the Grand Entrance of The Royal Goddess of Universe, Daughter of Lord God Abrahamus, The Sun-God, and Goddess Mhariella of Planet Nibiru. NIBIRUNIANS, UNIGALITIZINES, ANNOUNCING THE ARRIVAL OF YOUR GODDESS, THE GODDESS OF LIGHT, GODDESS NAKKI..." the announcer proudly introduced and announced the arrival of Goddess Nakki.

Again, the Trumpets played its tunes, this time with drums and cymbals in harmony, its beat echoing in the heart of God Anuk for every second beat that counts, every second tick of time, in his heart beats the FINAL COUNTDOWN of what he had planned days before, in his mind, this event and merriment is only a façade of what yet to come un-expectedly that will shock the whole Planet Of Nibirunians, for him it is the cruelest time of his existence, yet He could not do anything because if THE ENEMY learnt that He knows what they up to, it may cause a change in the series of event which might endanger the life of her beloved, Goddess Nakki, for up to now in that precise moment he's thinking, He hasn't gotten' any clue as to WHO REALLY ARE THE ENEMIES, AND THE MASTERMIND OF THE ENEMY.

All eyes fixated at the entrance aisle of the Royal Palace Grand Chamber and Ceremonial Altar Assembly Hall awaiting the grand entrance of Goddess

Nakki, everybody's on their feet holding their breath and not blinking, everybody so it seems don't like to miss a second of the unfolding event, even THE ENEMY OF ENEMY who were there waiting for their signal to enact their plan seems temporarily forgot their purpose, they too along with all the others inside the Ceremonial Altar Assembly Hall got carried by their emotions of excitement witnessing a historical event, yet even so, it will be more historical if they will successfully stage their plan.

Soon, the trumpets, drums and cymbals began to sound in a fading sound of music, and when all the instruments completely stop playing, they began to see outline of shapes forming in the entrance aisle. God Anuk who was waiting at the other end of the aisle near the Ceremonial Altar has mixed emotions of what's going on, He wants to celebrate and be happy, yet his heart is in agony and fear.

Commander Levonne shouted on top of his voice, commanding an order, a signal that his Legionnaire Royal Guard Escort is waiting. "... LEGIOOOOONNAAAAAAIREEE, FORWARD MARCH..."

And in uniformly movement and cadence, the Palace Royal Guard Escort of Goddess Nakki began to enter the aisle of the Royal Palace Grand Chamber and Ceremonial Altar Assembly Hall, it was such a remarkable sight of parade of Palace Royal Guard Legionnaires in their red and blue colorful Gala Uniforms, they were marching with two column composing of Twelve Legionnaires each squad, at the front center was Commander Levonne. They were marching so that the last two Legionnaire opposite each other upon reaching a certain point will stationary march in cadence with main group until such time all Legionnaires marching are positioned evenly occupying the whole stretch of the aisle creating a passageway with the Legionnaires on the sides, and again comes the command of Commander Levonne which make God Anuk even more anxious for he didn't know if Commander Levonne was among those who attended the last minute meeting call with THE ELDERS, in his heart are worrisome thoughts for if Commander Levonne will give the command THE ENEMY have been waiting, there will be chaos inside the Ceremonial Hall and he is too far away to protect his beloved, Goddess Nakki.

"...LEGIONNAIIIIIIREEEEEEEE.......HALT..." commanded again by Commander Levonne and they all stop marching still facing the Ceremonial Altar, eyes front, their hands on their side straightly align with their body, and they remained standing motionless. Commander Levonne executed himself "ABOUT FACE" command in snappy and smart manner, then marched again back to the entrance of the Royal Palace Grand Chamber and Ceremonial Altar Assembly Hall, where Goddess Nakki was suppose to enter, when Commander Levonne reached the door of the entrance hall, he executed 'ABOUT FACE" again and shouted on top of his voice.

"...NIBIRU LEGIONNAIRES, ROYAL GUARDS, GALACTIIIIIIIC SALUTE..." and in uniform and smartest motion, the Royal Guard Escort Legionnaire positioned in the aisle executed LEFT FACE and RIGHT FACE motion so that they now face each other, then all together in unison and at precise movement, draw their flaming laser sword and executed THE NIBIRU ROYAL SALUTE by drawing their sword from their left sides then raised to their chest for a brief moment then raised upward again in a 45 degrees inclination above their head forming an UMBRELLA OF FLAMING LASER SWORD OF PYRAMID.

It was a fabulous exhibition that everyone inside were enjoying the spectacle, but not for God Anuk, who again was terrified when He saw the Palace Royal Guard Escort Legionnaires draw their sword above their head in a Combat Ready Battle Formation, his heartbeat increased like a sound of drumbeat being hit in the heat of a battlefield, for if Commander Levonne is not an ally, but support his adversaries, he knows that they are already one step ahead of him, for the Legionnaires have already drawn their sword, occupied and guarded the important passage where Goddess Nakki will walk and pass towards the Ceremonial Altar.

God Anuk then felt bemused, he remembered his DREAM hours ago, what if that dream was conveying him a message, what if instead of him at the middle of the aisle is someone, what if its Commander Levonne was the character in his dream that enter the room, and he was the groom with radiating face, and that his dreams was conveying that Commander Levonne will abduct Goddess Nakki under the orders of THE ELDERS.

"...It is a perfect plan for THE ENEMY..." he told himself, for in his mind already played the next scene where Commander Levonne will escort ahead of Goddess Nakki walking slowly towards him at the end of the aisle where he supposed to accept her hand and together will walk towards the Ceremonial Altar where the Shaman is, but, when they, Commander Levonne and Goddess

Nakki are in the middle of the aisle passage way, Commander Levonne will then command all the Royal Guard Legionnaires the final signal to attack and hostage Goddess Nakki, which no one inside the room could prevent and help because Goddess Nakki was already surrounded, and even him, if He tries to help and fight the Legionnaires, he will be outnumbered.

"…OH MY GODLY FATHER, SUPREME GOD SIRIUS, HELP AND GUIDE ME IN THIS DARKEST DAY OF MY HOUR…" God Anuk murmured unto himself, he could see already the radiating light of Goddess Nakki in the entrance door of The Royal Palace Grand Chamber and Ceremonial Altar Assembly Hall, which makes his heart even more beating thunderously.

God Anuk wants to run and stop Goddess Nakki from entering the Royal Palace Grand Chamber and save her from impending tragedy and misfortune, "…but WHAT IF?..." and he pondered again quickly, "…what if I am wrong, I will be foolish myself, and I will be the one who will cause the Grand Stupidity of all time, I will ruin our Grandest Sacred Wedding Ceremony, and will be the laughing-stock of all Nibirunians for eon of time, and will be recorded in the Book of Time as The Culprit or The One who ruined The Grand Universal Wedding of the GODS…"

God Anuk was reasoning himself yet on the other side of his mind, he knows for sure something bad is going to happen, and yet He can't pinpoint the cue where THE ENEMY will reveal themselves, for if He reveals himself beforehand that He knows THE ELDERS plan, they might abandon their plan and He, and all Nibirunians would never know who the real enemies are, worst He will not a have a chance to find who is the MASTERMIND OF THE ELDERS causing all THE DILEMMA in THE WEDDING, and who's THE ENEMY OF ENEMY. "…I must have to wait more…PATIENCE IS A VIRTUE" he convinced himself.

Everybody in the Royal Chamber feels so much excitement in their heart especially when the Royal Palace Grand Chamber door was slowly opened after Commander Levonne commanded GALACTIC SALUTE to the Royal Guards Escort, and reveals the presence of Goddess Nakki for her Grand Entrance.

The whole audience gasp and sighs, murmuring in awe and admiration after the door was fully opened, there in the entrance door behold their Goddess Nakki in her glorified splendor, radiating like a Galactic Universe standing in a Nibirunian pose, sparkling, dazzling and scintillating with so much beauty and grace, a magnificent and marvelous sight, that anyone looking wholeheartedly would be bewitched by her sophistication of aura and exquisiteness, as if cosmos has arrive radiating and full of enchantment, like stars in the universe that twinkles and sparkles, they were all amazed of what they were witnessing

"…BEHOLD NIBIRUNIANS, YOUR GALACTIC GODDESS, THE GODDESS OF LIGHT, GODDESS NAKKI…" announced again loudly by the announcer

"SOMETHING IN NOTHING"
BY MONAC
(POETIC BREEZE, POETIC FROTH PART 1 – POEM NO. 125)

Rest in the sweetest wine
What is known is known
In the blood of universe
There is SOMETHING IN NOTHING

Distant truth of knowledge
Mind conforms parallel to universe
Everything works on purpose
A puzzle of what should be known

A divine creation of works
Precision is cunningly wit
Cosmic product of reason and will
Only faith and hope can ever explain

In it's awesome wonderful way
It reveals in our imagination magnificently
Any being has its own reason to dwell
For out of nothing there is something!

And then comes the intro of the sweetest sound of music enveloping the whole Royal Palace Grand Chamber enthralling all entity that is within, the graceful hand of The Maestro Wolfgang Amadeus Mossarto compassing the notes and rhythm of his Masterpiece, "The Marriage of Figaro", which is a favorite music play of Goddess Nakki, adding enchantment inside the Royal Palace Grand Chamber with all the melodic sound blending harmoniously in a heavenly ambiance in conjunction with Goddess Nakki's alluring and beguiling Galactic Universal Glory and Beauty.

God Anuk stands mesmerized and numb, so much perplexity was going-on on his mind wreaking havoc in his thoughts, he wanted to shout and end all his agonizing confusion, to end THE DILEMMA and confront THE ENEMY in-front of all Nibiru's Society that are being misled and lead to believe that this Grand Sacred Union of their wedding is a part of a grand plan of Universal Peace and Inter-Galactic Planetary Co-Existence with other planets, especially the Blue Planet called Earth, in his mind it is not the case"…IT'S ONLY A SHOW FOR THE ENEMY…" he murmured

With the Royal Guard Escort Legionnaires still in Royal Salute Formation, their swords imposing upward above their heads 45 degrees angle inclination forming a Flaming Sword of Pyramid shape, Commander Levonne suddenly withdraw his laser sword with his right hand and put it in his chest, with the laser sword's flaming blade pointing upward also in 45 degrees inclination, signaling the commencement of The Grand Entrance of Goddess Nakki to the Palace Royal Chamber Hall, and slowly Commander Levonne in marching cadence and pace march forward passing the first two Royal Guard Escort Legionnaires with their flaming sword in the air forming a shape of pyramid, the entourage of Goddess Nakki following him.

God Anuk's eyes transfixed at the other end of the aisle where his beloved Goddess Nakki is, as if an eon of time separate them from each other, yet he can see that space-craft carriage of Goddess Nakki is moving forward slowly, and again He murmured "…OH MY GODLY FATHER, SUPREME GOD SIRIUS, HELP AND GUIDE ME IN THIS DARKEST DAY OF MY HOUR…".

For in his mind if Goddess Nakki will pass the aisle passage way with no harm, THE UNIVERSAL GOD is with him, and that will be his Heavenly Sign that no matter what will happen, he believes in his heart, GOOD WILL TRIUMPH OVER EVIL, and that He will proceed according to his plan,

THE ESCAPE of Goddess NAKKI, even-though he knows it will cause so much pain in his heart, yet it will serve its purpose for the betterment and safety of his Beloved Goddess Nakki and the Seed of Breathe He had planted inside his beloved's womb, and if Fate does so will allow Goddess Nakki pass the passage way unharmed, it will confirm and answer his judgment that Commander Levonne is not an enemy.

The whole audience inside the Palace Royal Chamber Hall upon seeing that the space-craft carriage of Goddess Nakki was slowly moving and entering, all burst into cheering and clapping of their hands, for them it was a magnificent sight and spectacle, it brought pride and honor into their hearts knowing they have a Nibirunian Goddess with so much splendor, a majestic in her own aura and appeal.

A dozens of Cherubim's comes first ahead of Goddess Nakki scattering different kinds of colorful and scented flowers petals, all the galaxies exotic flowers being spread out in the air causing so much fragrance and aroma that fills the whole Royal Chamber Hall bringing so much delight and sensation in each and everyone's nostrils, the petals as if dancing in the air falling down covering the aisle, which makes the parade even more lustrous and captivating, and then comes Goddess Nakki in a Goddess posture standing gracefully and admirably on a round disc space-craft carriage slowly hovering and moving forward following the dozen Cherubim who are scattering petals of flowers, a Scepter of Light suspended slightly above her right side head carrying by a Seraphim.

Even so when Goddess Nakki have entered the aisle passage way of Palace Royal Chamber Hall amidst cheering and clapping of hands, the Nibirunians Elite of Elites couldn't raise their eyebrow because of what they are witnessing, they thought Vice Gandaheh will showcase a new make-up invention for additional beautification, and yet what they are witnessing was contrary to what they are expecting, because as Goddess Nakki comes closer and more visible to their naked eye, they couldn't believe what they are seeing, they were all standing in awe and admiration, short to fall envious of Goddess Nakki's presence and aura of beauty and grace, for behold, Goddess Nakki didn't employ any kind of make-up into her face, it was plain Nibirunian beauty, yet no one inside the Palace Royal Chamber Hall could deny the MAJESTIC BEAUTY GODDESS NAKKI possess, it was oozing with all sort of radiating Galactic energy.

Goddess Nakki standing a Goddess pose on top of her hovering round-disc space-craft carriage commands such beauty and grace, her voluptuous and curvaceous silky smooth exotic fair skin body was alluring and captivating, her heart shape perfect diaphanous face radiates in simplicity with her beguiling sweetest smile, her curly long shiny golden-white hair glowing like a radiating supernova mystically enchanting, her long perfectly shape legs showcasing strong yet sensual upper hips and buttocks, all the more she possess, Goddess Nakki exude The Universal Galactic Beauty as Vice Gandaheh describe her, UNIVERSAL GODDESS, BEAUTIFUL IN ALL PERFECTION.

When the entourage of Goddess Nakki reached halfway the aisle passage way of the Palace Royal Chamber Hall, God Anuk again felt strange because He suddenly remembered his DREAM, and then again he murmured to himself "...OH MY GODLY FATHER, SUPREME GOD SIRIUS, HELP AND GUIDE ME IN THIS DARKEST DAY OF MY HOUR...".

Commander Levonne stop walking when He passed midway, and the whole entourage of Goddess Nakki stops as well, but Goddess Nakki remained standing radiating in all her glory and splendor on-top of her round-disc space-craft carriage still hovering about one feet above the polished floor of the Palace Royal Chamber Hall, as planned by The Palace Royal Wedding Planner, Raychelle, and as the melodious and heavenly music of The Maestro slowly fading, the Announcer speak in proudest voice "...NIBIRUNIAAAANNNSSS, BEHOLD, AND WITH ALL DUE RESPECT, I AM PROUDLY PRESENTING TO YOU, GODDESS OF LIGHT, DAUGHTER OF PLANET NIBIRU...NIBIRUNIANS, I PRESENT TO YOU ALL, YOUR BELOVED GODDESS, GODDESS NAKKIIIIII..."

Suddenly all the light went out at the same time the heavenly sound of music stop, the Royal Guard Escort Legionnaires flaming laser swords became the back-light, silhouetting shadows. God Anuk wanted to jump and run to his beloved Goddess Nakki to rescue her, but just as He was to take-off, something beautiful and stunning happened. It was so spectacular that it was the first time the Nibirunians had ever seen in their eon of existence, and they all stand there in amazement and admiration of what transpired to Goddess Nakki, for even THE ELDERS leader, Lord God Cainos couldn't believe that such beauty would occur, and his being was enveloped by such envy of what he was seeing that he vowed to himself to possess such remarkable possession and power.

"...IT'S A MIRACLE..." one audience shouted, and all the words of amazement roars in the air, "...MARVELOUS..." says another audience, "... THIS IS PHENOMENON..." came other audience's remarks

God Anuk was also stunned in amazement, and he can only gaze and utter "...OH MY LOVE AND BELOVED, WHAT WONDERS IN UNIVERSE YOU CAME TO POSSESS..."

Goddess Nakki in all her glory radiating with different colors of light began to ascend in the air with her round-disc space-craft carriage, she was standing yet it was clearly visible that her long perfect slender legs and feet was above the round-disc suspended yet her body stand straight in a Nibirunian pose of beauty and grace, she was floating in the air above the round-disc space-craft carriage about half foot, and six energies of lights was orbiting her body non-stop in different galactic colors like an electrons that encircling a neutron, Goddess Nakki become like a nucleus of profound energy like a Carbon-14 with half-life of 5760 years, she was standing as GODDESS as she is, the central and brightest part of a galaxy or nebulae, her body radiating with awesome power of light in different colors, glittering and sparkling radiance of intense luminosity.

The whole Nibirunian audience stands in utmost bewilderment, it is the first time they see such an incredible display of power and energy, and Goddess Nakki continued to soar above the Palace Royal Chamber Hall dome, that even Commander Levonne was at-lost of what to command, if he will have to continue marching or let the Royal Guard Escort Legionnaires AT EASE and join also the stunned Nibirunians watching Goddess Nakki floats in the air, and be captivated as well by such astonishing display of power energy and beauty.

"...LEGIONNAIREEEEEEEEEEEEEE, AT EASE..." finally Commander Levonne commanded the Royal Guard Escort, and instantly all the Legionnaire at the same time in one swift and precise motion, put back their laser sword to its scabbard, and joined the Nibiruninans watched in amazement as Goddess Nakki and the round-disc space craft carriage underneath her glide across the space toward where God Anuk is.

IT WAS SPECTACULAR SIGHT OF NUMEROUS CIRCLE OF LIGHT FLOATING IN THE AIR WITH DIFFERENT COLORS AND

ENERGIES ORBITING AND ENCIRCLING NON-STOP GODDESS NAKKI'S BODY RADIATING IN SUCH AWESOME RADIANCE LIGHTING THE WHOLE PALACE ROYAL CHAMBER HALL LIKE A SUN THAT LIGHTS A GALAXY.

There was so much jubilation, cheering and clapping of hands, but to THE ENEMY, it was a different story and perception, and they whispered unto each other how to counter-act such power of Advance Knowledge of Technology, because it signifies threat and worrisome for if Goddess Nakki possess such power and energy, they don't know and comprehend the extent it can do to prevent them from staging their plan, they will have to find leverage to control her, and possess that special new power and knowledge they had just witness, for them perhaps a new technology they could use to incorporate in their armaments in preparation of their Great Agenda of Revenge, the annihilation and destruction of Blue Planet Earth.

One of THE ELDERS become so edgy and tense of what he was seeing, he glanced where the Generals and Commanders are positioned, and caught the eye of SUPREME COMMANDER HITLEOROUS, THE HEAD OF UNIFIED HIGH COMMAND OF UNIVERSAL GALACTIC DEFENSE INTER-GALAXY PRISONER-GARRISON, their eyes locked as if talking to each other, then THE ELDER made an slightest gesture of his head as if signaling something.

SUPREME COMMANDER HITLEOROUS, THE HEAD OF UNIFIED HIGH COMMAND OF UNIVERSAL GALACTIC DEFENSE INTER-GALAXY PRISONER-GARRISON excused himself from the presence of the other Generals and Commanders on the pretext that He is going out to lavatory to attend to his personal call of nature, yet in his mind plays important roles He must act and portray for the success and the realization of their groups much awaited Secret Plan.

In his mind dances the thoughts of opportunity for him to prove his worthiness of Command Management Implementation and Execution, and be recognized as one of the best in the hierarchy of UNIFIED HIGH COMMAND, and that this opportunity laid down in his career serves as an stepping stone of promotion to get out from the stink and stench of what he often called THE DUNGEON, WHICH IS THE UNIVERSAL GALACTIC DEFENSE INTER-GALAXY PRISONER-GARRISON, the butt of all jokes for all the Supreme Generals for whosoever was assigned to Command and Manage that Inter-Galaxy Prisoner-Garrison is nonetheless a PRISONER himself, a CAST-AWAY or what they jokingly called "EXILED", for the Prisoner-Galaxy was located at the desolate and inhospitable barren Southern End of the Planet Nibiru away from the Cities and Colonies, and famously feared because it was guarded by Laser Weapon Armed Robonoid, who mercilessly kill with-out question asked, no heart and no feelings, no emotions of any sort. ROBONOIDS programmed to guard and kill those they find enemy including those who want to escape the cruelty and stench of THE DUNGEON, in-which Supreme Commander Hitleorous dreaded and hate, but love as well for his advantage, for he knows the devastating Combat Power Capability they possess, for Him, the mission laid down upon his shoulder by the Secret Society Group was an important event of his life and career, it is his ticket to STARDOM, to emerge from the depths of The Dungeon and place himself at the Portals of the Elites. He must have only to follow precisely and diligently the Secret Plan and his mission at all cost, to make an impression to the higher ranking members of their group called THE SECRET SOCIETY.

SUPREME GENERAL JHESUSAN upon noticing the exit of Supreme Commander Hitleorous, feared in his mind what He and God Anuk had been long suspecting is already beginning, for he had long believe that Commander Hitleorous was a fanatic member of the renowned group called the Secret Society. A legendary known group inside Nibiru's Clans of Elite, that has also fanatic members inside the Unified High Command, composed of High Ranking Officials and Junior Officers whose leader was unknown but with common purpose of Idealism, The Destruction of Blue Planet Earth.

He looked at where God Anuk was but couldn't see him because of the frenzy Goddess Nakki caused among the crowd and audience watching and standing in awe and bewilderment. And when Supreme General Jhesusan finally saw God Anuk, it was impossible for him to approach his childhood friend and warn him of what he had observed and suspected. In his mind echoing the words "...THE BATTLE HAS JUST BEGUN..." and He decided himself of what to do.

One day prior The Grand Sacred Wedding, Thousands of fully armed ROBONOIDS in FULL BATTLE GEAR had arrived along with their Head Commander, Supreme Commander Hitleorous, in the outskirts of The Nibiru Royal Palace, under the order and authorization of SUPREME GENERAL

BHUDASIAN, HEAD OF THE UNIFIED HIGH COMMAND OF UNIVERSAL GALACTIC DEFENSE ADVANCE SCIENTIFIC RESEARCH CENTRAL COMMAND, with the consent and approval of SUPREME GENERAL SUN RAH, THE HEAD OF UNIFIED HIGH COMMAND OF UNIVERSAL GALACTIC DEFENSE PLANET NIBIRU PALACE SECURITY CENTRAL COMMAND, to be use as BACK-UP FORCE in-case of any enemies unforeseen and surprise Galactic Attack that will try to disrupt The Grand Sacred Wedding.

IT IS WHAT THE UNIFIED HIGH COMMAND OF UNIVERSAL GALACTIC DEFENSE AERO-POLICE AND SPACE-FORCE, UNDER SUPREME COMMANDER NAPOLEONOUS, TERMED AND CALLED "ADDITIONAL SECURITY COUNTER-ATTACK MEASURES" BACK-UP FORCE.

Unknown to Nibirunians Society, THE UNIFIED HIGH COMMAND OF UNIVERSAL GALACTIC DEFENSE ADVANCE SCIENTIFIC RESEARCH CENTRAL COMMAND UNDER SUPREME GENERAL BHUDASIAN had long been experimenting of HYBREED WARRIORS which their Great Planet can use in-case of any Galactic War or as a First Line of Defense against any aggression of their Planet from any other Planets known to them in Galaxy.

In the Book of Time, they had learned their lessons eons of time ago during the 1st Galactic War against a Planet of The Milky Way Galaxy called The Blue Planet Earth, where according to their Historical Records, The Blue Planet Earth during that Galactic war employed a new breed of creatures not known to the ordinary Nibirunians Unigalitizines, which they had suspected of Highly Advance Species of Humanoids, for it possess High Intelligence of Reasoning yet cunning and vicious when angered, and will defend its domain with ruthless accuracy of planning and execution, more even, will fight fearlessly even up to their last breath, they are FEARLESS and don't fear even Death, yet glorified it as a way of Honor and Glory of their existence and ending. These traits they had learned from these new species become the basis and basic tactic copied and applied by the Royal Guard Legionnaires when defending and escorting their Gods and Goddesses."HONOR AND GLORY EVEN IN DEATH"

THE UNIFIED HIGH COMMAND OF UNIVERSAL GALACTIC DEFENSE ADVANCE SCIENTIFIC RESEARCH CENTRAL COMMAND during that time tried to duplicate those creatures, and yet their test result always ends up a failure. They tried to research more of these new species of Blue Planet Earth and abducted thousands and thousands of these creatures for experimentation and further research, and yet, one after another, after numerous extensive research and operations of the core on the new species yields only atoms and molecules, sliced and torn body parts, mangled and butchered, were thrown like an animal waste in the abyss of universe becoming a cosmic dust.

Their failure didn't stop their quest to find out the core of this new species called HUMANOIDS, for they possess special quality and uniqueness compared to other Blue Planet Earth Creatures they had encountered, so they resort to new kind of experimentation, they will have to study the manner and characteristics of these new creature by observing their behavior and the way they live their day to day life, and hope to find that MISSING LINK of their experimentation.

And that's when they created a new branch of their Galactic Defense called THE UNIFIED HIGH COMMAND OF UNIVERSAL GALACTIC DEFENSE INTER-GALAXY INTELLIGENCE, a new branch created to serve its main sole purpose of SPYING and GATHERING INTELLIGENCE DATA, and as a result also created a sub-body called SPY-LEGIONS, THE ARMED AND MUSCLE OF THE UNIFIED HIGH COMMAND OF UNIVERSAL GALACTIC DEFENSE INTER-GALAXY INTELLIGENCE, not only Combat Ready but also functions as Alien Spies of Earth (ASOE) and sometimes ABDUCTOR OF HUMANOIDS as well.

In order to facilitate high-speed GATHERING OF INTELLIGENCE DATA ANALYZATION AND RECORDING, THE UNIFIED HIGH COMMAND that time built a SUPER-SPY MACHINE DEEP-SPACE CRAFT CALLED BLACK KNIGHT, and stationed it orbiting the Blue Planet Earth non-stop but can travel back and forth to their Planet Nibiru's location deep in Galactic Universe wherever they are, through a Galactic passage and highway they called THE GATEWAY of BLACK HOLES OR WORM HOLES.

For thousands of years they had gathered so much Intelligence Records of the HUMANOIDS, and it seems that as per their Data Research and Observation Analysis, these so-called SPECIES OF HUMANOIDS have the ability to control other creatures roaming the Blue Planet Earth. They have seen how these Humanoids tamed and herd big monster creatures what they called DINOSAURS, and also other living creatures, and use it to their day to day work advantage, even so they observe as per their Intelligence Data Record that they use and employ also these creatures during war which was remarkable as per their ANALYZATION REPORT CONCLUSION, for as years gone by, these so-called HUMANOIDS are so RESILIENT and INTELLIGENT that the acceleration of their brain intelligence was overwhelming, that as they advance their knowledge and civilization, it seems as well as per their Intelligence Gathering and Report, that the HUMANOIDS had slowly in time PERFECTED THE ART OF WAR, that again terrified the Nibirunians.

After a thousand years of the Great Experimentation and RESULTS OF FAILURE of duplicating this HUMANOID and not finding the core of its existence and essence, THE MISSING LINK, they turned to other sort of experimentation to match the advancement of the Civilization of the Blue Planet Earth and the Humanoids capability of DESTRUCTIVE WARFARE.

They began to harbor idea of mixing their advance technology of NANOCELLS into the body of HUMANOIDS which later on sanctioned by THE UNIFIED HIGH COMMAND to facilitate the advancement of their experiment and not go to waste. After the first set of test carried out, it became a hit and sensation among the hierarchy of Higher Command for they had seen their FUTURE ARMY, THE ROBONOIDS as they call it. They combined human species and robotics technology to create Robonoids, and with NANOCELL TECHNOLOGY, it become more apparent to them that this HYBREED WARRIOR they had created will become the most powerful army in the Galactic Universe, for these Robonoids creature they had created won't feel any pain, nor complain, it will only follow what it was programmed to do, TO KILL AND ANNIHILATE, for the ROBONOIDS have a microchip embedded at the back of their head to control and program them.

The ROBONOIDS were combat and battle tested when the Planet Nibiru was in the Constellation of Orion, in there they unleashed their ARMY OF DOOM and captured the Planet of the Star People, of which God Anuk was the son of the Ruler of that planet. They then incorporated to their Great

Civilization the captured planet's culture and into their society, making them new colonies in the Great Planet Nibiru.

Upon realizing the potential of the ROBONOIDS AS HYBREED WARRIOR, and as an ARMY OF DOOM, the Secret Society and THE ELDERS began to have keen interest for their own SECRET AGENDA, and devised plans for their vested interest and advantage. They held meetings after meetings in THE ELDERS CHAMBER OF TRUTH and concluded that they need to build POWERFUL ARMY from this HYBREED WARRIOR of ROBONOIDS, but must come from Blue Planet Earth's Species of Humanoids, and the program of ROBONOIDS must start with a HUMAN CHILD of 10 years old to 15 years old for extensive training of fearless combat and then install in their BLOOD the NANOCELLS so that in time as they grow mature they become more robotic of advance thinking, and with the MICRO-MEMORY-CHIP (MMC) embedded at the back of their head, they will become THE CORE OF THE NIBIRUNIAN ARMY, POWERFUL AND SOPHISTICATED WITH ADVANCE NANO-TECHNO-INTELLIGENCE, A RUTHLESS ARMY THAT WILL BECOME THE UNIVERSAL FIGHTING SOLDIERS.

It was the beginning of a new era, The SPY-LEGIONS and SUPER-SPY MACHINE DEEP-SPACE CRAFT CALLED BLACK KNIGHT began MASS ABDUCTION of Blue Planet Earth's HUMAN CHILDREN and transporting them back and forth to their Planet Nibiru across the vast galaxies and universe passing through THE GATEWAY of Black Holes and Worm Holes, straight into the WILDERNESS of what they called THE DUNGEON, to train in various aspect of Galactic Combat Tactics and transform their body and mind into robotic humanoid with MICRO-MEMORY-CHIP (MMC) AND NANOCELLS TECHNOLOGY becoming the most feared ARMY SOLDIERS in the Galactic Universe, for which they were called THE ROBONOIDS.

Supreme General Jhesusan excused himself as well among the Supreme Generals and made his way out of the frenzied crowd, and followed Supreme Commander Hitleorous where he was going. It was a bold and courageous decision on his part knowing he may expose himself to dangerous circumstances, yet in his mind He must find out what Supreme Commander Hitleorous is up to and satisfy his curiosity for he suspect that something fishy is happening right in-front of his own eyes, He want to help and protect his dearest childhood friend, God Anuk, from unscrupulous individuals that might try to harm him, and to make sure that THE GRAND SACRED WEDDING OF PLANET NIBIRU WILL BE SUCCESFUL, and fulfill the transfer of Kingdom-ship and Nibiru Throne to Goddess Nakki.

When Goddess Nakki deemed herself that she had fully satisfied the enjoyment of the crowds and audiences with her spectacles, she began to descend towards where God Anuk is standing. The crowd roared and cheered even more when they realized that Goddess Nakki was heading towards God Anuk. Goddess Nakki was very pleased of the audiences' appreciation and support because she knows and understands well in her heart and mind that she got the command of Nibiru's Society and her Subjects.

"...Order in the Palace Nibirunians, Order in the Palace, please get back to your seats and let us continue the ceremony orderly..." the Announcer announced to the ecstatic crowd and audiences

The Royal Palace Chamber Hall spotlights now beamed to where Goddess Nakki is, hovering above the Nibirunian audiences and slowly descending and approaching towards God Anuk, she was beaming with prowess and smiling gaily, her hands in upward posture, her perfect alluring body standing majestically captivating each and everyone inside the Royal Palace Chamber Hall. And when her space-craft carriage hovered beside God Anuk, everyone inside the Royal Palace Chamber Hall awaits the very moment God Anuk will receive his beloved, they were all caught up with excitement, gasping for their breathe as if expecting something more extra-ordinary to happen.

But it is not the case for some of THE ELDERS who are awaiting for different extra-ordinary to happen, for they are awaiting that cue and signal where they will make their own grand entrance to reveal themselves and announce their plan of taking over the THRONE of Planet Nibiru, to stage and fulfill their grand plan of their long much awaited REVENGE and VENGEANCE against the Blue Planet Earth. They are becoming impatient and look at each other's eyes communicating, for until now the realization of their Secret Plan was nowhere at sight, for them the waiting is like also an eon of time, they are awaiting the entrance and arrival of Supreme Commander Hitleorous and The Robonoids as a sign and cue for their taking over, THE COUP D'ETAT OF NIBIRU'S THRONE.

God Anuk cleared his spot of exciting audiences so that Goddess Nakki will have a smooth landing near him, as the announcer keeps on announcing and encouraging all the audiences to get back to their seats, Goddess Nakki continues her descending towards God Anuk, and when she finally arrived and landed in-front of God Anuk, the crowds are already calm and seating.

The announcer speak and announced "Nibirunians, Unigalitizines, with all due respect, may I present to you…behold, your Queen, Daughter of Universe, Goddess Nakki"

The audiences clapped their hands, and settled down, their eyes inquisitive as if anticipating of something more spectacular to come.

When Goddess Nakki stepped down from her round-disc aircraft carriage, all the audiences are stunned of what had transpired, even THE ELDERS were so amazed of what they had seen, truly an incredible and spectacular show and display of power and energy. The Nibirunians witnessed how the round-disc aircraft carriage of Goddess Nakki transformed into her wardrobe, of stunning display of awesome lights and sparkling jewels.

Vice Gandaheh live up to Goddess Nakki's expectation as expert in the Art of Universal Galactic Beautification, for truly her creation of inspired NanoTechnology created not only Goddess Nakki's aircraft carriage, but also serves as her wardrobe, upon Goddess Nakki stepping down from the round disc-aircraft carriage, instantly, the round-disc aircraft carriage transformed into a robotic serpent, and slowly crawl from Goddess Nakki's right legs encircling until it reached the upper torso, covering the perfect alluring breast of Goddess Nakki, then turned passing at the back of Goddess Nakki's head, with the head of the robotic serpent like a Cobra imposing above Goddess Nakki's head serving like a crown, with its eye radiating a red light like laser beam, that wherever Goddess Nakki turns her head, the robotic serpent eye radiating red-light laser beam also pinpoints, as if ready to strike and unleash a great power of devastating energy from its gaping mouth, with its two fangs protruding like a dagger of Diamond sparkling.

The whole Royal Palace Chamber Hall was filled with clapping hands and cheering, deep inside Goddess Nakki's heart was jubilation for she felt so much happiness and appreciation from her Subjects who are all already standing up giving her an standing ovation, not only as a sign of respect but of great admiration, perhaps even envy among Nibiru's Elite women. She then tried to find Vice Gandaheh among the audiences, and when she finally sees Vice Gandaheh, and caught her attention, she smiled and throw a kiss signifying her utmost pleasure of Vice Gandaheh's creation that brought tears of joy in Vice Gandaheh's eyes, and triumphant in her heart, for she never thought what she had created will have a grand effect on Goddess Nakki's lustrous beauty, it give her satisfaction that she had lived to Goddess Nakki's expectation of her, and that in all her capacity and talent, she did created a wedding gown so unique and brilliant, yet possess as well so much power and energy.

Some of The Elders who are members of the Secret Society felt terrified in their heart. They felt fear of Goddess Nakki's possession, for deep in their mind, the Cobra Serpent Head in Goddess Nakki's head was imposing and menacing, as if warning them that Goddess Nakki is ready to strike anytime to unleash her cosmic power of energy.

God Anuk then bowed down to the audiences, and gesture his right hand to take Goddess Nakki to their seats where the Shaman who will administer their wedding is waiting. And again, the Nibirunians cheered wildly, acknowledging, as if already celebrating the grand cosmic wedding with triumphant finale.

The Announcer again announces, "Order in the Royal Palace, Order in the Royal Palace" to which the Nibirunian audiences complied with, and one by one they sit and settled for the grand occasion.

And then comes again the sweet melancholic sound of music being played by the Galactic Symphonic Orchestra under Maestro WOLFGANG A. MOSSARTO, and all the audiences inside the Royal Palace Assembly Hall were mesmerized, including Goddess Nakki and God Anuk.

PLANET NIBIRU ROYAL PALACE ESCORT LEGIONNAIRE'S ARMOUR CROSS-SHIELD

PLANET NIBIRU GALACTIC ARMY LEGIONNAIRE'S ARMOUR CROSS-SHIELD

* * *

"... NOW I AM HERE,
PURSUING WHAT IS RIGHT
SEARCHING FOR WAYS
THAT WOULD HOLD ME SO TIGHT
TO FACE THE FUTURE
I WILL ALWAYS BELONG
AND TO EMBRACE THE MOMENTS

I DEARLY LONGED ..."

* * *

* * * THE 2ND COMING * * *

*** CHAPTER – 4 ***

THE ENEMY OF ENEMY

There was a legend and myth recorded in the Nibirunians Book of Time that once upon a time, eon of years ago, in a distant Planet called Blue Planet Earth in the Galaxy of Milky Way, the Nibirunian ancestors and forefathers experimented by mixing their DNA through copulation with different creatures inhabiting that planet until such time they had perfected what they called Species of Humanoids, to make these new life forms as SLAVES for the sole purpose of mining and excavating the Blue Planet Earths vast minerals and natural resources for their Planet Nibiru's needed energy, it was the time of Ruler-ship of Goddess Nakki's Great Great Grand Father, the late LORD GOD ADANIS and his Queen wife, the late GODDESS EVANUS.

It was a dangerous and chaotic time on Blue Planet Earth as different kinds of animals and creatures roams its wilderness, as a result of vast experimentation conducted by the NIBIRU'S UNIFIED HIGH COMMAND OF UNIVERSAL GALACTIC DEFENSE ADVANCE SCIENTIFIC RESEARCH CENTRAL COMMAND. There were giant beings with one eye on the forehead called Cyclops. Horses with half human body called Centaurs. Serpents with half human upper body, sea creatures called mermaids, a fish with half woman body, even humans with dog's head, cat's head, a Lion with a human head called Sphinx, and so on. There were also giant creatures such as Dinosaurs, Reptiles and Amphibians which are savages and carnivorous.

One fine day in the Planet of Nibiru, God Adanis decided to visit and roam Blue Planet Earth along with his trusted and elite Legionnaires, the Palace Galactic Royal Guards as escorts, and along with him was then Supreme Commander of the Royal Guards, Supreme Commander Michael, and his right hand, Commander Gabriel, and twelve elite Galactic Royal Guard Legionnaires aboard the Royal Space Shuttle called VIMANA.

PLANET NIBIRU ROYAL GALACTIC DEEP SPACE CRAFT VIMANA

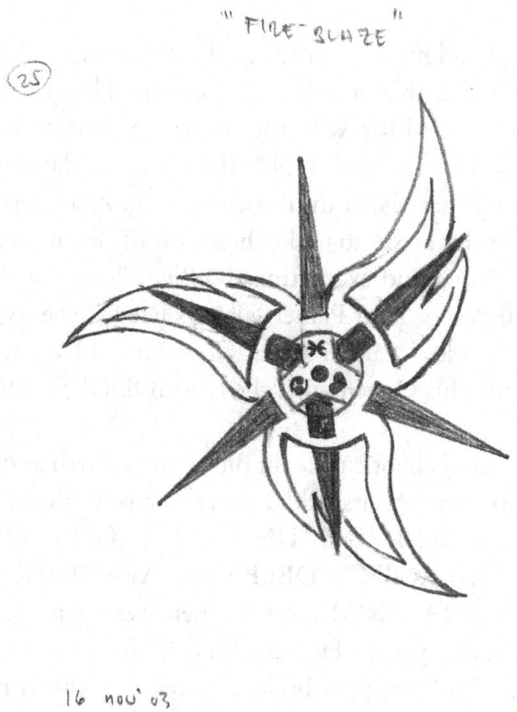

In their wandering of Blue Planet Earth's surface going from places to places exploring the vastness and its untamed beauty of wilderness, they observed numerous PYRAMIDS and TEMPLES being built in different corners and remote places of the Blue Planet Earth, some were in the highest peak of mountains of land called Americas, others are in the deserts of a place called Egyptiuz Africanis. And they also saw giant creatures called Dinosaurs being herd and use by Cyclops Humanoids to haul, transfer and arrange enormous size of stone tablets cut in granite, under the watchful eye of Legionnaires guarding and acting as Governor of each mining camp and the Pyramid building camps, they also saw un-intelligible humanoid forms of enormous size which they called the TITANS of those days which were being employed and exploited as well by the Legionnaires building GIANT WALLS AND FORTRESSES, AQUEDUCTS, CASTLES AND ENCAMPMENT and COMPLEX CAVES under direct orders of SUPREME COMMANDER LUCIFER, THE TASK COMMANDER OF EARTH MINING, AND DURING THE GREAT THOUSAND YEARS EXPERIMENTATION AND EXPLORING EARTH, THE COMMANDER OF GALACTIC SPECIAL FORCES EXPEDITIONARY COMMAND OF PLANET NIBIRU TO BLUE PLANET EARTH.

Lord God Adanis and his Commanders debated intelligently of what purpose those PYRAMIDS around the world in conspicuous places they had seen being built, and they argued that it could be a TEMPLE, A LANDING PAD, A TOWER STRUCTURE FOR NAVIGATIONAL MARKINGS, or perhaps as Lord Adanis suspect, AN ENERGY REFILLING STATION FOR SPACE CRAFTS OR, AS HE FEARS IT, A WEAPON OF SOME KIND, and whatever the purpose those structures He had seen, he was thinking of giving Supreme Commander Lucifer a Citation or Commendation for his valuable work and service to Planet Nibiru, for Lord God Adanis saw with his own eyes the enormous task and responsibility that was laid upon on Commander Lucifer's shoulder. "…He deserves the accolade of Planet Nibiru…" Lord God Adanis pondered

Lord God Adanis in his keen interest of exploring Blue Planet Earth, observed that the new life forms of SLAVE SPECIES have great resolute of fortitude and strength of mind, for He noticed that even in their great misery of working hours and hours of excavating and mining the Blue Planet Earth minerals, even in the midst of cruelties of the Nibirunians in-charge of supervising the mining operations, the humanoids don't complain and protest their conditions, and most of all, in spite of their hardships, find time to be happy and have satisfaction after a day's work with their own kind of species copulating which makes their population growing in numbers, and growing strong.

Lord God Adanis asked himself of what substance, qualities and behavior these new species possess in their DNA that makes them unique. He thought that these new species whom they have experimented and created in their LIKENESS AND FORMS by thousand years of experimentation of copulation until they perfected such species, possess that special quality in which in his Godly mind don't comprehend well. THE SPECIES called HUMANOIDS possess the character of Individualistic Performance, Will of Advancement, Behavior of Adaptability, Instinct of Self-Progress, Animalistic Inner-side, Survival Skills, KILLER INSTINCT, and yet also possess Love and Affection, Compassion, and many more attributes he couldn't find in any other life forms he encountered during his keen and astute observation while roaming the Blue Planet Earth, and wondered to himself that these new Species whom they created in their Likeness compared to other beings of other Planet in the Universe He had visited, and their Planet Nibiru frequented were really something SPECIAL and UNIQUE. Lord God Adanis in his deep pondering about these Species called Humanoids of Blue Planet Earth concluded that, there is a Missing Link that He wants to know, to fully understand the core and substance of these creatures.

He then decided to put to TEST these new species of creatures of life forms called HUMANOIDS to proof his doubts and satisfy his curiosity, and get answers for that Missing Link He wants to solve, for He him-self cannot comprehend well how these creatures of Human Species possessed that Gift of Divine Will to Survive. Lord God Adanis devise a plan to conduct his experimentation test, for if the humanoids will pass his EXPERIMENTATION TEST He will let them undergo, then He might consider absorbing and integrate this new species as new life forms of colonies in their Planet Nibiru's Society and Subjects, for the perfection of their Galactic Universal kind, The Nibirunians, Universal Galactic Citizens or UNIGALITIZINES as they called themselves.

Lord God Adanis ordered Supreme Commander Michael to steer their deep-space shuttle VIMANA to head the course going to the ISLAND CITY OF ATLANTIS where the OVER-ALL IN-CHARGE TASK COMMANDER OF BLUE PLANET EARTH'S MINERALS MINING OPERATION, SUPREME COMMANDER LUCIFER, along with his GALACTIC

SPECIAL FORCES EXPEDITIONARY COMMAND MADE AS EARTH'S BASE AND THEIR PALATIAL DWELLING.

"… Aye aye Lord God Adanis, steering control hard starboard now, heading course Zero Zero Zero Degrees to Atlantis City…" replied Supreme Commander Michael who has the conning of the deep-space shuttle Vimana, He then ordered his Communication Officer, Commander Gabriel to send an advance message to Security Command Center of Atlantis City that they are going there in an un-scheduled visitation, but instructed Commander Gabriel not to put anything in Passenger and Cargo Manifest, to conceal the arrival of Lord God Adanis so as not to create news and disrupt the Mining Operation Management, it is simply a quiet and un-official visitation.

Supreme Commander Michael by his Navigational calculation, they will arrive in Atlantis City located in an ocean called Atlantic Ocean between two continental land where the great mining camp under Supreme Commander Lucifer, in about half an hour for they are already half of the Blue Planet Earth away, as per his Navigational Electronic Chart Monitor, their space shuttle Vimana is already above the land called AUSTRALIS, he touch his navigational electronic screen and plotted Navigational Route Plan of coordinates and waypoints, passing Asian Minor, Africaniz and Europa, he then put the space shuttle Vimana on auto-pilot upon completion of his coordinates programming, and announced inside the shuttle through the phone-chip attached to his Space Helmet.

"…Hear me, Hear me, this is your Flight Commander announcing Royal Space Shuttle flight on auto-pilot and auto-landing mode now, E.T.A (estimated time of arrival) to destination, about half an hour, fasten all your seatbelt, put on our Space Helmet and activate Flight Auto-Sleep Mode, preserve your body energy, this is your Flight Commander, Supreme Commander Michael, signing out…" and all who heard what Supreme Commander Michael had just announced including Lord God Adanis obeyed and complied with.

"…How much is the distance?..." a commanding voice asked firmly, his heart and mind filled with excitement, because in his lifetime existence, he felt that his long overdue recognition in-which he has been dreaming of ever since He become the Supreme Commander of the GALACTIC SPECIAL FORCES EXPEDITIONARY COMMAND on Earth will finally be Galactically honored, at least that's what his thoughts playing on his mind. He never considered that one fine day, The Nibiru's Royal Space Shuttle Vimana will come, dock and visit his Blue Planet Earth Base Camp Atlantis City, it was un-announced and surprise visit by Nibiru's Royal Space Shuttle, and that the Royal Space Shuttle will never leave The Planet Nibiru without it's Royal Highness on-board, the Lord God Adanis, and yet in the Passenger and Cargo Manifest electronically received, there was no mention of who are coming, it only says that "To Supreme Commander Lucifer, Royal Space Shuttle departed Planet Nibiru, ETA HALF AN HOUR, Space craft on auto-pilot and auto-landing mode, request permission to dock with OK clearance and assistance, REPLY ON AUTO-ACKNOWLEDGE!"

Supreme Commander Lucifer felt immense joy and excitement in his heart and mind, yet not at ease with the surprise visit. What will be their purpose? Who are inside the Vimana? Did they come to HONOR me, of my great contribution as TASK COMMANDER of these great mining on Blue Planet Earth for our Planet Nibiru's consumption of ENERGY, all these inkling thoughts playing again and again in his mind, at the very least, the Royal Space Shuttle coming and docking is already a great honor for me, he thought, it will be his symbolic bastion and pride for his Family and Ancestors.

"…500 aeromiles, Supreme Commander…" come the reply immediately "… their speed slowing down, their space shuttle on AUTO-PILOT AND AUTO-LANDING MODE…"

"…very well, initiate AUTO-LANDING PAD AND AUTO-SPACE CRAFT LANDING ASSISTANCE…" commanded Supreme Commander Lucifer

"…Aye aye Supreme Commander, initiating AUTO-LANDING PAD AND AUTO-SPACE CRAFT LANDING ASSISTANCE…" replied one of his Legionnaire, his Command Center space-craft landing operator

"…initiate SPACE-CRAFT APPROACH EMERGENCY CONTINGENCY…" again Supreme Commander Lucifer commanded, and another Legionnaire acknowledges his command

"… AUTO-LANDING PAD AND AUTO-SPACE CRAFT LANDING ASSISTANCE clear and operational, SPACE-CRAFT APPROACH EMERGENCY CONTINGENCY ready and on stand-by Supreme

Commander…" reported back of his Executive Officer, (Ex-O), the ever loyal to him Commander Draculatis

"…very well, everything is going smooth, how much their distance and speed now, please update me…" Supreme Commander Lucifer asked his Executive Officer, his eyes fixed to the giant monitor screen showing the landing pad area, and the emergency contingency team on-alert, ready and stand-by.

"…200 aeromiles, coming on Dead Slow Ahead, 1000RPM…" replied Commander Draculatis

"…OK, I acknowledge…" replied Supreme Commander Lucifer and when the Royal Space Shuttle appeared on their monitor screen slowly descending, he commanded again, '…initiate pyramid landing gear…on my count, 5, 4, 3, 2, 1…activate…"

And as the Royal Space Shuttle slowly vertically descending to the landing pad, suddenly the landing pad opens and slowly a small pyramid comes out, meeting the Vimana in mid-air interlocking the bottom flat underside and concave center of the Space Shuttle Vimana, and when the interlocking was completed, slowly the pyramid goes down until the Space Shuttle Vimana was secured on deck of the Space-craft landing pad.

"…well done my ever loyal Legionnaires, Planet Nibirus Royal Palace Space Shuttle landed successfully, now let's go and welcome our un-expected visitors and what they up to…" Supreme Commanded Lucifer grinningly uttered, but before they go out to meet their visitor and guest, he give orders to all his Legionnaires to be COMBAT READY, in his mind, these are risky and dangerous times.

"WHAT IF?..." he asked himself, "WHAT IF THEY HAVE KNOWN OF MY GREAT PLAN?" in his mind comes this disturbing thoughts, and when he sees that all his Legionnaires are in FULL BATTLE GEAR, he shouted on top of his voice, "…MY LEGIONNAIRES, BE ALERT AND READY…" to which all his Legionnaires acknowledge with one unified shout "…HURRAH…"

Supreme Commander Lucifer then signal to open the Atlantis City Base Camp of its Space Craft Landing Pad Arrival Bay access door, and proceeded to march in uniform motion, with him at the front, proud and confident, in full battle gear yet decorated Galactic Uniform.

Meanwhile, upon docking of the Royal Palace Space Shuttle on the Atlantis City Base Camp space craft landing pad, the space helmet of all passenger inside the space craft were automatically filled with cloudy luminous smoke, which awaken Lord God Adanis and all his companions inside. And when all of them had fully recovered, they prepared themselves to meet the unsung hero of their Planet Nibiru, Supreme Commander Lucifer and his Legionnaires, but before going out as well, Supreme Commander Michael cautioned Lord God Adanis to be very careful and exercise extreme caution in dealing with Supreme Commander Lucifer, for he knows how cunning and foxy this Supreme Commander is, and proceeded to order all his Twelve Legionnaires along with his right hand, Commander Gabriel, to be alert and ready, and not to leave Lord God Adanis in-sight, and must protect him according to decorum, the elite Royal Palace Galactic Royal Guard Creed "Honor and Glory even in Death, Defender of Kingdom's Throne, Defender of Nibiru's Royalties."

Supreme Commander Michael draw his laser sword and raise above the head of Lord God Adanis, to which all his Legionnaires follows, and in one unison shout, shouted "...HONOR AND GLORY, EVEN IN DEATH..."

Supreme Commander Michael and his Legionnaires put back their laser sword to its electronic scabbard, and then aligned themselves in rectangle battle formation with Lord God Adanis in the center, protecting him, six by six on each side, Supreme Commander Michael in middle front and Commander Gabriel in the rear center, uniformly slowly marching coming out from the opened ramp of the Royal Space Shuttle rear entrance as if in a grand parade.

Supreme Commander Lucifer positioned himself and his Legionnaires in a Parade of Honors Formation, composing of One Company with Four Platoons, and each Platoon composed of Four Squads of Eight Element each, excluding the Platoon Legionnaires Sergeant, and it's Lieutenant Commander. All in all, Commander Lucifer is commanding a total of One Hundred Forty Legionnaires including his trusted Executive Officer, Commander Draculatis and Three more Commanders, which during their formation, His four Commanders, standing straight and align one meter apart from each other at his back.

And when the slowly and uniformly marching Palace Galactic Royal Guards Escorts came to right angle and abeam of Supreme Commander Lucifer and his Legionnaires, his Executive Officer, Commander Draculatis shouted and commanded "…EARRTHHHH LEEEGIOONNAAAAAIRE, GALACTIIIIIIIIIIC SALUTE!!!…", and in one swift uniformed motion, all Legionnaires of Supreme Commander Lucifer including him draw their laser sword from their right hand, place it on their chest and raise above their head forty-five degrees inclined, all laser swords radiating with FLAMING LASER BLADES, signifying their GALACTIC SALUTE and respect to their visitor, His Royal Highness, Lord God Adanis.

Supreme Commander Michael acknowledge Supreme Commander Lucifer's Salute of Parade of Honors, and commanded his Legionnaires while still in battle formation and slowly marching, "…NIBIRU LEGIONNAIRES, ROYAL GUARDS, GALACTIC SALUTE…" and at the same time, in one swift motion as well, draw their laser sword, briefly put in their chest, and raise it straight above their head, all their laser sword in FLAMES OF ACID LASER FIRE, signifying their acknowledgement of Supreme Commander Lucifer and his Legionnaires Salute of Honors, and also signifying their dominion over them by raising their laser sword straight above their head, to which Supreme Commander Lucifer caught his attention, and make his heart annoyed and irritated, even-so, Supreme Commander Michael also noticed what Supreme Commander Lucifer and his Legionnaires had shouted, "…EARTH LEGIONNAIRE?..." in his mind stirred a questionable and disturbing thoughts of instinct, a gruesome premonition that brought chills in his heart and mind.

After the welcome Parade of Honors and Salute, there was Grand Festivities in Atlantis City. Commander Dionysius and Commander Temptress, as instructed by Supreme Commander Lucifer took charge of all the merriments and events, and presented to their guest and visitors fine Species of Humanoids. They personally hand-pick from different regions of Blue Planet Earth beautiful and voluptuous female humanoids as sacrificial sexual favors to their visitors deity including Lord God Adanis.

Legends says that these female humanoids whom Commander Dionysius and Commander Temptress personally hand-picked would later become important persona of their time as a result of getting impregnated by the visiting Legionnaires, their children would later become the KINGS and

QUEENS of their lands like Babylon, Manchuria, Aztec, Egyptians, Africans, Mongols, Turks, Celtics, Saxons, and many more.

In these legends comes one myth and story of controversy that for eon of time was still a mystery. It was told that Lord God Adanis impregnated one female humanoid and bore him a daughter named Magandalena, but the child was never found and seen again before the First Galactic War erupted, it was a myth that questions the validity of the Royal Lineage of Goddess Nakki.

"DEMI-GOD, COMMANDER TEMPTRESS"

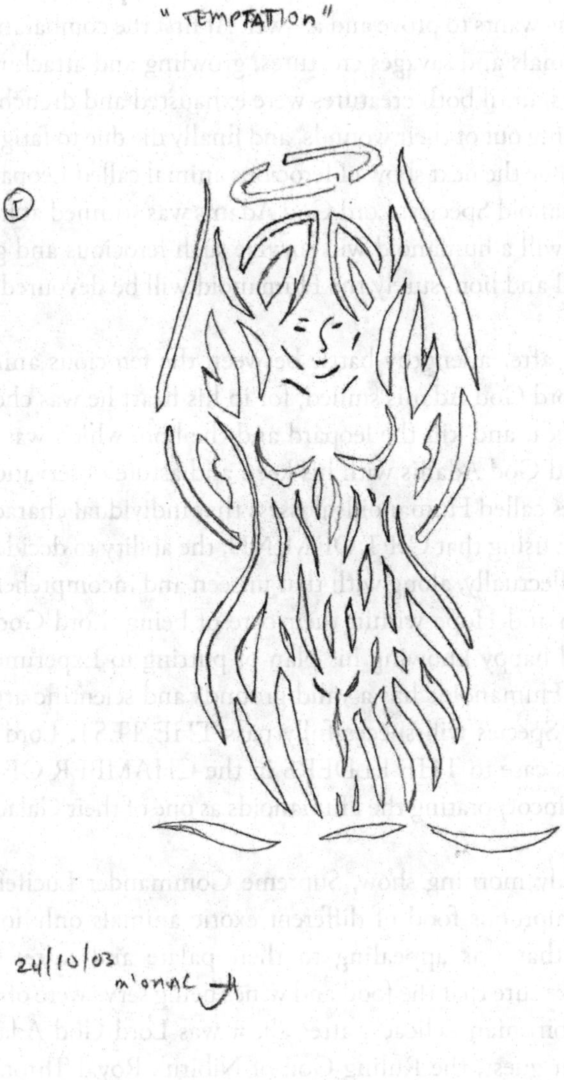

In the morning after the night of sexual festivities, another show was presented again by Supreme Commander Lucifer to his guest and visitors, it was a show that caught the attention of Lord God Adanis, for in it shows an act of barbarism, and yet it was a show that answers his questions of Humanoids Missing Link he wants to prove and answer. At first the combatant in the arena were giant animals and savages creatures, growling and attacking each other with savageness, until both creatures were exhausted and drenched with their own blood oozing out of their wounds, and finally die due to fatigue and loss of blood. Then come the next show of ferocious animal called Leopard and Lions, against a Humanoid Species. Lord God Adanis was stunned at first for he was thinking how will a humanoid will survive such ferocious and giant animals such as leopard and lion, surely the Humanoid will be devoured to pieces.

Yet in the end after a lengthy battle between the ferocious animals and the Humanoid, Lord God Adanis smiled, for in his heart he was cheering for the humanoid to beat and kill the leopard and the lion, which was exactly what happened. Lord God Adanis with his keen and astute observation concluded that the Species called Humanoids possess that individual character of WILL TO SURVIVE using that GIFT OF MIND, the ability to decide intelligently and think intellectually, along with that unseen and incomprehensible Divine Power of Faith and Hope within their core of being. Lord God Adanis was so smiling and happy knowing his plan of putting to Experimentation Test the Species of Humanoids has a valid grounds and scientific argument, that if the Human Species will successfully pass THE TEST, Lord God Adanis will present his case to THE ELDERS in the CHAMBER OF TRUTH, of absorbing and incorporating the Humanoids as one of their Galactic Colonies.

After the bloody morning show, Supreme Commander Lucifer presented a banquet of sumptuous food of different exotic animals only found on Blue Planet Earth that was appealing to their palate and taste, Commander Draculatis make sure that the food and wines being serve were of finest quality and match Nibirunian delicacy, after all, it was Lord God Adanis who was their important guest, the Ruling God of Nibiru's Royal Throne, they must have to satisfy and make impression of him as strictly commanded by Supreme Commander Lucifer.

In the afternoon, Lord God Adanis after indulging himself with the foods and wines offered by Supreme Commander Lucifer, decided to tell Supreme Commander Lucifer his plans of incorporating the Humanoids into Nibiru

Society as one colony, if they will pass the Experimentation Test He devised. Lord God Adanis devised a plan of putting two humanoids, one male and one female, into simple test of OBEDIENCE.

He told Supreme Commander Lucifer that He is planning to put the two humanoids into their Planet Nibiru's Garden of Edena, and will ask and command them not to eat the fruit of Tree of Knowledge of Good and Evil and the Tree of Life, where-as they could eat everything, but not the fruit of the two tree being commanded, and if they shall so pass the test, it means the humanoids can easily be govern and administer, and that they can be absorb into Nibiru Society for advancement and perfection of their great civilization, but, if the humanoids will dis-obey what they are commanded to do, then they shall put to death and forever be condemned to dwell in hardships and hard labors in the face of Blue Planet Earth. Supreme Commander Lucifer was listening attentively to what Lord God Adanis was explaining to him, but at the back of his mind, something was brewing within his pride and egoistic self.

Legends and myths as told from generations to generations that what happened next was indescribable, there was a misunderstanding and altercation during the after lunch meeting of Lord God Adanis and Supreme Commander Lucifer, there was a hearsay that Supreme Commander Lucifer didn't agree of Lord God Adanis plan to put the humanoids to Intelligence Test, and to integrate the Humanoids into Planet Nibiru society if they shall so pass this SECRET TEST, and Supreme Commander Lucifer for whatever REASON in his mind and heart didn't agree and argued angrily with Lord God Adanis, and after a lengthy and heated debate, finally Supreme Commander Lucifer lose his temper and claimed He is the only God of these new Species called Humanoids, and goes to proclaim his REBELLION against Lord God Adanis, and to all the Gods and Goddesses Of Planet Nibiru.

The Book of Time somewhat have a hidden pages that don't divulge as to what really happened during that time, although at present under Goddess Nakki's reign, there are select few who knows and have knowledge of these hidden pages of Book of Time. The only witnesses during that time who could give accounts as to what really happened were the two Royal Guard Escort Legionnaires survivors that was escorting Lord God Adanis in that tragic and fateful day, whom Supreme Commander Lucifer spared their life to navigate the Royal Palace Space Shuttle back to Planet Nibiru as a SIGN and MESSAGE OF REBELLION. And yet when the surviving two Royal Guard

Escort Legionnaires were being interrogated, they were in terrible fear and shocked of what they have witnessed and seen that sometimes they couldn't speak intelligently, and so frightened as if they have lost their sanity, and in the long run condemned to damnation by the Nibirunians Galactic High Tribunal of Investigation to eternal frozen death, thrown and vanished in the abyss of galactic universe as wandering corpse of cosmic dust, they were condemned not as punishment but to alleviate them from their horrific nightmares and painful experience that is making them insane corroding their innermost sense of sanity into insanity. The Galactic High Tribunal of Investigation perhaps wants to conceal and cover-up as to what really happened to quell the anger of The Nibirunians Unigalitizines.

The whole Planet of Nibiru was on the verge of Civil War because during that era, they themselves, THE ELDERS, and the Gods and Goddesses couldn't agree with each other and make solutions how to deal SANELY with what happen to Lord God Adanis and his trusted escort Royal Guards Legionnaires, for if they will report what they had found out, and will be known to all the Nibirunians Unigalitizines what really transpired, their Galactic Society will collapse, all the foundation of Universal Good Governance will be questioned and tarnished with Evil Deeds, so that what the Galactic High Tribunals Reported in the final investigation report was ALL FALSIFICATION OF DOCUMENTS AND EVIDENCE, of what they called WHITE LIES, The Galactic High Tribunals had reported that Lord God Adanis and his companions of Royal Palace Escort Legionnaires encountered a much sophisticated and savage Species called HUMANOIDS, that monstrously killed and murdered them.

Yet, the truth is, all evidence of what befalls them was found inside the Royal Palace Galactic Space Shuttle cargo bay at the stern part, which was splattered all over by the bloods of the Legionnaires, they were all massacred cruelly and monstrously killed. Supreme Commander Michael was beheaded but his body was full of traces of cuts and wounds of laser swords that proves they never give up and battled THE ENEMY up to their last breath, Commander Gabriel body was terrorized and full of laser burnt that one can't recognized, the other ten Legionnaires body were never recovered and nowhere to be found, their Heads severed and found pierced to their laser sword's end and the handle planted in pots of Blue Planet Earth's soil, placed standing around Lord God Adanis body which was crucified upside down as if mocking the whole Planet of Nibiru. It was a grotesque sight and shocking moment for all Nibirunians that ignites and started the 1st Galactic War.

The descendants of those who had perished in that debacle never forget what had happened during that blackest fateful day. They remained quiet and calmed, resolved, and planned secretly for eon of time, awaiting that perfect timing of their REVENGE. Some of these descendants rise to power and occupied high positions in Nibiru's Society, some are Generals in the Unified High Command, and some are members of the ELDERS and the so-called NIBIRU'S POWERFUL ELITE GROUP OF SECRET SOCIETY.

And now, in the grand sacred wedding of Goddess Nakki and God Anuk, they are their attending, disguising and masquerading their identity, awaiting that final cue of revealing themselves, to seize and take over the Throne Of Planet Nibiru, so that no one will oppose their much awaited realization of REVENGE, the annihilation and full destruction of Human Race, and the condemnation to frozen eternal death of those DEMIGODS, lead by Commander Lucifer who betrayed their Planet Nibiru, and defiled their Lord God Adanis and his Royal Palace Guard Escort Legionnaires, for as per Galactic Defense Inter-Galaxy Intelligence Report under Supreme Commander Ceazarous, THE REBELS led by Supreme Commander Lucifer and some of his loyal Legionnaires, the Demigods that include Commander Draculatis, Commander Dionysius and Commander Temptress survived the 1st Galactic War and were still alive, hiding in the shadows of Blue Planet Earth, treating themselves as Gods of Blue Planet Earth.

"REVENGE"
BY MONAC
(POETIC BREEZE, POETIC FROTH PART 1 – POEM NO. 133)

QUICKLY,
BEFORE IT'S TOO LATE
LONELY MOON,
SLOWLY CREEPING IN
AMIDST,
HARROWING DARKNESS
SOMEONE IS LAUGHING
IN ANGER.
TEARS,
COMES IN FURY
A MADDENING THUNDER
OF BEAUTY
BEHIND,
IS A LIGHT
OF REVENGE
THE SWEETNESS
OF SEEING YOU
IN PAIN!

***

"DOOR OF PASSAGE
BEYOND ABYSS OF DREAMS
TO WHERE LOVE
IS REAL AND ETERNITY
LET COSMIC ENERGY
BREATHE THE LIFE WITHIN
AND SEEK DESTINY
WITH REALITY"

***

* * * THE 2ND COMING * * *

*** CHAPTER – 5 ***

THE ESCAPE

As excitement builds within the walls inside the Royal Palace Chamber Hall because of the Grand Galactic Wedding Ceremony, and the frenzied audiences brought upon by Goddess Nakki's spectacular show and display of her grand entrance, unknown to the Nibirunians who were wildly and enthusiastically cheering the spectacle, another dramatic and intense scene is unfolding beneath the maze and labyrinth dungeons of the Royal Castle, where Supreme Commander Hitleorous made a dashing run to meet his troops of one hundred self-handpicked ROBONOIDS who are mustering and waiting in one of the Royal Palace dungeons.

He knows that time is running out and he must act at once to re-program the Robonoids "Micro-Memory-Chip" embedded in their heads so as to obey what they will be command of, and not harm the Nibirunians Unigalitizines, unless they are force upon to fire their deadly laser weapon. He and the Robonoids in Full Battle Gear and Combat Ready should enter the Royal Palace Chamber Hall with-out the Nibirunians or any other member of Royal Palace Security doubting of their intention and His mission as ordered from the Top Rank of their organization and Secret Society, after all, as per Royal Galactic Wedding Plan, the Robonoids are there as additional security counter-measures for any unforeseen galactic attack that will distract the Grand Wedding of Goddess Nakki and God Anuk as sanctioned and approved by the Unified High Command of Royal Palace Security Command under Supreme General Sun Rah and Supreme Commander Hannibalkan, he just have to fulfill dutifully his mission in order to place his name amongst the elite of Nibirunians high ranking hierarchy command, and the fulfillment of his long awaited dreams, to be promoted as Supreme General.

It will be his entrance along with his troops of one hundred self-handpicked Robonoids that will be the cue of THE ELDERS and their followers and alliances to reveal themselves during the wedding of Goddess Nakki and God Anuk, to stage their plan of COUP D'ETAT, and take over the throne of Nibiru Planet before the Shaman proclaim Goddess Nakki and God Anuk universally wed as couple, husband and wife for eternity. He should be at Royal Palace Chamber Hall positioning himself near the Shaman so that when the Shaman ask if there is anyone against the wedding before he proclaim them as grand galactic couple, he is there to shout "I AM".

And whatever the consequences it will bring out of his action, he knows for sure that the Secret Society he pledge his allegiance will be there for him to reveal themselves and take over the throne of Nibiru Planet, and all their agenda and plans for eon of years will come to reality, and most of it all, his place in annals of Book of Time as the one who gives the final signal to THE ELDERS and their alliances to reveal themselves and seize the throne and power of Nibiru Planet, in his mind dances the sweetest thoughts of his promotion to Supreme General.

Meanwhile, Supreme General Jhesusan was at first at lost to what's going on, and then fully realize the danger that lies ahead with Supreme Commander Hitleorous and the Robonoids around. He knows that they are a part of the Galactic Wedding Plan as part of additional security counter-measures, yet his mind convinces him that something is wrong. He must have to find at once what is the hidden agenda why the Robonoids are there when in-fact there is no really threat of unforeseen attack during Goddess Nakki and God Anuk wedding, as per intelligence data gathered and reported by the UNIFIED HIGH COMMAND OF UNIVERSAL GALACTIC DEFENSE INTERNAL INTELLIGENCE under Supreme Commander Alexandrous and UNIFIED HIGH COMMAND OF UNIVERSAL GALACTIC DEFENSE INTER-GALAXY INTELLIGENCE under Supreme Commander Ceazarous.

He believes in his heart and mind that something dangerous and disastrous is brewing, and that his childhood dear friend God Anuk and his wife to be Goddess Nakki are in great danger of losing their life, perhaps even all of the Nibirunian Unigalitizines are in danger of being hurt by the Robonoids, for this reason he must have to act fast and locate where is Supreme Commander Hitleorous and confront him of his motives, why he brought along with him thousands of Robonoids, and self-handpicked one hundred elite Robonoids as part of Royal Palace Chamber Hall additional security counter-measures, when there is no really threat, even more he was terrified of what he came to understand.

He now believes that Supreme Commander Hitleorous and his troops of one hundred self-handpicked Robonoids are the real threat and enemy within, and are a part of greater conspiracy within the Unified High Command high ranking officials, along with THE ELDERS and their alliances, awaiting for their final cue to reveal themselves during the grand galactic wedding of Goddess Nakki and God Anuk, in order to seize and control the power and throne of Planet Nibiru for them to once and for all enact what their Secret Society had planned eon of years, THE ANNIHILATION OF HUMANOIDS AND DESTRUCTION OF BLUE PLANET EARTH AS PART OF THEIR VENGEANCE, TO AVENGE THEIR FOREFATHERS HUMILIATING DEFEAT AT THE HANDS OF THE EARTHLINGS DURING THE 1ST GALACTIC WAR, AND THEIR LONG OVERDUE REVENGE AGAINST THE DEMI-GODS WHO HELP THE HUMANOIDS, LED BY SUPREME COMMANDER LUCIFER, ALONG WITH HIS LOYAL LEGIONNAIRES.

It becomes clear now to Supreme General Jhesusan what a big conspiracy he had found out, and he must play cat and mouse at the moment in order to assess the situation, so as not to divulge to the enemy what he come to know and understand. He don't know yet the scope of who were the real enemies are, and who were the ally's amongst the High Ranking Officials of Unified High Command, he just have to play his cards, and at the moment, he knows what Supreme Commander Hitleorous was up to. He knows now that Commander Hitleorous will bring the Robonoids within the walls inside the Royal Palace Chamber Hall in order to position them surrounding the Royal Palace Security Guards and the Royal Escorts under Commander Levonne, so that when the right time comes, Supreme Commander Hitleorous will give the final signal of COUP D'ETAT, and that with the Robonoids in strategic places, all Royal Security Guards and Royal Escorts forces will be powerless and can be easily dis-armed.

Supreme General Jhesusan, in the midst of jubilation amongst Nibirus Unigalitizines lost track where Commander Hitleorous went to, He's heart is beating fast while traversing the hallways of the Royal Palace, shook his head, his eyes searching every corner of the hallways alley, and tried to imagine to locate the where-about and location of Supreme Commander Hitleorous, and the one hundred elite Robonoids.

In his mind dictates, surely there must be a way to find Supreme Commander Hitleorous.

He is running against fate and destiny, and cannot waste any single second of time, he must have to act fast in-order to save his childhood friend, God Anuk, including Goddess Nakki, and the whole Planet Nibiru as well, from the hands of THE ELDERS and the Group called Secret Society, who are power hungry and only want vengeance and revenge, and are just a grasp away of fully realizing their Grand Plan of Destruction to reality by seizing the Throne of Power of Nibiru planet by staging Coup D'état during the Grand Galactic Wedding of Goddess Nakki and God Anuk. They are just waiting for the arrival of Supreme Commander Hitleorous and the Robonoids.

He went straight to the Royal Palace Intelligence Command Office, and upon entering ordered at once the lone Legionnaire on-duty to scroll-on the luminous computer web monitor screen, and locate the location of Supreme Commander Hitleorous and the one hundred elite Robonoids. The Leggionaire on-duty, Centurion Sheen Ezriel, monitoring the Royal Palace Intelligence Command Office and it's web feeds of CCTV all over the Royal Palace was at first shocked, for He thought he was caught by Supreme General Jhesusan watching in one of the web screen monitor the whole spectacle, enjoying the grand show of Goddess Nakki and God Anuk. Centurion Sheen Ezriel at once stand up and raise his hand in close fist and throw a Nibirunian salute to Supreme General Jhesusan.

Again, Supreme General Jhesusan shouted on top of his voice and commanded, "Centurion, at ease, back to your post, but locate me at once where is Supreme Commander Hitleorous, and the one hundred robonoids, search the Royal Palace CCTV'S web feeds the last 30 minutes, hurry start your search now"

Centurion Sheen Ezriel replied, "Aye Aye Supreme General" and hurriedly went back to his post and sit down, and began scrolling and searching every CCTV'S security webcams feeds on the luminous computer screen the last 30 minutes.

Supreme General Jhesusan caught a glimpse on one of the web screen monitor of what's happening inside the Royal Palace Grand Assembly Hall, it was the web monitor screen Centurion Sheen Ezriel was watching.

Supreme General Jhesusan asked Centurion Sheen Ezriel, "Legionnaire, How long you had been watching the Grand Wedding of Goddess Nakki and God Anuk?"

Centurion Sheen Ezriel was quite nervous but told the truth that He was watching the whole wedding ceremony since the beginning, reasoning that He was also all the time monitoring other CCTV'S security web camera feeds.

Supreme General Jhesusan wants to explode in anger and condemn the Legionnaire on duty of why not doing his job properly by noting and watching the Royal Palaces CCTV'S SECURITY CAMERA of any Security Breach, but saw in his mind an opportunity to use to good purpose what the Legionnaire on-duty was doing a while ago, watching the Grand Wedding Ceremony and not doing his job supervising and watching the CCTV'S Security Camera.

Supreme General Jhesusan again commanded Centurion Sheen Ezriel, but this time commanded him calmly, but with urgency in his voice, "Okay Legionnaire, open the Security Camera inside the Royal Palace Assembly Hall, locate the CCTV Security Camera positioned at the front and covering the view where the Unified High Command High Ranking Officials are sitting. Centurion Sheen Ezriel touch the luminous computer screen, follows the prompt commands, and windows after windows of CCTV'S Security Camera web feeds comes to view on the screen monitor.

Supreme General Jhesusan pointed one web feeds, it was the CCTV'S Security Camera positioned to cover and record the view as to where the Unified High Command High Ranking Officials were sitting, He immediately touched the screen monitor, and there appear on the web screen the cheerful and happy faces of Unified High Command High Ranking Officials in their colorful Gala Uniforms, enjoying the spectacle of the wedding ceremony, oblivious to what's going on and to what He had found out in his reasoning mind, and yet He can't blame them, for up until now He himself don't know yet who are amongst them the real ally, and who are their enemy within.

He was about to order Centurion Sheen Ezriel to scroll the webcams feeds to the last 30 minute recording when again He notice a glimpse of important scene where the Unified High Ranking Officials are sitting, He notice that aside from him and Supreme Commander Hitleorous that was not there sitting, He saw another vacant seat amongst the Supreme Commanders, and if He is not mistaken, it was SUPREME COMMANDER HANNIBALKAN, THE HEAD OF UNIFIED HIGH COMMAND OF UNIVERSAL GALACTIC DEFENSE PALACE ROYAL SECURITY, that was also not around and missing.

All the more his suspicion of conspiracy was coming to details, and that He has reason to believe Supreme Commander Hannibalkan is an accomplice by Supreme Commander Hitleorous to stage their grand entrance with their Robonoids with-out being questioned as Supreme Commander Hannibalkan holds the key of Supreme Commander Hitleorous safe access and passage with his one hundred self-handpicked elite troops of Robonoids into the walls and vicinity of the Royal Palace Assembly Hall where the Grand Galactic Wedding Ceremony of Goddess Nakki and God Anuk is being held at the moment, and even perhaps the safe access going inside the very Royal Palace Assembly Hall, where the enemy leaders are waiting themselves for their grand act as well. He's mind is rationalizing whether to sound the Royal Palace Emergency Alarm Signal of Security Breach, and disrupt the wedding so as to warn God Anuk and Goddess Nakki of impending danger, but at some point in his mind as well is arguing if he does so, there is a possibility that he will lose the chance to pinpoint the Grand Master of the Secret Society amongst THE ELDERS who was manipulating and controlling some of the High Ranking Officials in Unified High Command including Supreme Commander Hitleorous and Supreme Commander Hannibalkan, for their hidden agenda and vested interest, and causing un-harmonious relationship between rankings in the Unified High Command.

In his mind triumph the need to know and expose the leaders amongst the Secret Society in order for him, and his UNIFIED HIGH COMMAND OF UNIVERSAL GALACTIC DEFENSE TACTICAL ARMADA CENTRAL COMMAND where he was in-charge, with the help and cooperation of his close-friend and ally, SUPREME COMMANDER NAPOLEONIOUS, THE HEAD OF UNIFIED HIGH COMMAND OF UNIVERSAL GALACTIC DEFENSE AERO-POLICE AND SPACE-FORCE, to quash and prevent their ruthless plan, and arrest those who are involve to be brought to justice and punish accordingly, perhaps, will be sentence by Galactic High Tribunals to eternal frozen death and be vanish in the abyss of galaxy and universe as cosmic dust.

Supreme General Jhesusan, upon realizing He must have to double-up his actions and decisions, commanded the lone Legionnaire on-duty inside the Royal Palace Intelligence Command Office who was Centurion Sheen Ezriel, and ordered him to go to the Royal Palace Chamber Hall as fast as He could, to hurry up without creating any raucous situation so as not to suspect him by the enemy, and pass important and urgent message discreetly of "SECURITY BREACH, ENEMY WITHIN, COMMANDER HITLEOROUS WITH ROBONOIDS" directly to Commander Levonne, and warn him of impending debacle, and must protect at all cost God Anuk and Goddess Nakki adhering to SWORN OATH of Royal Palace Escort Legionnaires Code which is "... HONOR AND GLORY, EVEN IN DEATH...".

The Legionnaire on-duty, Centurion Sheen Ezriel, upon hearing Supreme General Jhesusan's command and what He wants of him to do, at first was perplexed and confused, but in the end when He fully absorb and realize the importance of his mission, sees an opportunity for him to utilize and grab the important mission laid upon in his shoulder by Supreme General Jhesusan, for the advancement of his career in the Unified High Command.

He listen carefully and wholeheartedly to what Supreme General Jhesusan was instructing him to do, and in his heart He promise to do what he was asked to do 100%, even to exceed what He was asked and command of, in his heart and mind, it is his duty as Legionnaire to defend the Sovereignty of Nibiru's Throne and look after the safety of their Gods and Goddesses, even if it will cause his death, after all He is a Legionnaire, and must abide to their sworn oath and code, "GLORY AND HONOR, EVEN IN DEATH", yet at the back of his mind, if He will play his cards masterfully and achieve the success of his mission, an opportunity awaits for him for a promotion to become a Commander.

Supreme General Jhesusan after instructing elaborately the Legionnaire, Centurion Sheen Ezriel, of his mission, commanded him to go hurriedly, and found in his heart the consolation of thanking the Legionnaire, for He came to know and understand that Centurion Sheen Ezriel is an ally, and advised him to take all extra effort to be cautious and careful so that He will achieve his mission successfully.

Supreme General Jhesusan then utter words of encouragement just as the Legionnaire, Centurion Sheen Ezriel was about to leave the Royal Palace Intelligence Command Office, "LEGIONNAIRE, GLORY AND HONOR EVEN IN DEATH, DEFEND OUR PLANET NIBIRU'S THRONE AND SOVEREIGNTY AGAINST OUR ENEMIES, WHO WANTS TO DISRUPT AND DESTROY OUR GREAT CIVILIZATION, YOUR MISSION IS SO VERY IMPORTANT, IN YOUR SHOULDER LAYS THE SUCCESS OF TELLING COMMANDER LEVONNE AND HIS TRUSTED ROYAL PALACE ESCORT LEGIONNAIRE ALONG WITH HIM INSIDE THE ROYAL PALACE TO PROTECT THE NIBIRU'S THRONE AND CROWN, WARNING HIM OF IMPENDING TRAGEDY, AND MUST PREVENT ACCESS AT ALL COST TO SUPREME COMMANDER HITLEOROUS, ALONG WITH SUPREME COMMANDER HANIBBALKAN, AND THEIR TROOPS OF ONE HUNDRED ELITE ROBONOIDS TO ENTER THE ROYAL PALACE ASSEMBLY HALL WHERE THE GRAND GALACTIC WEDDING CEREMONY OF GODDESS NAKKI AND GOD ANUK IS BEING PERFORM"

"DO WHAT YOU COMMANDED TO DO, AND I WILL SEE TO IT PERSONALLY YOUR PROMOTION TO COMMANDER IF YOU WILL ACCOMPLISH SUCCESFULLY YOUR MISSION" Supreme General Jhesusan added in order for the Legionnaire to be inspired and act decisively performing his mission.

Centurion Sheen Ezriel stand straight and firm in-front of Supreme General Jhesusan, executed salute and shouted on top of his voice, "I AM A LEGIONNAIRE, PROTECTOR OF THE GODS AND GODDESSES, PROTECTOR OF NIBIRU THRONE AND IT'S CROWN ROYALTIES, I WILL ABIDE TO MY CREED AND OATH, GLORY AND HONOR, EVEN IN DEATH" and with that remarks of allegiance, after Supreme General Jhesusan acknowledge his salute hurriedly went out of the Royal Palace Intelligence Security Office, and find his way into the Royal Palace hallways leading to where the Royal Palace Assembly Hall is, deep within his mind, is the thoughts of fear, for he knows the danger that lies ahead of his mission, and yet beneath his heart, the courage and bravery of being a Legionnaire.

"I WILL DO WHATEVER IT TAKES TO FULFILL MY MISSION, I SWEAR ON THE BLOOD OF MY FAMILY, AND TO THE OATH OF MY DUTY" thus the Legionnaire, Centurion Sheen Ezriel promised himself

Supreme General Jhesusan went back to what he was doing, he touched again the luminous computer screen of Intelligence Security Office, and comes the view of different CCTV feedcams, he saw in one feedcam window screen that Centurion Sheen Ezriel was already in the sky elevator going to the Royal Palace Assembly Hall, he touch another feedcam window screen where the Grand Wedding was being held, and look quickly to find out what's happening inside and assess the situation of how much time left he have in order to locate Supreme Commander Hitleorous, and his one hundred elite Robonoids, keeping in his mind also, Supreme Commander Hanibbalkan.

Supreme General Jhesusan saw that the audiences attending the Grand Galactic Wedding are now sitting and listening attentively to the music being played by the Galactic Symphonic Orchestra under Maestro WOLFGANG A. MOSSARTO, and with the graceful hand of Maestro Wolfgang playing again the musical piece of "The Marriage of Figaro", as He knows it is the favorite piece of music concerto by Goddess Nakki, in his heart comes the honor and excitement of playing the music with utmost care of sweet melodious sound of hymns and rhythms, the Nibirunians Unigalitizines are somewhat caught into oblivion of sound of music, as what Supreme General Jhesusan observed.

He scrolled the Security Camera webcam feeds in the screen monitor and located where Goddess Nakki and God Anuk are positioned, He noted in his mind that they are in the front where The Shaman is, awaiting only to finish the musical piece being played by the Galactic Symphony Orchestra under the graceful hand of Maestro Wolfgang, before proceeding to the proper rites of the their Galactic Wedding, where-in The Shaman will proclaim Goddess Nakki and God Anuk universally wife and husband, and the complete transition of Nibiru Throne and Kingdomship Power will be rest in Goddess Nakki's head, and which the Nibirunian Unigalitizines have been waiting for a long time.

Supreme General Jhesusan upon realizing He has still time, again, touch the luminous computer wall screen infront of him, and try to locate the CCTV webcam feeds of Royal Palace Assembly Hall exit where he suspect might Supreme Commander Hitleorous went out. He scrolled the feedcams and when He found what he was trying to find, he immediately touched the window, and again comes on the window screen the CCTV feedcam where the Unified High Command Ranking Officials were sitting. He touch one command button in the screen, and the feed-cam in the window screen is playing slowly going backward. He saw himself when He got up of his seat and went to the side exit door of the Royal Palace Assembly Hall.

Supreme General Jhesusan felt a sudden surge of urgency in his heart to locate Supreme Commander Hitleorous, he quickly scrolled backward manually with his finger tip the feed-cam on the screen, and when He does come across of what He wants to see, He stop immediately, touch the figure who was exiting the Royal Palace Assembly Hall at the back exit, and type the word command, (LOCATE).

The wall computer was about to yield results of information on the where-about and location of Supreme Commander Hitleorous, when suddenly the Royal Palace Intelligence Office luminous wall computer back-down, and all power inside was cut-off.

Supreme General Jhesusan quickly hide at the back of the room, where the electrical power switchboards unit are, He knows that something wrong is going on, and that in his reasoning mind, there is danger prowling. He knows that after one minute, the emergency power will automatically switch-on, but will only supply power to emergency lightings, and it will takes another two minutes more to fully charge and restore all system so that the Royal Palace Intelligence Command Office wall computer can be use again.

Supreme General Jhesusan remained calm standing to where He was hiding, He's right hand gripping his service laser pistol, readying himself of any danger against his life, and true to his expectation, after one minute the electric power supply switch-on and the emergency lighting inside the Royal Palace Intelligence Command Office lighted. He remained focus and didn't move, he's eyes observing any shadow movement, He wants to make sure that everything is okay and under control, that there is no one intruding of what He was doing.

And after two minutes, just as He was calculating the time in his mind, the Royal Palace Intelligence Command Office luminous wall computer came to life and automatically switches on.

Again, Supreme General waited another one minute to make sure nobody's around, in his mind time is ticking and that every second ticks equates the safety of Goddess Nakki and God Anuk, and the whole Planet Nibiru and its Unigalitizines from the hands of Supreme Commander Hitleorous and the Robonoids, with the leaders and members of their Secret Society Group awaiting their entrance as cue and final signal of revealing themselves for their much awaited Coup D'état, to seize the Throne and Command of Planet Nibiru.

When the Royal Palace Intelligence Command Office luminous wall computer was fully restored, and began processing again information data's, Supreme General Jhesusan came out to where He was hiding and walk fast in-front of the luminous wall computer, and just as the computer wall window screen shows the last images and data's of CCTV security feed-cams before the power shutdown, a voice speaks from nowhere that startled Supreme General Jhesusan.

"Don't move Supreme General, stay where you are, and don't do anything foolish" the strange voice told Supreme General Jhesusan, as if commanding him. Supreme General Jhesusan was so shocked and frustrated, but He remained compose and calm, in this darkest moment of his life, He cannot act foolishly.

And the voice speaking added as if warning him, "I have my laser pistol point at you Supreme General, I will not hesitate to fire and kill you if you will act stupid, please turn around slowly with your hand above your shoulder"

Supreme General Jhesusan recognized the voice speaking. He knows that it was the voice of the HEAD OF UNIFIED HIGH COMMAND OF UNIVERSAL GALACTIC DEFENSE ROYAL PALACE SECURITY.

And as Supreme General Jhesusan slowly turn around himself to face the enemy, He speak and said, "I recognize your voice, I know you, Supreme Commander Hanibbalkan, I never thought the Royal Palace will trust a viper inside"

Supreme Commander Hanibbalkan gripped his laser pistol, He was irritated and hurt emotionally by what Supreme General Jhesusan said of him, and prepare himself for confrontation, and as Supreme General Jhesusan completely turned around facing him, He shouted "Silence, Supreme General, you don't know what you are talking, I respect you but don't push me too far, I will not hesitate to kill you"

Supreme General Jhesusan sees an opportunity to distract Supreme Commander Hanibbalkan of his thoughts and quickly added, "Tell me Supreme Commander, What is the "GREAT PLAN" that I do not know of? I am not ignorant here not knowing your evil plans along with Supreme Commander Hitleorous and your Secret Society Group, or is it that they are just using you for their own agenda?"

Supreme Commander Hanibbalkan wants to lose his temper and explode, he is contemplating inside his mind whether to kill at once the Supreme General He admire for being a good High Ranking Senior Officer, and go on with his mission, for He knows in his mind that Supreme Commander Hitleorous and the one hundred elite Robonoid troops could not enter the Royal Palace Assembly Hall with-out him de-activating the Electro-magnetic Security Alarm, and as the HEAD OF UNIFIED HIGH COMMAND OF UNIVERSAL GALACTIC DEFENSE ROYAL PALACE SECURITY, He has the access to activate and open the Royal Palace Assembly Hall electro-mechanical attic dome, where, as planned at THE ELDERS CHAMBER OF TRUTH just before the wedding starts of their conspiracy plan, Supreme Commander Hitleorous and the one hundred elite Robonoids will make their entrance from the top coming from outside as soon as the Royal Palace Assembly Hall electro-mechanic attic dome open, for it was included as well in the Grand Wedding Plan as part of spectacle, disguising as part of the show, so as not to cause panic amongst Nibirunians.

"Stop talking, shut your mouth Supreme General" commanded Supreme Commander Hanibbalkan.

And added angrily "...don't push me Supreme General, and don't ever underestimate my capability, for right now I own your life, it's only in my finger tip, it will just be a flash of seconds if I shoot you with my laser pistol, and you will be on fire as hell"

Commander Hanibbalkan grinning, continued speaking as if mocking Supreme General Jhesusan "…thanks to Supreme General Ahllakdan for this advance weapon LASER PISTOL He invented, and I am sure you know well how your body will end up if I shoot you, like an incinerated ASH"

Supreme General Jhesusan upon hearing Supreme Commander Hanibbalkan of his warning stand still and keep quiet, but his gaze intensely locked on Supreme Commander Hanibbalkan's eyes and said.

"…How big is the CONSPIRACY PLAN? Is Supreme General Ahllakdan part of this Secret Society Group that plans to overthrow the Nibiru's kingdom and throne by staging Coup D'état during the grand galactic wedding…, enlighten me Supreme Commander so that I may understand fully well your intentions, perhaps in the end I may join your noble cause and be a part of this great history of our Great Planet Nibiru unfolding."

Supreme General Jhesusan was contemplating inside his mind of fooling Supreme Commander Hannibalkan that He wants to switch allegiance, perhaps it will distract Supreme Commander Hannibalkan's attention and that in the process He could overturn the event and fate of impending destruction that lies ahead.

"Oh you're so naive and foolish Supreme General" answered back Supreme Commander Hanibbalkan, and mockingly added

"…You are really underestimating me, beware that you might miscalculate and misjudge me, I am no fool, I know what's on your mind and thinking right now, but you cannot prevail Supreme General, and WE will not fail, this is the moment we'd been waiting for, it was been planned eons of time, by our ELDERS, by those who care enough to see the great future that lays ahead of our Great Planet Nibiru, and understand the motivation of boiling anger inside each and every one of the descendants of those who perish during the First Galactic War, that driving force of REVENGE and VENGEANCE, to annihilate that Blue Planet Earth living intelligent species called Humanoids, and to hunt down the TRAITOR and REAL ENEMY that cause all these misfortune of our Planet Nibiru's history. Do not forget your history Supreme General, I myself a descendant of Supreme General Dinnisius, who was killed in the Great First Galactic Battle. I do not forget our past, Supreme General, and so must YOU"

Supreme General Jhesusan was taken-aback of what he had heard from Supreme Commander Hanibbalkan, He then realize the scope of their Planet's dilemma, it is profound and of deep sentiments, that He himself cannot blame the Unified High Command Junior Ranks joining the Secret Societies Agenda and Noble Cause, after all, He reasoned out, everybody was affected by that tragic event of Lord God Adanis death along with his trusted Royal Palace Guard Escort Legionnaires headed by Supreme Commander Michael and Commander Gabriel, who were murdered by Supreme Commander Lucifer and his Blue Planet Earth Expedition Legionnaire Forces. It was the START of the darkest hours of Planet Nibiru, as recorded in their history in the Book of Time. It triggered the First Galactic War that sent their Great Planet into humiliating defeat at the hands of the Earthlings, with the help and orchestration of THE DEMIGODS led by Supreme Commander Lucifer.

He paused for a moment, and pondered in time, then answered back with caution and reverse-psychological statement.

"Supreme Commander Hanibbalkan, I deeply understand the motives your organization wants to achieve, and I am convinced now that what you are fighting for is worth your mission, but I cannot tolerate such act of insubordination and Military Junta inside the Royal Palace undermining the Royal Throne. Your organization's aim of avenging our ancestors from their defeat against the humanoids is of course a noble act, but there is a right way to do it, and not just like this, with you and Supreme Commander Hitleorous being use by THE ELDERS and their SECRET SOCIETY GROUP of their own hidden agenda"

It is now a battle of the wits, Supreme General Jhesusan was hoping that Supreme Commander Hanibbalkan will bite and accept his opinion and proposal, perhaps will soften his heart and distract his attention, for in his mind, He could outduel Supreme Commander Hannibalkan if given opportunity, He's only about three meters away from his enemy, and He could easily grab and wrestle with him, but, if only not for that laser pistol pointed at him which could obliterate him in lightning fast if He miscalculate and misjudge Supreme Commander Hanibbalkan.

"I am telling you, do not provoke me Supreme General Jhesusan, I know what are you up too, I read your files, and I know your capabilities, I will not hesitate to kill you, the only reason now that you are still alive is because of my respect and admiration for you being a good high-ranking officer, so don't irritate me, I am here to finish my mission and go on, but I cannot let you foil our plan of Coup D'état against the Nibiru Throne, it is already been decided, and once we achieve what our organization wants to achieve, I will leave the verdict to Galactic High Tribunal of your fate, I will not spoil my hands with the blood of your life, BUT DO NOT PROVOKE ME, your life right now is just in my finger tip, one false move you make and I will squeeze the trigger" again Supreme Commander Hanibbalkan sternly warned Supreme General Jhesusan

Supreme General Jhesusan listening to Supreme Commander Hanibbalkan finds delight and fear in his heart, delight because He manage to stall time against Supreme Commander Hanibbalkan, for he knows time is running out fast for him to do what He should do to warn the Royal couple, and fear because He could lose his life anytime, but his heart is full of hope, and if He will play his card right, He will live and call it another day, perhaps Centurion Sheen Ezriel, the Legionnaire whom He commanded to find Commander Levonne would make it and relay his urgent warning message, and avert the impending intrusion, time is running fast, and He is very hopeful Centurion Sheen Ezriel will outrun Supreme Commander Hitleorous and the one hundred elite Robonoids if He could delay Supreme Commander Hanibbalkan from fulfilling his mission of opening the Royal Palace Assembly Hall electro-mechanical attic dome, for it was clear now to him where Supreme Commander Hitleorous and the Robonoids will make their entrance, He just have to delves in his thoughts ways to distract Supreme Commander Hanibbalkan from fulfilling his mission.

Supreme Commander Hanibbalkan sensing He was being played and fooled by Supreme General Jhesusan move cautiously closer to the Royal Palace Intelligence Command Office luminous computer control panel.

"Out of the way Supreme General, move slowly to your right, hands still above your shoulder, and I warn you, don't act stupid, or you'll end up in ashes" strongly commanded Supreme Commander Hanibbalkan

And as Supreme Commander Hanibbalkan move slowly towards the Royal Palace Intelligence Computer Control Panel with his laser pistol pointed at him, Supreme General Jhesusan slowly move back two pace to his right with his hands up above his shoulder, waiting for that perfect timing He will launch his assault on Supreme Commander Hanibbalkan.

"Don't dare move on me Supreme General Jhesusan" warned again by Supreme Commander Hanibbalkan, as if anticipating Supreme General Jhesusan will attack him, in his mind are worries that Supreme Commander Hitleorous and the One Hundred Robonoids are already outside the Royal Palace Assembly Hall attic waiting for him to activate and open the Royal Palace Assembly Hall electro-mechanical attic dome so that they can enter and fulfill their mission successfully, and not annoy their leaders who are waiting inside, THE ELDERS along with some Unified High Command High Ranking Officials will put the final stage of their plan of Coup D'état on Nibiru's Throne, for him as well it's a race against time.

And when Supreme Commander Hanibbalkan comes close to the Royal Palace Intelligence Computer Control Panel, He immediately touch the computer wall screen, with his eyes intently gazing at Supreme General Jhesusan, watching his nemesis of any provoking moves against him, his heart beating fast knowing his mission is very important and holds the key of their success, for if He fails to open the Royal Palace Assembly Hall electro-mechanical attic dome, it will be disastrous and the realization of their dreams and eons of year planning will fail, and He will be blame for eternity, and might cause his death as punishment, He knows for sure he will be vanish in the abyss of universe as frozen cosmic dust.

"No, I must not fail" Supreme Commander Hanibbalkan murmured to himself, "I swear on the blood of my family, and to you Great Great Grandfather Supreme General Dinnisius, I swear, I will not fail, I will carry on and avenge your death."

Supreme General Jhesusan keenly observing Supreme Commander Hanibbalkan of his movements, his eyes not flinching awaiting that perfect timing He will launch his assault on Supreme Commander Hanibbalkan, it is a matter of life and death, but He had already made his decision, in his mind comes the safety of his dear friend, God Anuk and his soon to be wife, Goddess Nakki, and the preservation of Nibiru Kingdomship against these Secret Society Group trying to disrupt their Great Planet's harmonious and peaceful civilization.

"HONOR AND GLORY, EVEN IN DEATH" these are the words that dances in his mind, He can't allow Supreme Commander Hanibbalkan activate and open the Royal Palace Assembly Hall electro-mechanical attic dome, it will be his great failure if that happens, an unwanted speck in his lustrous Galactic Military career, and in this particular moment brought upon his path as dignified soldier and High Ranking Officer of Planet Nibiru, He is ready to face the consequences, even if it will cause his death, He will stop Supreme Commander Hanibbalkan of his mission at all cost.

Supreme Commander Hanibbalkan still pointing his laser pistol with his left hand at Supreme General Jhesusan tried to re-program the computer command for the Royal Palace Assembly Hall electro-mechanical attic dome and activate it to open with his right hand, all the time his eyes keep looking back and forth to Supreme General Jhesusan and to what he was doing.

Little did Supreme Commander Hanibbalkan knows that he was being observed carefully and keenly by Supreme General Jhesusan to launch his attack, and, just as he was to assault Supreme Commander Hanibbalkan, Supreme General Jhesusan caught a glimpse of Centurion Sheen Ezriel in one of the Royal Palace CCTV webcam in the computer wall screen, making his way towards Commander Levonne.

Supreme Commander Hanibbalkan didn't escape from his eyes what Supreme General Jhesusan had seen in the computer wall screen and exclaimed to himself "Centurion Sheen Ezriel, what is he doing in the Royal Palace Assembly Hall?..."

And just as he was to touch the command button for activating the Royal Palace Assembly Hall electro-mechanical attic dome to open, Supreme General Jhesusan seized that precise moment he had been waiting for where Supreme Commander Hanibbalkan was temporarily lost from his thoughts, he quickly assaulted him and managed to knocked away the laser pistol in his left hand, and they fumbled to the floor trying to outduel each other with their own might and strength, both knows the importance of who is going to prevail between the two of them, it is a duel of RIGHT and WRONG, GOOD and EVIL, it is their battle of LIFE and DEATH.

Meanwhile, Centurion Sheen Ezriel managed to pass the Royal Palace Security without any commotion or any fuss, and was now inside the Royal Palace Assembly Hall trying to locate where Commander Levonne is.

He is so nervous and hoping that nobody from the Galactic High Command Ranking Officers will take notice of him, He was thinking of his Commanding Officer, Supreme Commander Hanibbalkan that He might see and punish him, whom He thought was there among the audiences watching Maestro Wolfgang Mossarto playing his last piece of "Divine Sound of Universal Hymn", little did He know at that precise moment, his Commanding Officer, Supreme Commander Hanibbalkan was not there and that He is facing his own dilemma fighting and battling Supreme General Jhesusan in the Royal Palace Intelligence Office, outdueling each other.

Centurion Sheen Ezriel approach the closest Legionnaire posted as Royal Palace Security Guard near the side gate of the Royal Assembly Hall where He entered, whom He recognize at once as one of his buddy in the Royal Palace Legionnaires Barracks, it was Centurion Keevin.

"Attention" He commanded with low voice in-front of Centurion Keevin, and immediately Centurion Keevin responded by standing straight and was to execute Galactic Salute but Centurion Sheen Ezriel quickly hold Centurion Keevin hand and told him to be at ease, and when Centurion Keevin recognized him, they smiled at each other and talked.

"What are you doing here?" asked Centurion Keevin, and proceeded to add "… you're supposed to be on-duty at Royal Palace Intelligence Office, if Supreme Commander Hanibbalkan will find out you're here and not doing your job, I am sure you will be in Court Marshall after this wedding, and my guess, you will be shipped immediately to UNIVERSAL GALACTIC DEFENSE INTER-GALAXY PRISONER-GARRISON COMMAND, and suffer the isolation of The Dungeon as your punishment, under Supreme Commander Hitleorous, and you would not like that"

"Shut your mouth" replied by Centurion Sheen Ezriel, "…now hear me well, it's a long story BUDDY, and I am running out of time, I must find Commander Levonne and pass to him urgent message from Supreme General Jhesusan, before Supreme Commander Hitleorous arrive here with his one hundred Robonoids"

Centurion Keevin puzzled by what he heard from Centurion Sheen Ezriel ask again "Comrade, tell me what is it, before I will tell you where Commander Levonne is"

Centurion Sheen Ezriel upon hearing Centurion Keevin of what he had said as if enquiring about his mission becomes suspicious of Centurion Keevin whether he is an enemy or an ally, and cautiously told Centurion Keevin that his mission is to find Commander Levonne and tell him of the entrance of Supreme Commander Hitleorous and the one hundred Robonoids as part of the Grand Wedding Show as it is included in the Wedding Plan.

Centurion Sheen Ezriel lied about his mission, but He knows in his heart that what he is doing is a noble cause, and that he can't compromise what He was commanded to do so.

"Wow, that will be spectacular I am sure" exclaimed Centurion Keevin, then added, "…Commander Levonne is at the front near the Royal Palace Altar where God Anuk and Goddess Nakki is" with his right hand pointing the direction.

Centurion Sheen Ezriel realize that Commander Levonne was of course near the Royal Palace Assembly Hall Altar where the Shaman will perform the marriage ceremony, to protect God Anuk and Goddess Nakki during the wedding rite, and that in order to get there He must have to traverse the center aisle of the Royal Palace Assembly Hall leading to the front where the Royal Palace Assembly Hall Altar is. He is so certain that it will be a critical decision he will make, walking in the center aisle with all eyes on you, and might even cause his death if the enemy will find out what He is up to, and why He was there.

Centurion Sheen Ezriel quickly think and squeeze his mind of what He will do in order that the enemy will not detect him, and came up with idea to borrow Centurion Keevin's uniform, and He would disguise as one of the Royal Palace Escort Legionnaire.

He pulled Centurion Keevin out of the sight of the audiences into one alley and told him to remove his uniform, and that they will exchange clothes. Centurion Keevin at first was very reluctant, but when Centurion Sheen Ezriel told him how important his mission is, and that he must have to find Commander Levonne at once to deliver the important and urgent message without causing any commotion, and that He must not stand against his plan otherwise He will file report against him, and perhaps in the end, Centurion Keevin will be the one to be punish and ship to UNIVERSAL GALACTIC

DEFENSE INTER-GALAXY PRISONER-GARRISON, and suffer the isolation and boredom of The Dungeon.

Centurion Keevin upon realizing what Centurion Sheen Ezriel had told him about his mission and the consequences if He will not cooperate, decided to obey Centurion Sheen Ezriel, and immediately removed his garments and uniforms, it was an awkward situation for both of them standing naked, but both managed to exchange uniforms and wear them instantly.

"You look good on my uniform" Centurion Keevin grinningly told Centurion Sheen Ezriel, "…it fits you well" he added.

"Thank you" replied Centurion Sheen Ezriel, but his mind was already pre-occupied of what He will do next, finding Commander Levonne and fulfill his mission dutifully.

And with that in mind, He asked Centurion Keevin to go back to his post immediately before somebody take notice of him not in his guarding post, to which Centurion Keevin heed at once and go back to his guard post.

Centurion Sheen Ezriel looking like a Royal Palace Escort Legionnaire, readied himself, took a deep breath and began walking slowly, in a cadence manner going to the center aisle.

"It's now or never, I must be brave and courageous, I am a Legionnaire, protector of Royal Gods and Goddesses, defender of Nibiru Throne and Sovereignty, HONOR AND GLORY EVEN IN DEATH" thus He murmured to himself.

And as He marched in a cadence and military pace walking in the center aisle towards the Royal Palace Assembly Hall Altar, the hymns and music being played by Maestro Wolfgang Mossarto somewhat coincide with his cadence, and all the audiences enjoying the sound of music being played were mesmerized and thought what he was doing was part of the musical play.

Centurion Sheen Ezriel was so nervous walking, he could feel the drum-beat in his heart, and although He's marching with his eyes looking straight, He could see from his Legionnaire helmet visor that he is getting attention, and audiences eyes are observing him, murmuring what surprises might again enthrall them, for out of nowhere He came in and his marching cadence coincide uniformly with the sound of music Maestro Wolfgang Mossarto and The Royal Palace Galactic Symphonic Orchestra was playing.

In his mind, he is calculating he's about 20 pace away from the Royal Palace Assembly Hall Altar, and he could see that the Royal God Anuk and Goddess Nakki are in-front kneeling in the altar where the Shaman is standing awaiting for the sound of music being played by Maestro Wolfgang to end and finish, and perform the wedding ritual.

He could now also see Commander Levonne stationed nearby at the side of the Royal Palace Assembly Hall Altar with two Legionnaire beside him, and the other Legionnaires spread all over around the Royal Palace Assembly Hall guarding, part of his mind was dictating him to run as fast as he could and tell Commander Levonne the impending debacle and Coup D'état the enemies will stage, yet half of his mind was also arguing that He should remain compose and relax, that He should finish the marching cadence he was doing until such time that He will reach where Commander Levonne is, so as not to alert the enemy and give impression that they already know what are the enemies plan.

"PATIENCE IS A VIRTUE" he murmured to himself, "…I must act naturally, and finish this marching cadence as if part of the wedding show, I will not fret, 15 marching cadence steps away and my mission is complete, after all, there is no sign of Supreme Commander Hitleorous and the one hundred Robonoid troops, I must act and complete this marching show, and be a part of this wedding ceremony" thus he told and convinced himself.

Commander Levonne, like all the other audiences watching and hearing Maestro Wolfgang Mossarto and The Royal Palace Galactic Symphonic Orchestra playing "The Divine Galactic Sound of Music", was enjoying the hymns and melancholic sounds, when all of a sudden, He felt a sudden fear in his heart, an urgency that He should act and decide at once what to do, for out of the corner of his eyes, He saw one Legionnaire marching in the center aisle in cadence with the music Maestro Wolfgang was playing, marching towards the Royal Palace Assembly Hall Altar where God Anuk and Goddess Nakki are located awaiting for the Shaman to perform the wedding rite and proclaim them as Husband and Wife, Grand Couple of Planet Nibiru.

Commander Levonne knew one hundred percent sure in his heart and mind that whatever was happening was not part of the wedding plan. He himself reviewed the Wedding Planner's wedding plan as part of the Royal Palace Security Protocol being him as in-charge of the Royal Palace Legionnaires Escort.

"This is not right" he told himself, and base on his calculation and judgment, the Legionnaire marching in cadence with the music being played was about 10 pace away from where God Anuk and Goddess Nakki are kneeling down in the Royal Palace Assembly Hall Altar.

He was about to take action, when again He noticed that the Legionnaire marching in the center aisle towards the altar don't have a laser sword or any weapon, and recognized that the uniform worn by the marching Legionnaire was one of those assigned and posted at various entrance gate of the Royal Palace Assembly Hall, and not the uniform of his men assigned to the Royal Palace Legionnaire Escorts.

"This is strange" thus again he murmured himself. He was baffled of what he was seeing, He wants to act fast, but also in his mind lingers doubts whether it was an additional part of the wedding plan he overlooked, He wants to make sure before he acts accordingly because he don't like to distract the wedding and spoil it's solemnity. Everybody is attentive and enjoying the show, and nobody is taking notice of the Legionnaire marching in the center aisle, thus was his assumption.

"He must be up to something, he could be the bearer of Nibiru's Royal Throne Crown and Scepter, or the Wedding Zeal perhaps, there must be a purpose as to why he is there, I must have to find this out at once" thus Commander Levonne was convincing himself, and by then, it's only about 5 pace and steps away before the Legionnaire reach the Royal Palace Assembly Hall Altar where God Anuk and Goddess Nakki are kneeling down, and everyone is oblivious to what's happening, as if anticipating another spectacular show.

Commander Levonne wants to draw his laser pistol service arms, and charge to where the marching Legionnaire was, and stop him from getting nearer to the Royal Couple being wed, but he was hesitant, for he sees no reason to stop the Legionnaire from executing his graceful marching, there is no threat of weaponry as he reason out with himself, and yet, even his two Legionnaire standing beside him were confused and keep looking at each other as if questioning one another WHO was the Legionnaire marching and what is he doing there, they even noticed Commander Levonne to be somewhat agitated by the situation, and could feel his restlessness and un-easiness, they too wants to charge but stay calm and alert, awaiting their Commander's order.

Everybody inside the Royal Palace Assembly Hall were very attentive and paying much attention to what's going on, they don't want to miss every details of the ceremony, and what the marching Legionnaire will do in cadence with the mesmerizing music that was being played by The Royal Palace Galactic Symphonic Orchestra with Maestro Wolfgang Mossarto at the helm, conducting to the grand finale, they want to see more spectacular show that will linger in their sanity for eon of years to talk with, they want this Grand Galactic wedding as memorable as it should be, and satisfy their vanity.

Even the Unified High Command High Ranking Officers, and their Lower Ranking Officers, were so engrossed of what they are seeing, their eyes transfixed to the Royal Couple being wed and the marching Legionnaire, as if awaiting for something to happen, a surprise perhaps of another Galactic show of Cosmic Energy.

But not for the ONE'S who were inside the Royal Palace Assembly Hall masquerading themselves as allies and friends. These are the powerful Entities of THE ELDERS and their Secret Society Group Members with their own motives of Grand Galactic Agenda, patiently sitting down watching the wedding ceremony they called wedding parody, awaiting also the grand entrance of Supreme Commander Hitleorous and the elite One Hundred Robonoid troops as the final signal of their group's Coup D'Etat against the Planet Nibiru's Royal Throne, to seize and control the Royal Throne Power and fulfill their Eon of Years Galactic Plan of "CODENAME: ENGLUEBOLDERGY2015" (acronym for ENERGY, BLUE, GOLD, 2015), which is the annihilation of Humanoids of BLUE Planet Earth and taking control of its vast wealth of ENERGY and minerals especially GOLD by year 2015 as mandated by their "Behind The Scene Leaders", including the much-awaited and long-delayed vengeance and revenge against the DEMI-GODS led by Supreme Commander Lucifer and his Legionnaires who survived the First Galactic War, who at that time with the help of Commander Draculatis steal the Nanocell Technology from NIBIRU'S UNIVERSAL GALACTIC DEFENSE ADVANCE SCIENTIFIC RESEARCH CENTRAL COMMAND, and in time perfected its function and usage, that keeps them alive for eon of years hiding in the shadows of Blue Planet Earth, roaming and wandering as Gods of their own. It was also among this reason on why their Spy Satellite Black Knight under Commander Marlonus was sent to Blue Planet Earth through the Wormholes and Black Holes, to spied and gather intelligence data on the where-about and locations of Supreme Commander Lucifer and his surviving Legionnaires, and capture them for interrogation about the NANOCELL TECHNOLOGY which they had perfected so well as per UNIFIED HIGH COMMAND OF UNIVERSAL GALACTIC DEFENSE INTER-GALAXY INTELLIGENCE DATA UNDER Supreme Commander Ceazarous, before condemning them to eternal frozen death in the abyss of Galaxy.

For these powerful Entities of THE ELDERS and their Secret Society Group Members, the Grand Galactic Wedding of God Anuk and Goddess Nakki represent the perfect timing and enactment of their hideous plan. They know that all the ruling clans and elites of every Nibiru's Colonies will be present attending the Grand Galactic Wedding, for them it is an opportunity that should not bypass for if they will be successful in staging their plan and agenda, it will be easier for them to enforce into Nibiru's Society of Ruling Class and their subjects, the Nibiru Unigalitizines, what their Secret Society Group wants to achieve.

Every second tick was like eon of time awaiting, THE ELDERS and their cohorts awaiting patiently for the grand entrance of Supreme Commander Hitleorous and stage their own agenda, Commander Levonne awaiting that sign whether the marching Legionnaire at the center aisle going to the altar will launch an attack against the Royal Gods being wed before He could decide what to do next, The Shaman awaiting patiently as well for Maestro Wolfgang Mossarto and The Royal Palace Galactic Symphonic Orchestra playing "The Divine Galactic Sound of Music" finish their music before He could perform his Wedding Rituals and Rites, and of course, Goddess Nakki and God Anuk awaiting like eternity for the Shaman to proclaim them as GALACTIC ROYAL COUPLE, HUSBAND AND WIFE, SUPREME RULER OF PLANET NIBIRU, even the Nibiru Unigalitizines and the audiences watching and attending the Grand Galactic Sacred Wedding were patiently awaiting all events and spectacles unfolding before them as if expecting more shows and surprises to come. It was a moment like a TIME BOMB awaiting for that BIG BANG EXPLOSION and get on with the Show of Life.

And when everybody seems locked-up in tranquility, and still of time, an unexpected surprises comes unfold, suddenly the Royal Palace Assembly Hall electro-mechanical attic dome slowly opens, unfurling a vast skies of glittering lights of stars, and the whole audience inside the Royal Palace Hall Chamber were again mesmerized of what they deemed as part of the Galactic Wedding Show, by that time, Centurion Ezriel was one pace away from where God Anuk and Goddess Nakki was kneeling, and when Centurion Ezriel was about to reach them one step away suddenly performed a snappy military cadence of right turn heading towards Commander Levonne is, and just as Centurion executed right turn marching towards Commander Levonne, the melancholic tune and hymns of Maestro Wolfgang Mossarto and The Royal Palace Galactic Symphonic Orchestra playing "The Divine Galactic Sound of Music" slowly as well fades.

It was a perfect coincidence brought upon by TIME, where FATE and Destiny hangs in the Balance of Reality.

All of a sudden, there was a massive uproar and clapping of hands, the whole audiences were cheering and shouting triumphant chanting. God Anuk and Goddess Nakki greatly puzzled of what had just happened stand up together at the same time, and slowly turned around to see for themselves what the audiences were cheering and clapping about, for both of them were puzzled and looked upon each other when they saw the SHAMAN's face turned red and cowered in FEAR just as the audiences wildly cheered.

Commander Levonne upon realizing the danger ahead because of what was transpiring rushed to God Anuk and Goddess Nakki's location, but was met by Centurion Ezriel along the way.

Centurion Ezriel gestured a quick Galactic Salute to Commander Levonne and immediately told him his urgent message coming from Supreme Commander Jhesusan, and upon hearing the urgent message ordered his two body guards to sound the signal of Royal Palace Red Alert for all Royal Palace Escort Legionnaire to convene around the Royal Gods being wed to protect them from harm, and from the fate that was dictating that moment.

It was a sight the whole Nibirunians Unigalitizines thought a part of the Galactic Wedding Show, another event of surprise adding to luster of God Anuk and Goddess Nakki's grand sacred wedding. The audiences were wildly cheering and clapping the MILITARISTIC entrance of Commander Hitleorous and the elite Robonoid troops in their COMBAT READY BATTLE SUIT, coming from the top outside the Royal Palace attic dome, floating and flying like birds in the air with space carriage of flying saucers at their feet carrying and ferrying them in the air, almost similar to what Goddess Nakki use when she entered the Royal Palace Hall.

God Anuk felt a sudden surge of fear inside his mind and heart for He knows that what was transpiring was not a part of the Wedding Plan, and was in-fact the realization of the enemies staging of Planet Nibiru's Throne Coup D'état, which He was anticipating weeks ago, as advised to him by his dear childhood friend Supreme General Jhesusan. And yet, when God Anuk gets a glimpse where Supreme General Jhesusan should have sit, He couldn't see his dear childhood friend amongst the High Ranking Officers.

God Anuk gripped the hands of Goddess Nakki and was about to lead her ESCAPE, but then, Commander Levonne and the Royal Palace Escort Legionnaire arrived and surrounded them, forming a battle protection shield.

When Supreme Commander Hitleorous was about halfway in the air going down to where God Anuk and Goddess Nakki, and the Royal Palace Escort Legionnaires are located, He draw his laser sword and raise it in-front above his head as if signifying a battle charge, his laser sword flaming and burning of intense yellow and red color. And just as Supreme Commander Hitleorous raised his laser sword, the elite one hundred Robonoids following him split into 4 groups of twenty five Robonoids, making a formidable four flanks, and maneuvering encircling the whole Royal Palace Assembly Chamber Hall.

The crowd and audiences even wildly cheered what was going on they thought was part of the Wedding Show, there was so much clapping of hands and jubilation, the uproar of merriment and laughter's filled the Royal Palace Assembly Hall with so much joyful noise that Commander Levonne couldn't hear what God Anuk was telling him to do.

Commander Levonne and the Royal Palace Escort Legionnaires braced themselves for battle confrontation with Supreme Commander Hitleorous and his one hundred elite Robonoids, yet, as per Galactic War Code of Ethics, Commander Levonne must observe Galactic High Command War Protocols, they can only fire their laser weapons when provoked and fired upon.

Commander Levonne assessing the situation couldn't see any reason of hostility, it seems that Supreme Commander Hitleorous and his one Hundred Robonoids are just like making a parade formation, and the Robonoids are not holding their weapons, in-fact, all their laser weapons and swords are kept in the holders and scabbards, only Supreme Commander Hitleorous was holding his weapon of laser sword and yet holding it above as if executing a Galactic Salute.

And when all the one hundred elite Robonoids completed their formation hovering midway above in the air forming a phalanx and barricading the whole Royal Palace Assembly Hall, with Supreme Commander Hitleorous in the center, it was a battle formation God Anuk knows too well.

Amidst cheerful jubilation of the crowds and audiences admiring the Robonoids formation as if imposing a security assurance, God Anuk shouted on top of his voice to Commander Levonne.

"Commander Levonne, don't provoke any fight, or we will all die, just cover me and Goddess Nakki, maintain your battle shield formation, and slowly we will moved at the back end entry of the Royal Palace Altar, we will help Goddess Nakki ESCAPE, this is a well plan Coup D'état on the Throne of Planet Nibiru. THE ELDERS and the Secret Society wants to overthrow the power and rulership of Goddess Nakki, so that they can exact revenge on Blue Planet Earth's humanoids, the realization and execution of their long much-awaited plan CODENAME: ENGLUEBOLDERGY2015"

Commander Levonne couldn't hear well what was God Anuk shouting to him because of the cheerful jubilations inside the Royal Palace Assembly Hall, the noise of clapping hands and laughter's of the audiences echoing across the Royal Palace Assembly Hall was so intense.

And then the voice of the Announcer hosting the event came aloud pacifying the audiences and guest alike to calm down "NIBIRUNIANS, NIBIRUNIANS, SILENCE AND CALM DOWN" to which the audiences followed and the Announcer announces again.

"...return to your seats and we will continue the ceremony. Let us delay no more the Grand Sacred Wedding of God Anuk and Goddess Nakki, let the Shaman perform the Universal Galactic rites and rituals that we may declare today the Rulership and hand-over the SCEPTER of Nibiru's Throne unto our beloved Queen, the Daughter of Universe, Goddess Nakki."

And just as the Announcer finished the announcement, Supreme Commander Hitleorous lowered down his Laser Sword and put on his laser sword holster, then descended slowly towards the Royal Palace Assembly Hall Altar where the Shaman is, with Commander Levonne and the Royal Palace Escort Legionnaires still forming battle formation shield protecting God Anuk and Goddess Nakki.

Commander Levonne sensing a battle confrontation shouted and commanded his Legionnaires "Legionnaires, protector of Royal Palace Sovereignty and Nibiru's Throne, GLORY AND HONOR EVEN IN DEATH, brace and prepare your-selves, WAIT FOR MY COMMAND"

And all Royal Palace Escort Legionnaires surrounding God Anuk and Goddess Nakki shouted and answered, "HURRAH, WE ARE THE LEGIONNAIRES, PROTECTOR AND DEFENDER OF ROYAL CROWN SOVEREIGNTY AND NIBIRU'S THRONE, GLORY AND HONOR EVEN IN DEATH" and all Legionnaires readied themselves, placed and gripped their battle laser swords in their scabbard.

God Anuk upon hearing what the Legionnaires had just shouted gripped the hands of Goddess Nakki and embraced her tightly, his heart in anguish knowing TIME and FATE at that moment is against them, and that the enemies who wants to take control of Nibiru Throne were already positioned awaiting that final signal for them to reveal themselves and stage the Coup D'état, and seize the power and rulership of Planet Nibiru. He knows in his heart the enemies will never let them succeed in their marriage, and would not accept the Kingdomship under Goddess Nakki, for the enemies deemed Goddess Nakki as descendants of Magandalena, the humanoid who was offered to Lord God Adanis as sexual favor during his visit to Earth.

Goddess Nakki was so confused of what was happening, her tears building up in her eyes, she comprehend that God Anuk was embracing her tight as if signifying something, in that moment of anguish and confusion, Goddess Nakki couldn't utter any words, she could feel the fast beating sound of God Anuk's heart like a drum beat, she thought something is wrong and wants to cry, she now fully grasp and understand what her beloved God Anuk was trying to explain to her about the impending debacle during their wedding.

"Oh my Goddess, my love for all eternity, THIS IS IT, whatever happens today, remember always I LOVE YOU, and for all reasons, I am doing this for you, for the seed and breathe of love I planted in your womb, take care of our child, there will come a TIME when everything will be perfect for us, for now, let us bear the cruelty of fate, I had devised a plan of your ESCAPE to BLUE PLANET EARTH, away from THE ELDERS who wants to seize the power and throne of Nibiru Kingdom, and plans to vanish you" God Anuk telling Goddess Nakki, his voice trembling and full of emotions.

Goddess Nakki burst into tears, her heart in so much pain, she was searching her mind and heart, what was it that FATE offers and intervene, and didn't allow her marriage, her grand union to God Anuk finish at least, in her moment of happiness suppose to be, turns into so much pain and sorrow. She is languishing, and her emotions betrays her strength, she was weakened by the inglorious moment, she just cling unto God Anuk's warmth and assuring embrace, crying and sobbing.

Just as God Anuk will utter soothing words to soothe Goddess Nakki's wailing heart, then came the announcement from the announcer, but this time, it's coming from a different voice.

"BREATHE OF LOVE"
BY MONAC
(POETIC BREEZE, POETIC FROTH PART 1 – POEM NO. 161)

Rejoice indeed rejoice
The secrets revealed
Amidst its grandeur
Aphrodite gasped

Door of infinite bliss
Pearl of glory invites
Scabbard of hardened flesh
Bring the serpent of life

Pierce that line in-between
The gate to life
It promises joy beyond
The sweetest of them all

Rejoice indeed rejoice
When secrets engulf
All reasons lost
Passion it brings forever

Entwined as one
Burst of blissful seeds
It promises dreams
A joy of love

Rejoice indeed rejoice
Deep beneath the secrets
A BREATHE OF LOVE comes
The sweetest fruit as one!

"Nibirunians, Unigalitizines, today is a historical time for our beloved Planet Nibiru, for today is the culmination of THE ELDERS and the SECRET SOCIETY to fulfill its eon of time planning of avenging our forefathers defeat against the Humanoids of Blue Planet Earth. THERE WILL BE NO GRAND GALACTIC WEDDING BETWEEN GOD ANUK AND GODDESS NAKKI."

Upon hearing this announcement, the Nibirunians sitting as audiences were bewildered and puzzled, and started talking to each other, shouting what's going on, asking what trouble the Royal Palace had gotten into. Chaos was brewing as more and more Nibiruninians demands answers.

Supreme Commander Hitleorous, awaiting that final perfect timing couldn't wait any longer, He withdraw his laser sword and raise above his head flaming, signifying the final cue of their Grand Plan of taking over the Planet Nibiru's throne and command, and when He lowered his flaming laser sword infront of him, it was the symbolic command the one hundred elite Robonoid Troops awaiting, it was the command of "BATTLE CHARGE", and all of a sudden, all the one hundred elite Robonoids withdraw their laser pistols and began descending rounding up the audiences, the Royal Guards were shocked and couldn't do anything because they were already surrounded and captured by the Robonoids, some proceeded to accompany Supreme Commander Hitleorous charging to where God Anuk and Goddess Nakki were standing.

Commander Levonne again shouted to his Royal Palace Escort Legionnaires surrounding and protecting God Anuk and Goddess Nakki to wait for his command, his heart is pounding because He knows it will be a bloody battle that could never be avert, and He knows whatever will happen, He and his Royal Palace Escort Legionnaires will protect God Anuk and Goddess Nakki, even if it cause their death. "GLORY AND HONOR EVEN IN DEATH" he murmured to himself.

And then came again the voice and announcement but this time, the voice was dictating.

"COMRADES, SEIZE THE POWER OF PLANET NIBIRU'S THRONE, SEIZE THE ROYAL SCEPTER AND HAND OVER TO THE ELDERS, SEIZE GOD ANUK AND GODDESS NAKKI, THAT THEY MAY BE JUDGE ACCORDINGLY BY THE GALACTIC HIGH TRIBUNAL

COURT FOR TREASON, AND BE PUNISH OF THEIR CRIME. NIBIRUNIANS, UNIGALITIZINES, DO NOT BE STUPID TO DO ANYTHING, BE STILL, CALM YOURSELVES, WE ONLY WANT THE POWER AND COMMAND OF PLANET NIBIRU, WE DO NOT WISH YOU ALL ANY HARM, BUT DO NO GIVE US REASON TO KILL YOU, FOR WE WILL NOT HESITATE TO DO SO" thus the voice speaking in microphone announced and commanded, and Supreme Commander Hitleorous upon hearing what had been announced charge to attack the Royal Palace Escort Legionnaires protecting God Anuk and Goddess Nakki.

Goddess Nakki felt the sudden urge to fight, and kissed feverishly God Anuk and said "My God Anuk, whatever will happen I will not let them ruin our grand marriage, I will fight them and whatever happens, always remember in your heart I WILL BE YOURS FOR ETERNITY, THAT'S MY VOW UNTO YOU….and she struggle to let go of God Anuk's embraced.

God Anuk sensing Goddess Nakki will fight the enemies, hold her back and said "NO, GODDESS NAKKI, MY LOVE, DON'T FIGHT THE ENEMIES, TODAY IS NOT THE BATTLE, THE BATTLE TO BE WON IS IN BLUE PLANET EARTH, I MUST LET YOU ESCAPE AND GO TO BLUE PLANET EARTH TO WARN THEM, THEIR LEADERS OF IMPENDING CATASTROPHIE AND DEBACLE THEIR PLANET WILL ENCOUNTER, PLEASE BELIEVE ME MY LOVE, I HAVE DEVISE A GALACTIC DEEP SPACE SHUTTLE-CRAFT THAT WILL TAKE YOU SAFELY THERE, IT IS VERY IMPORTANT THAT YOU MUST ESCAPE AND ARRIVE AT BLUE PLANET EARTH, AND WARN THE HUMANOIDS, FOR IF WE WILL FAIL, MAY THE GOD OF UNIVERSE FORBIDS, IT WILL BE THE GRAND DESTRUCTION OF BLUE PLANET EARTH AND THE ANNIHILATION OF HUMANOIDS, IT WILL BE THE END OF YOUR PEOPLE MY LOVE, IT WILL BE THE END OF YOUR ANCESTORS"

Goddess Nakki couldn't believe what she had just heard from God Anuk, for God Anuk was implying she came from Blue Planet Earth, that her ancestry was link to the Humanoids, and in the midst of chaos, her mind is screaming for answers of questions she just couldn't comprehend, she was lost at words.

Commander Levonne upon seeing Supreme Commander Hitleorous and twelve Robonoids were coming and charging at their position commanded instantly "LEGIONNAIRES, DEFENDER OF NIBIRU THRONE AND SOVEREIGNTY, PROTECTOR OF GODS AND GODDESSESS, GLORY AND HONOR EVEN IN DEATH, ARM YOURSELVES, PREPARE FOR BATTLE, PREPARE TO DIE HONORABLY, BE BRAVE, BE COURAGEOUS, DIE WITH ME, GLORY AND HONOR TO OUR DEATH"

And all Legionnaires surrounding and protecting God Anuk and Goddess Nakki shouted "HURRAH", withdraw their laser weapons and laser armour cross-shield, brace themselves for battle confrontation with attacking Supreme Commander Hitleorous, and along with him twelve elite Robonoids ready to squeeze the trigger of their laser weapons, very eager to kill without mercy.

The Nibirunian audiences held up by the Robonoids were all petrified and horrified of what they are seeing near the Royal Palace Assembly Hall Altar, where Supreme Commander Hitleorous and twelve Robonoids attacking the defense of the Royal Palace Escort Legionnaires under Commander Levonne protecting the Royal Couple, God Anuk and Goddess Nakki, they were all caught up with shock and unpleasant surprise, their breathe sobbing with cries and frustration knowing they couldn't do anything to help save their Queen Goddess Nakki and King God Anuk, they just embraced each other and hold hands together awaiting what FATE and DESTINY will dictate and unfolds.

Even the Galactic Unified High Command High Ranking Officials couldn't do anything of the situation, they were also detained and held up by the Robonoids with their laser cannons pointing at them, all they could do was hope and pray that THE GODS OF UNIVERSE will intervene and avert the course of action, and somehow a MIRACLE will come which might save the life of God Anuk and Goddess Nakki from Supreme Commander Hitleorous and his twelve Robonoids charging, it was a sight and spectacle no one suspect to come, it was a complete surprise, another tragedy that will be added and recorded to their Planet's turmoil history.

Supreme Commander and the twelve Robonoids formed a single column with Supreme Commander Hitleorous at the center, all their laser cannons pointing at the Royal Palace Escort Leggionaires surrounding and protecting the Royal Couple, and when they are about ten paces away, they stop charging, their finger tip ready to squeeze the trigger and unleash the highly charge laser beams of their laser cannons that will obliterate and burn the Legionnaires, including God Anuk and Goddess Nakki to ashes.

And just as Supreme Commander Hitleorous commanded the twelve Robonoids alongside with him the command "AIM and FIRE", Commander Levonne managed to command his Legionnaires first, "Legionnaires, defense formation, activate ELECTROMAGNETIC SHIELD"

As the Robonoids and Supreme Commander Hitleorous squeeze the trigger of their weapons, and the burst of their weapons laser beams and fireballs were fired unto the Legionnaires, creating a massive bright lights of bursting different colors exploding, the whole Nibirunians watching the scenario were shocked, crying and shouting, they couldn't believe what they are seeing with their own eyes, the MASSACRE of the Royal Palace Escort Legionnaires and their Royal King and Queen, God Anuk and Goddess Nakki.

The sight was gruesome and unbearable to watch for the Nibirunian audiences, all the foray of laser ammunitions were fired by the Robonoids and Supreme Commander Hitleorous, in their mind there is no way the Legionnaires and the Royal Couple could escape such power of weapons, all they could see was smoke and burst of laser beams, surely they thought all of them will burn to ashes.

PLANET NIBIRU ARMY LEGIONNAIRE'S ARMOUR ELECTRO-MAGNETIC SHIELD

And when Supreme Commander Hitleorous and the twelve Robonoids stopped firing their laser weapons ruthlessly, and all the exploding laser beam lights, smoke and dust settled in, all the Nibirunians inside the Royal Palace Assembly Hall at first were shocked, then puzzled and bewildered when they finally grasped what had just happened, and realized the final outcome, all of a sudden they all burst into cheering, shouting and clapping their hands, as if the show was over, and the show's ending was triumphant for the lead performers.

Much to amazement of Supreme Commander Hitleorous, and THE ELDERS along with their cohorts, the members of their group called SECRET SOCIETY, who were also there watching the battle, and awaiting the proclamation of taking over the Nibiru Throne, behold, indeed, there was a MIRACLE that happened. Supreme Commander Hitleorous couldn't believe what He was seeing with his own eyes, He was greatly puzzled and astonished.

There in-front of him was a massive electro-magnetic balls of light engulfing and protecting the Royal Palace Escort Legionnaires and the Royal Couple. The Royal Palace Escort Legionnaires managed to activate their body-armor ELECTROMAGNETIC SHIELD that each armor magnetic energy linked and merged with all magnetic energy emitting by each Legionnaires armor-shield forming a big round-ball of electro-magnetic defense shield, thus, stopping all the laser beams and cannons fired unto them by Supreme Commander Hitleorous and the twelve Robonoids.

When everything was settled and quiet, Commander Levonne seized the opportunity, that moment where Supreme Commander Hitleorous was astonished and stunned of what had just happened, and couldn't utter any word of command for the twelve Robonoids who were then busy reloading their weapons with assorted laser ammunitions.

Commander Levonne knowing time is on his side shouted without hesitation to his Legionnaires "DREATHGON LEGIONS, BATTLE OFFENSE, FIRE AT WILL AT ENEMY; UMBRIEL LEGIONS FALL BACK, PROTECT GOD ANUK AND GODDESS NAKKI ESCAPE, RETREAT AT THE BACK DOOR, WE WILL COVER YOU"

PLANET NIBIRU ROYAL ESCORT LEGIONNAIRE'S ARMOUR CROSS-SHIELD

PLANET NIBIRU'S DREATHGON

PLANET NIBIRU ARMY LEGIONNAIRE'S LASER BOW

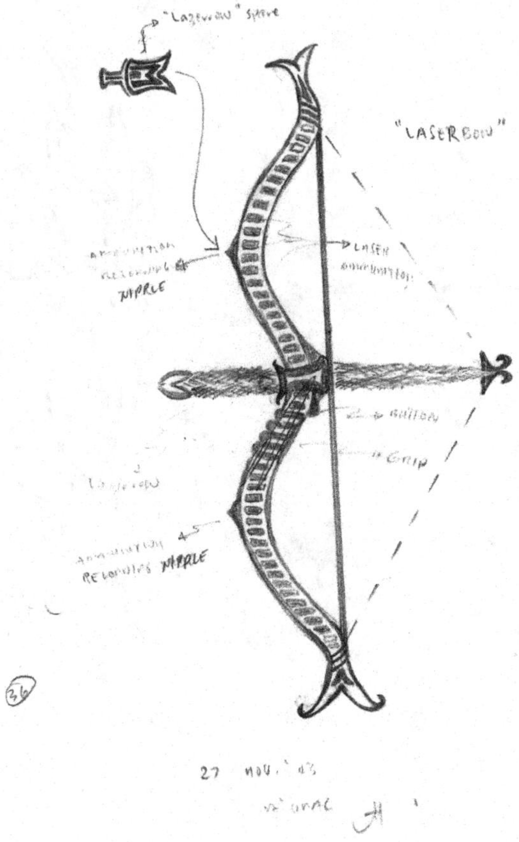

And in a flash of seconds comes the sortie of fire cannons from the Squad of Royal Palace Escort Dreathgon Legionnaires laser weapons hitting ten Elite Robonoids that instantly burned to ashes, Supreme Commander Hitleorous and the remaining Robonoids surviving the Royal Palace Escort Dreathgon Legionnaires Squad's assault scrambled to take cover, and fired back their weapons. Twenty Elite Robonoids came to reinforce and help Supreme Commander Hitleorous fight back Commander Levonne and His Dreathgon Legionnaires Squad whom by that time were already maneuvering taking cover.

Meanwhile, Royal Palace Escort Umbriel Legionnaires Squad as commanded by Commander Levonne escorted and protected God Anuk and Goddess Nakki escape to the back door of Royal Palace Assembly Hall, and in the mayhem, the Nibirunian Unigalitizine audiences terrified of what they have seen rushed to escape and save themselves, it was a chaotic scene, the Robonoids assigned to watch the detained audiences fired their laser weapons and killed those Nibirunians trying to escape, the Grand Galactic Wedding that supposed to bring laughters and merriment turns into bloody BLOOD-BATH.

Heart-wrenching sadness engulfs Goddess Nakki's heart as she sees from her own eyes the killing and murder of her Subjects, the Nibirunians who came and grace her supposed wedding, and while escaping alongside God Anuk, she vowed to herself, there will come a time she will punish those who commited the gruesome atrocities, and disrupted her Galactic Grand Sacred Wedding to God Anuk, "surely there will be retribution when time comes", she murmured herself, "I WILL HAVE MY OWN REVENGE…IN TIME"

Sea of tears was flooding Goddess Nakki's eyes, streaming her cheeks, she couldn't believe herself what she had seen and learned, her heart and mind in anguish, dictating her to fight back, but God Anuk hold and embrace her tight, and the words of God Anuk about the importance of her ESCAPE to Blue Planet Earth echoing in her sanity and vanity, adding more to her grief and bewilderment, the thoughts of her LINEAGE, that she possess the BLOOD OF MILKY WAY, THAT HOSTILE AND ENTICING BLUE PLANET EARTH'S INTELLIGENT CREATURES CALLED SPECIES OF HUMANOIDS WAS HER PEOPLE AND ANCESTORS.

She was crying and in anguish, yet in her mind were questions that needs answers, "…HOW COULD IT BE, WHAT MYSTERY AND SECRETS

BEQUEATH MY ENTITY, WHO AM I?" Goddess Nakki lingers in her mind such reverberating questions while trying to escape the onslaught of their enemies, she doesn't know well the ESCAPE PLAN to Blue Planet Earth of her beloved God Anuk, but she convinced herself, in order for her to better understand and know her entity, she must TRUST God Anuk, and find her MISSING LINK OF LINEAGE to Blue Planet Earth, and when the right TIME comes, she will REDEEM herself, and reclaim her glory not only in Planet Nibiru, but to Blue Planet Earth as well.

"RIDDLE OF INGENUITY"
BY MONAC
POETIC BREEZE, POETIC FROTH PART 2 – POEM NO. 297)

Oh darkness, twin of light
Hide not the face of immense
Beauteous radiance of Infinity
Entity shines in mystery

Great secrets embedded within
Bestowed with glistening parody
Unveil the drama of existence
Ominous Phantom of Creativity

Mystifying truth of Enigma
The riddle of universal ambiguity
Abyss grips the hidden travesty
Unperturbed mockery of reality

Abode of profound perception
Unlock the multifarious beauty
Flickering amidst distant shadows
Silhouetting the ancient comedy

Beyond speck of cosmic rays
Wondrous glory of uncharted realm
Explosion of sparkling Divinity
Precise concept of ingenuity!

Supreme Commander Hitleorous seeing the carnage and bloodshed, the slaughter of Nibirunians Unigalitizines by the Elite Robonoids He personally handpicked, felt astounded, and shocked of the debauchery, in his mind was the word "DISASTER", he quickly reached to his pocket, and grasped the control program device of the Robonoids microchips embedded in their heads, He then reprogram the Robonoids not to kill the civilians, the Nibirunians Unigalitizines, but instead program the Robonoids to kill all Royal Palace Escort Legionnaires, including Goddess Nakki and God Anuk who were trying to escape.

Instantly, the Elite Robonoids killing the Nibirunians Unigalitizines who were trying to escape stopped firing their weapons, divert their attention and fired at will to the Royal Palace Escort Legionnaires Dreathgon Legion Forces led by Commander Levonne who were by that time already taking covers near the Royal Palace Assembly Hall Altars Stone Tables and Pillars, protecting and covering the back door where the Royal Palace Escort Umbriel Legion Forces along with God Anuk and Goddess Nakki entered for their ESCAPE.

Indeed, it was a day of carnage, a bloody blood-shed that again tarnished the tumultuous history of Planet Nibiru. Scores of Unigalitizines murdered bodies were strewn all over the Royal Palace Assembly Hall, slump lifeless in their seats, others in the hallways and corridors, it was a grotesque and ghastly sight, that the Unigalitizine audiences who survived the senseless assault couldn't bear to see and accept, and were all terrified, screaming and crying, trying to comprehend what sorrow and anguish befalls them, some of them holding the lifeless body of their beloved love-ones killed by the Robonoids nonsensical and irrational assault. Indeed it was a tragedy nobody expected to happen.

On their way passing the labyrinth corridors and hallways of the Royal Palace secret passages, God Anuk with Goddess Nakki on his arms, stopped for a brief moment and shouted a plea to the Royal Palace Escort Legionnaires Umbriel Legion Forces, the frightful sound of laser ammunitions exploding and being fired in the Royal Palace Assembly Hall between Commander Levonne and his Royal Palace Escort Dreathgon Legionnaires Forces against the ruthless and power-hungry Supreme Commander Hitleorous and his handpicked elite Robonoids, echoing and rumbling a horrific sound of morbid terror and disillusionment, a hollow sound of deafening FEAR OF DEATH.

"Legionnaires, stay with me, we must protect Goddess Nakki's ESCAPE at all cost, we must reach the Royal Palace Galactic Deep Space Shuttle-craft launching plinth at once, and LAUNCH THE ESCAPE OF GODDESS NAKKI to Blue Planet Earth, don't let Supreme Commander Hitleorous and the Robonoids come and stop us, THIS IS EXTREMELY IMPORTANT, THE ESCAPE OF GODDESS NAKKI TO BLUE PLANET EARTH IS NOT ONLY FOR HER SALVATION, BUT THE SALVATION OF PLANET NIBIRU'S THRONE AND GALACTIC KINGDOMSHIP FROM THE HANDS OF TYRANNICAL ELDERS WHO WANTS ONLY WAR AND REVENGE AGAINST THE HUMANOIDS AND THE DEMIGODS. IT IS ALSO THE SALVATION OF THE BLUE PLANET EARTHS HUMANOIDS FROM BEING ANNIHILATED BY THE SECRET SOCIETY GROUP"

God Anuk then added "LEGIONNAIRES, ABIDE BY YOUR SWORN OATH AND CREED, GLORY AND HONOR EVEN IN DEATH"

And all Royal Palace Escort Legionnaires Umbriel Legion Forces shouted at the same time "AYE, AYE LORD GOD ANUK, GLORY AND HONOR EVEN IN DEATH"

Then as God Anuk turned around with Goddess Nakki to continue their way of escaping into the Royal Palace Galactic Deep Space Shuttle-craft launching plinth area where VIMANAS are stationed as well, God Anuk caught something oddly strange yet delightful in his eyes, for out of the corner of his eyes, God Anuk saw a young Legionnaire, a Centurion Rank holding tightly in his chest the PLANET NIBIRUS ROYAL THRONE SACRED SCEPTER.

God Anuk made a gesture asking the Centurion to come forward and present himself to him, in his mind and heart reign jubilation because He thought Goddess Nakki and Him had lost the PLANET NIBIRUS ROYAL THRONE SACRED SCEPTER, which acknowledged the Royal essence that whoever possessed it, is the sole and rightful Ruler of Planet Nibiru. God Anuk gave thanks in his heart Almighty God Orioness, the God of Sirius, the God of his home galaxy, the Constellation of Orion.

And when the Centurion comes close to God Anuk, He told him at ease and asked him what is his name, and how did He get in his possession the PLANET NIBIRUS ROYAL THRONE SACRED SCEPTER.

"...Centurion Ezriel is my name, my most Gracious High Lord God Anuk" thus the Legionnaire, Centurion Ezriel started his introduction and story to God Anuk while they are all walking fast, finding their way out of the Royal Palace Secret Passage, the LABYRINTHS and DUNGEONS of Planet Nibiru Royal Palace Secret underground passages.

"I myself couldn't believe what have I done, as to what fate and destiny ensued me" Centurion Ezriel began his account.

"I was happily watching your Grand Galactic Wedding Ceremony in one monitor web screen inside the Royal Palace Intelligence Security Office while I was on-duty assigned to check-out the various CCTV Security Monitors, when suddenly Supreme General Jhesusan arrived and entered the office." Centurion Ezriel paused for a moment, knowing what He said would ring a bell in God Anuk ears, for it is well-known in Planet Nibiru Kingdom the friendship and brotherhood affection of two great Unigalitizines, Supreme General Jhesusan and Him, Lord God Anuk.

Upon hearing what Centurion Ezriel had just said about Supreme General Jhesusan, quickly throw a questioning glance at Centurion Ezriel, puzzled on what Supreme General Jhesusan was doing in the Royal Palace Intelligence Security Office, and encouraged the Legionnaire, Centurion Ezriel to continue his stories and account of how he came to possessed the PLANET NIBIRUS ROYAL THRONE SACRED SCEPTER, but this time very eager to hear the story attentively because of Supreme General Jhesusan involvement, in his mind delve a surprise issue and questioned the loyalty of his childhood friend, Supreme General Jhesusan.

"Did He betray me and my beloved Goddess Nakki? Is He the one who activated the Royal Palace Assembly Hall Attic Dome to open so that Supreme Commander Hitleorous and his Robonoids could gain access entering the Royal Palace Assembly Hall and disrupt our wedding? Did He sold himself to THE ELDERS and their SECRET SOCIETY GROUP who wants vengeance and revenge to the Blue Planet Earth, and wants control of Planet Nibirus throne and Kingdomship? What are you up to my dearest friend? Why you didn't consult me?" these are the intriguing thoughts and questions that linger in God Anuks sanity while they are escaping.

"I must hear every details of this Centurion's story" God Anuk murmured himself and positioned Goddess Nakki to his rightside and Centurion Ezriel to his leftside, while the twelve Royal Palace Escort Legionnaire Umbriel Legion Forces lead by Commander Domenz surrounding them, alert and battle-ready to protect them from any in-coming enemy threat and assault.

"Continue your narration Centurion Ezriel" God Anuk then commanded and added "...tell us your story precisely what happened with your encounter with Supreme General Jhesusan, don't omit or fabricate, but tell the truth, and THE TRUTH SHALL SET YOU FREE"

As they find their way out of the Palace Dungeon, Centurion Ezriel continued his narration of his story.

"Like I said, I was surprised myself when Supreme General Jhesusan suddenly entered the Royal Palace Intelligence Security Office and demanded my attention at once. I thought He's going to punish me for not doing my job well because I was watching your Grand Galactic Sacred Wedding, of course, I don't want to miss any details of such important event in our Planet Nibiru's History, but I was astounded and really surprised when Supreme General Jhesusan told me to be at ease, and asked my help to operate the Intelligence Security Command computer. Supreme General Jhesusan was like in a hurry to find something, perhaps someone in the Security CCTV camera, He asked me to open the file records of the Security CCTV camera 30 minutes earlier when He arrived, and specifically demanded the records of the Security CCTV camera pointing directly where the Unified High Command High Ranking Officers were seating at, it seems Supreme General Jhesusan was trying to find someone among the High Ranking Officers." Centurion Ezriel paused for a while when He sees that the passage they are walking on came to a dead end, and look at God Anuk as if questioning what to do next.

God Anuk felt the importance of Centurion Ezriel story, He knows all the questions lingering in his mind about the questionable loyalty of his dearest friend is at stake, and that through the story of Centurion Ezriel He could find answers, and clear all his doubts, perhaps will tell the true motives of his dear friend Supreme General Jhesusan.

God Anuk gestured to Centurion Ezriel to step aside when they all stopped at the passage wall dead-end, then ordered Commander Domenz and his Royal Palace Escort Legionnaires Squad of Umbriel Legion Forces to be alert and cover them from in-coming enemy attack.

"Legionnaires re-group and cover well God Anuk and Goddess Nakki, get ready your armor-shield for activation of Electro-magnetic shield, be alert and abide to our code, Glory and Honor even in Death" commanded Commander Domenz as soon as He was ordered by God Anuk

God Anuk pressed a hidden button in one of the corridors support pillar, then instantly the dead-end wall open and yield an elevator shaft.

"This is a secret passage elevator shaft that will take us straight into the Deep-Space Shuttle launching pad where Goddess Nakki will have her escape. I already programmed the Deep-Space Shuttle destination coordinates, and its armory of automatic weapons" God Anuk explaining to Goddess Nakki and Centurion Ezriel
And as He ordered them to go inside the elevator shaft, suddenly an array of fire-cannon balls were fired at them killing instantly two Legionnaires, Commander Domenz ordered to fire at will against the in-coming enemy attack, grab two Legionnaires and they shielded themselves God Anuk and Goddess Nakki from in-coming volley of fire-cannons.

God Anuk and Goddess Nakki along with Centurion Ezriel managed to get into elevator shaft. God Anuk was shouting to Commander Domenz to get inside but it's too late, the array of in-coming enemy laser fires and cannons obliterate Commander Domenz and all his Legionnaires. They had sacrificed their lives for their safety and escape, just as Commander Domenz was hit by in-coming laser-cannon; He managed to look into the eye of Goddess Nakki as the elevator shaft was closing. He sacrificed himself so that the laser fire would not hit the closing elevator shaft, and could have killed Goddes Nakki.

Goddess Nakki was petrified and shocked, she cling to God Anuk's arms for she never thought and imagined that someone would die for her. She was too naïve of how ruthless and cruel the enemies are, she wanted to cry but deep in her heart, her emotional conscience was flooded with anger because of what she had seen and witnessed. Goddess Nakki vowed to herself the death of

Commander Domenz will not be forgotten, and she will exact revenge against the culprits of this senseless massacre.

As the elevator shaft ascending to the launching area where the Deep-Space Shuttle is, God Anuk asked Goddess Nakki if she is alright, and looked straight unto Goddess Nakki's eyes and said "Oh my beloved, be strong now, you have seen how ruthless and cruel our enemies are, they will not stop until we are dead, please be strong for me, and for that child you are carrying in your womb, trust me my beloved, your ESCAPE is very important, whatever the future holds between us, remember that I truly love you, and I will always will, wherever you are my love is with you, and I will be with you IN TIME" and just as God Anuk finished talking, tears streams out of his eyes, God Anuk couldn't subdue the tormenting agony of that moment for He knows when they reach the launching pad, there will be no time for parting words and kisses, but of tears and hope, perhaps FEAR.

Goddess Nakki upon seeing God Anuk eyes crying burst into tears as well, she knows the dying moments of their parting time is such an agony and unbearable, she couldn't utter a word at first but throw herself into God Anuk's arms and they embraced each other tightly, then she free herself from God Anuk arms and spoke, tears streaming down her cheeks.

"Oh my Dearest, my love, how tormenting this moment is, there is so much pain in my heart, and I can feel that agony in your heart as well, this pain of parting away from each other, how cruel it is indeed, but I trust you my love with all your plans, whatever happens in the future, remember also that my love for you is ETERNAL, and I will be strong for you, and to our off-spring, I will tell great stories about you" Goddess Nakki telling God Anuk in her sobbing voice "…and I will wait for you my love, I WILL PRAY UNTO OUR DIVINE GOD TO PROTECT YOU…"

Centurion Ezriel witnessing the tormenting moment couldn't hide his sadness as well and burst into tears because of what He was hearing from God Anuk and Goddess Nakki of their declaration of love for each other, and that undying HOPE for future which He knows is uncertain, for He was thinking that if they will survive the ruthless Robonoids laser weapons, surely they will not escape the punishment of Galactic High Tribunal if they will be captured by enemy, which is the ETERNAL FROZEN DEATH by vanishing and condemning them into the Abyss of Galaxy.

Again, God Anuk and Goddess Nakki embraced and hold-on unto each other's arms, they both know how crucial time is, and so precious at that very moment they are embracing one another in the elevator, they both know it will be their last embraced, and that whatever future holds for them, it is so uncertain when are they going to embrace each other again, whether they could see each other again, if only FATE would be so kind and generous for them.

God Anuk on hearing Goddess Nakki's trembling and sobbing voice suddenly felt the need to regain their composure, He must have to show Goddess Nakki that He is strong and have the courage to face all the realities unfolding so that she may as well be brave to face the future's surprises.

God Anuk sensing that the elevator will come to stop and soon would reach the Deep-Space Shuttle launching area, push Goddess Nakki gently away from him, and look deeply in her teary eyes, it was the strangest moment in his life, and lovingly spoken.

"My beloved, my ever-dearest Goddess Nakki, I don't know what future holds for us but I am sure your safety and salvation of our Planet Nibiru is in your hand, much so of the salvation of Blue Planet Earth, the Species called Humanoids, their salvation is in your hand as well, they are your people my love, SAVE THEM from the vengeance of the ELDERS and their SECRET SOCIETY GROUP, for if you fail to warn them of in-coming attack from our Planet and from the Spy-Legions, then it will be the end of your people my love, the Humanoids will be wipe-out from the face of the Blue Planet Earth, they will be all EXTERMINATED, so my love, my Goddess, be strong for me, and be strong for your people, this might be OUR LAST, but it doesn't mean the fight is over, the battle to be won is in BLUE PLANET EARTH, I am sending you there not to escape the enemies from here, but I am sending you there to prepare the Humanoids, your people, prepare them my love for the fight of their life, it will be the DARKEST HOURS of their life when our Planet Armies under the Lordship of the ELDERS will wage the 2nd Galactic War against them, perhaps the salvation of Blue Planet Earth might be as well the salvation of Planet Nibiru from tyrannical Rulers and Kingdomship, I am counting on you my Dearest, my Love…I will not say any GOODBYE my love, I am with you forever in your heart"

And God Anuk after telling Goddess Nakki the encouraging words, kissed her fervently, and passionately, it would be the SWEETEST KISS of their life, but deep inside their hearts, it was the SWEETEST PAIN of their life together.

Then suddenly the elevator came to halt, they have arrive at the Deep-Space Shuttle launching pad area that made them stop kissing each other, God Anuk embraced Goddes Nakki one last time, and told her "EVERYTHING IS NOT OVER MY LOVE".

Centurion Ezriel fearful of his life, uttered to God Anuk "My Lord God Anuk, my apology for intruding but please hurry, let's go now and prepare Goddess Nakki's ESCAPE, the enemies are after us, and they are just right behind" and beg God Anuk speaking "…if you will be so kind and gracious, can I go with Goddess Nakki to Blue Planet Earth, I am sure I could be useful to her Highness doing errands, I promise and swear on my Family's Honor, I will take good care of Goddess Nakki, I will abide to our Legionnaire's Code, Glory and Honor even in Death"

God Anuk upon hearing what Centurion Ezriel had just said contemplated fast in his mind, at the same time checking out the elevator security monitor if there are enemies outside waiting, and when He deemed sure that it's safe to go out, opened the elevator door, and they hurriedly run as fast as they can to the Deep-Space Shuttle launching pad.

Upon reaching the Deep-Space Shuttle, God Anuk opened at once the passenger cockpit from a remote control inside the launching control room.

Goddess Nakki then realize she's still wearing her wedding dress made by Vice Gandaheh, and remembered what Vice Gandaheh had told her about her wedding dress. It is made of Advance Scientific Technology of Nanocells, that it has program to transform from one dress to another if desired to, all She have to do is push a button if she wants it to be like an space-suit of radiating lights covering all her body.

When God Anuk saw Goddess Nakki transformed her dress into a deep-space suit with radiating lights, He knows in his heart, there is HOPE he could cling on for eon of time, He understood Goddess Nakki's desire to survive, perhaps for her people the Humanoids, perhaps for her Kingdom of Planet Nibiru, perhaps for HIM, for their ETERNAL LOVE to each other, and He was pleased deep inside his heart.

"COME-ON NOW MY GODDESS, TIME FOR YOU TO GO MY LOVE" God Anuk shouted

Goddess Nakki was also thinking on her own, if God Anuk will let Centurion Ezriel come with her, why it can be just her beloved to go with her to Blue Planet Earth, and she shouted back "MY GOD ANUK, COME WITH ME TO BLUE PLANET EARTH. LET US START ANEW IN THERE AND WE COULD PREPARE FOR WAR TOGETHER"

God Anuk felt so devastated and hurt of what her beloved had just spoken, for surely He could go with her, but the Deep-Space Shuttle launching program can only be launch by him in the launching control room, He had program the Deep-Space Shuttle in secrecy so that all his plans wouldn't be jeopardize if the ELDERS found about it through the Unified High Command of Universal Galactic Internal Intelligence Command, as what Lord Cainos was asking and querying him before their supposed wedding.

"I can't my love, I cannot go with you, I am the only one who knows the launching sequence program and password, I know how you feel my love, and it is really tormenting, but here we are my love, IT IS THE REALITY, you must go for US TO SURVIVE" God Anuk answered, then added.

"…Centurion Ezriel, I am granting your wish to come and go with Goddess Nakki to Blue Planet Earth, you are right, you could be useful to her especially doing errands when our SEED OF LOVE, OUR BREATHE OF LOVE starts to grow in her womb, take care of your Goddess, and the Planet Nibiru Throne Scepter you are holding now, I am entrusting it to your care, abide by your Family's Honor and Legionnaire's Code, someday I will repay you if it's God's will I survive this Galactic Dilemma of our Planet…"

PLANET NIBIRU GODDESS NAKKI'S ESCAPE DEEP SPACE SHUTTLE CRAFT

Centurion Ezriel felt overjoyed when He heard what God Anuk said and entrusted him, it was a task worth dying for He told himself and answered back God Anuk proudly and confidently in the tradition of a LEGIONNAIRE WARRIOR AND SOLDIER.

"AYE LORD GOD ANUK, HONOR AND GLORY EVEN IN DEATH, I WILL ABIDE TO MY CODE AND TO MY FAMILY'S HONOR" thus Centurion Ezriel answered God Anuk and executed the Planet Nibirunian Legionnaire's Military Salute.

As God Anuk acknowledge the salute of Centurion Ezriel, then comes suddenly the alarm which God Anuk knows too well for He himself program it, it was the alarm of INTRUDERS ALERT. He quickly went back inside the Launching Control Room and look at the CCTV's Security Monitor feedcam, He felt rush of energy and fear, the enemies have breach the Security Barrier and are now nearing them, worse in his fear, THE ROBONOIDS are coming.

God Anuk run quickly to where Goddess Nakki and Centurion Ezriel is, and ushered them both to board the DEEP-SPACE SHUTTLE at once.

Goddess Nakki wanted to show her beloved, God Anuk that she is strong as He is, that she can brave and face reality with courage and determination, but her feelings betrayed her, and when they finally are inside the Deep-Space Shuttle Passenger Cockpit, she couldn't hide her tears anymore, and she burst into tears.

God Anuk unmindful of Goddess Nakki's tears prepared the Deep-Space Shuttle Passenger Cockpit Time-Capsule that will hold Goddess Nakki and Centurion Ezriel asleep for the entire deep-space voyage, until such time the program elapse to open upon reaching its programmed coordinates of destination in Blue Planet Earth, if its survive the deep-space voyage and the onslaught of enemy's Deep-Space Attack Battle-Craft.

God Anuk put first Goddess Nakki inside the Deep-Space Shuttle Passenger Cockpit Time-Capsule, his heart in anguish.

PLANET NIBIRU'S GALACTIC DEEP SPACE ATTACK BATTLE-CRAFT

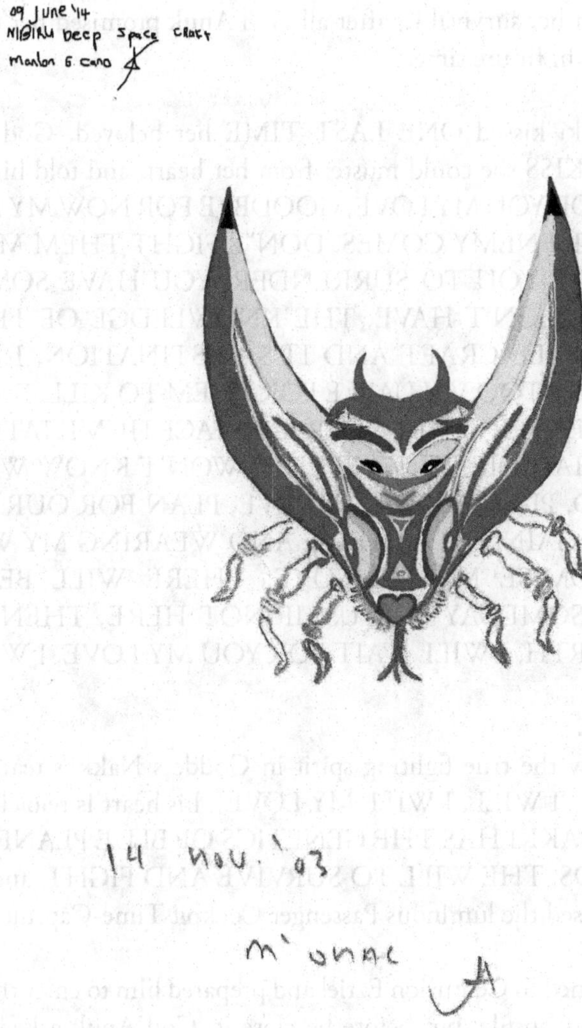

Goddess Nakki felt so oddly strange inside her heart as if she's fearful something bad and cruel will happen to her beloved, part of her mind dictating her to stay with her beloved and face the enemies whatever the consequences, even if it will cause her death, but another part of her mind as well was reasoning of how important her survival is, after all God Anuk promised her they will be together again in future time.

Goddess Nakki kissed ONE LAST TIME her beloved, God Anuk, the SWEETEST KISS she could muster from her heart, and told him "I WILL BE BRAVE FOR YOU MY LOVE, GOODBYE FOR NOW MY DEAREST, IF EVER THE ENEMY COMES, DON'T FIGHT THEM MY LOVE, I RATHER LIKE YOU TO SURRENDER, YOU HAVE SOMETHING THAT THEY DON'T HAVE, THE KNOWLEDGE OF THIS DEEP-SPACE SHUTTLE CRAFT AND IT'S DESTINATION, I AM SURE YOU ARE JUST TOO VALUABLE FOR THEM TO KILL, REMEMBER MY LOVE, BETTER SURRENDER AND FACE HUMILIATION NOW RATHER THAN DIE, IN TIME THEY WON'T KNOW WHATS ON YOUR MIND, PLAN AGAIN MY LOVE, PLAN FOR OUR LOVE TO RE-UNITE AGAIN, I STILL HAVE AND WEARING MY WEDDING DRESS, PROMISE ME MY LOVE, THERE WILL BE GRAND WEDDING SOMEDAY FOR US, IF NOT HERE, THEN IN BLUE PLANET EARTH, I WILL WAIT FOR YOU MY LOVE, I WILL WAIT, I PROMISE"

God Anuk saw the true fighting spirit in Goddess Nakki's teary eyes, and answered back "I WILL, I WILL MY LOVE", his heart is rejoicing for truly GODDESS NAKKI HAS THE GENETICS OF BLUE PLANET EARTH HUMANOIDS, THE WILL TO SURVIVE AND FIGHT, and with that, God Anuk closed the luminous Passenger Cockpit Time-Capsule.

God Anuk turned to Centurion Ezriel and prepared him to enter the Passenger Cockpit Time-Capsule, but before he close it, God Anuk asked Centurion Ezriel one question.

"Is Supreme General Jhesusan betrayed our Planet Nibiru, is he our enemy?" thus was the question Centurion Ezriel heard from God Anuk to which he replied "My Lord God Anuk, I swear on the blood of my Family's Honor, Supreme General Jhesusan did not betray us. He is not among our enemy, in-fact my Lord God Anuk, He was the one who ordered me to pass the urgent message to Commander Levonne of in-coming enemy attack, and to protect you and Goddess Nakki at all cost, I left Supreme General Jhesusan in the Royal Palace Intelligence Office Room scrolling the CCTV's Security feed-cams, if I am correct and not mistaken, He was searching for Supreme Commander Hitleorous and the Robonoids Troops"

God Anuk upon hearing what Centurion Ezriel told him about Supreme General Jhesusan muttered "OH DIVINE GOD, DON'T LET SOMETHING BAD HAPPEN TO MY DEAREST FRIEND" and thanked Centurion Ezriel, then closed immediately the Time-Capsule's door of Centurion Ezriel.

God Anuk then went back again to the Time-Capsule where his beloved Goddess Nakki was, He could see tears streaming down Goddess Nakki's cheeks and by that time Goddess Nakki was feeling the effect of grogginess to put her in deep-slumber during the entire course of deep-space voyage, and just as she closed her eyes for the last time, She saw God Anuk on the otherside of the luminous cover of the time-capsule crying as well, and she could read his lips saying "I LOVE YOU FOREVER" and her eyes slowly closed and her vision became blurry and dimmed.

God Anuk seeing Goddess Nakki had fallen asleep in deep-slumber for the Deep-Space Shuttle Craft deep-space voyage, throw a KISS-GOODBYE and hurriedly went to the conning cockpit and activated the automatic launching sequence program in ten seconds time, and activated as well the Deep-Space Shuttle Weaponry System, and when everything was set and ready, He closed all the doors of the Deep-Space Shuttle Craft and run as fast as He could inside the Launching Pad Control Room, and when He is inside safely He immediately program the launching protocol password, and the computer luminous monitor inside the Launching Pad Control Room became alive and lighted, sequencing the program data and the Deep-Space Shuttle Craft deep-space voyage route to its programmed destination.

"LOVE THAT IS FEARLESS"
BY MONAC

I believe, I believe in love
A love that conquers all
Nothing to hide, nothing to fear
No reservation and no hesitation

Only kindness and tenderness
Understanding each limitations
Embracing every shortcomings
With smile and patience

There will be no argument
Endearment will prevail
Into hearts and mind
Soothing words of affection
Surely will heal every wound

I believe, I believe in love
A love that conquers hate
Nothing to ashamed of
Nothing to lose faith

No ifs, no doubts
And no alibis
Firm and brave
Accepting all consequences

Be it of sweet-sorrow
It maybe a sweetest-pain
Perhaps, passionate joy
In every tears subside
Rain of happiness harboring

I believe, I believe in love
A love that conquers death
Worth fighting for
Worth dying for

No boundaries and no limits
And no questions asks
Even in the face of the end
Courage the shield and armor

Love will be the valor
And it will prevail
Whatever the circumstances
All it will seek and defend

Is to find and offer
A fire of romance
Smiles of utmost glory
A heart that is fearless
Love and honor even in death!

God Anuk was clenching his fist because He is so worried, He could see from CCTV's Security Monitor feedcams that the Robonoids are already coming near from the launching area, and just as the elevator door was opening, the sequencing of launching program have completed and God Anuk immediately push the button of Deep-Space Shuttle Craft launching countdown.

The launching alarm sounded and the computer sequencing program started counting "LAUNCHING IN TEN SECONDS…. TEN, NINE, EIGHT" thus the countdown started, but the Robonoids opened fired their laser weapons to the Deep-Space Shuttle Craft.

God Anuk seeing the Robonoids firing their laser weapons at Deep-Space Shuttle Craft was terrified, for He thought He had failed and that He had caused the death of his beloved Goddess Nakki, and the destruction of Blue Planet Earth's last hope, but to his surprised and amazement, the Deep-Space Shuttle Craft didn't explode yet retaliated with its laser-cannons and eliminated the Robonoids.

The Deep-Space Shuttle Craft Automatic Self-Defense Initiative (ASDI) encompassing Anti-Enemy Radar Detection and Auto-Launch Firing Program of any threat detected was automatically activated when the sequencing program protocol was completed, thus God Anuk realized upon seeing what happened to the Robonoids who were firing their laser weapons at the Deep-Space Shuttle Craft.

"SEVEN, SIX, FIVE, FOUR" continued the automatic launching countdown, and just as the launching countdown completed, and to God Anuk's much surprise, Supreme General Bhudasian and Supreme General Khrisnan, along with Lord Cainos and Lord Genaros entered un-expectedly the Launching Pad Control Room.

"STOP THE LAUNCHING PROTOCOL GOD ANUK" commanded Lord Cainos

Supreme General Bhudasian knows it is too late so He grabbed his laser-pistol from his holster and fired several shots at the Launching Pad Control Sequencing Program Monitor.

God Anuk again was shocked and terrified for He thought the automatic sequencing launching program was damaged brought upon by Supreme General

Bhudasian laser-pistol, but soon felt relief when He heard the thundering sound of Deep-Space Shuttle Craft Super-Sonic Engine Bolster roars and the Deep-Space Shuttle Craft begins to ascend from its launching plinth.

God Anuk was so happy inside his heart, at least there is a chance for Goddess Nakki's ESCAPE TO BLUE PLANET EARTH, He just hope that the Deep-Space Shuttle Craft would successfully defend itself and escape the Laser-Cannons from Planet Nibiru's UNIFIED HIGH COMMAND OF UNIVERSAL GALACTIC DEFENSE AERO-POLICE AND SPACE-FORCE DEEP-SPACE ATTACK BATTLE-CRAFT, under the Commandant-ship of Supreme Commander Napoleonious.

God Anuk again deep in his mind called unto his forefathers and ancestors DIVINE GOD to protect the Deep-Space Shuttle Craft, and its two passengers, his beloved Goddess Nakki, and the Planet Nibiru Throne Scepter bearer, Centurion Ezriel. All the while praying in his mind as the Deep-Space Shuttle Craft speeding into the vastness of Galaxy, its path lighting like a CHARIOTS OF FIRE dashing for eternity in the Darkness of Universe, God Anuk looked fiercely unto Lord Cainos eyes, as if demanding answers, perhaps condemning him of BETRAYAL OF TRUST.

Supreme General Khrisnan sensing that the Deep-Space Shuttle Craft is galloping its way into the darkness of Universe and escaping, called at once from his collar-phone Supreme Commander Napoleonious and commanded him to launch Deep-Space Attack Battle-Craft and intercept the escaping Deep-Space Shuttle Craft and specifically ordered in-front of God Anuk to OBLITERATE AND DESTROY IT WITH-OUT MERCY IN THE VASTNESS OF GALAXY, THAT THE REMNANTS OF THE DEEP-SPACE SHUTTLE CRAFT AND THE BODY OF GODDESS NAKKI BLOWN TO PIECES WILL BE FOREVER VANISHED AS COSMIC DUST IN THE ABYSS OF UNIVERSE.

Lord Genaros meanwhile commanded God Anuk not to resist his arrest, or else might cause his UNTIMELY DEATH, looking at him deeply as if telling him something beneath those piercing eyes, giving emphasis on the words "UNTIMELY DEATH".

"CHARIOTS OF FIRE"
BY MONAC

In a chariots of fire
I'm gonna' take you with me
I'm gonna' sweep you away
Into the known unknown
We'll find our destiny

In a chariots of fire
We'll sail the unknown universe
Hand in hand beyond as one
Together side by side
We'll dash our way into eternity

Chariot's on fire
No fear my love
It's the ride of a lifetime
We'll gallop the way on fire

Chariot's on fire
Like a comet we'll dash our way
Our story will shine in heavens
Lighting the sky with our love

Chariot's on fire
We'll conquer our fears
In a chariots of fire
Our love is our fire

Chariot's on fire
Love and ecstasy entwine
In a chariots of fire
Our love will bind us together
I'll take you beyond boundaries my love
Across the galaxies of stars
Our chariots of fire will shine in heavens
Stars will guide our way
Into the depths and space of happiness

We'll wander with our love and dreams
Don't you worry oh my Love
Into the darkness we'll light our fire
Boundless, there is no limit my love
Our chariots of fire will lead us
Into the realm of utmost bliss

Chariot's on fire
Galloping the glory of life
Where-ever way we go
Our love-story will shine

Chariot's on fire
Like a comet we'll dash our way
Our love-story burning in the sky
Lighting the universe with our love

Chariot's on fire
We'll seek our future's wake
In a chariots of fire
We may awake blissfully

Chariot's on fire
Love and ecstasy entwine
In a chariots of fire
We'll conquer the unknown Universe!

PLANET NIBIRU'S LORD CAINOS

God Anuk never uttered a word, He just stand still waiting for the enemies next course of action, in his mind echoing the words of his beloved Goddess Nakki (…IF EVER THE ENEMY COMES, DON'T FIGHT THEM MY LOVE, I RATHER LIKE YOU TO SURRENDER, YOU HAVE SOMETHING THAT THEY DON'T HAVE, THE KNOWLEDGE OF THIS DEEP-SPACE SHUTTLE CRAFT AND ITS DESTINATION, I AM SURE YOU ARE JUST TOO VALUABLE FOR THEM TO KILL, REMEMBER MY LOVE, BETTER SURRENDER AND FACE HUMILIATION NOW RATHER THAN DIE, IN TIME THEY WON'T KNOW WHATS ON YOUR MIND, PLAN AGAIN MY LOVE, PLAN FOR OUR LOVE TO RE-UNITE AGAIN, I STILL HAVE AND WEARING MY WEDDING DRESS, PROMISE ME MY LOVE, THERE WILL BE GRAND WEDDING SOMEDAY FOR US, IF NOT HERE, THEN IN BLUE PLANET EARTH, I WILL WAIT FOR YOU MY LOVE, I WILL WAIT, I PROMISE…)

Those words of Goddess Nakki echoing in his heart and mind, Full of HOPE and PROMISE, God Anuk clinches his fist hard, He is ready to explode and unleash his fury against Supreme General Khrisnan who ordered Supreme Commander Napoleonious of intercepting and attacking the Deep-Space Shuttle Craft with-out mercy, disregarding the precious life on-board of Goddess Nakki, his beloved, his Love of a Lifetime, for him it is DISRESPECTFUL and UNGENTLEMAN MANNER for a High Ranking Officer of Planet Nibiru, AN ACT OF COWARDNESS. He want to unleash his cosmic power and anger building within his Godly Being, if not only of that piercing glare of Lord Genaros that was somewhat warning him of not to do something stupid He might regret in the end, thus He tried to control his boiling anger in his heart, after all, he whispered in himself, "I am a God, I am Just and Fair, I fight a Godly Fight when I deem necessary, No, I do not wish to become a Diabolical and horrifying Monster like these four creatures in-front of me" thus God Anuk refrained and controlled his anger deep within his heart.

God Anuk then suddenly remember his dearest childhood friend, Supreme General Jhesusan whom He credited so much for all the valuable information He received from him, and that, until the critical moments of their life, his dearest friend Supreme General Jhesusan stood by him, He cannot keep himself from feeling sorry for He is wondering what had happened to his dearest friend. His last information about him was from Centurion Ezriel who told him that the last time Centurion Ezriel saw Supreme General Jhesusan was in the Royal Palace Intelligence Security Office room searching the CCTV's Security feed-cams of Supreme Commander Hitleorous location, but then He remembered well how surprisingly Supreme Commander Hitleorous and his Robonoid Troops entered the Royal Palace Chamber Hall that started the chaos and pandemonium inside the Royal Palace Chamber Hall disrupting His supposed to be Grandiose Wedding to Goddess Nakki.

God Anuk's mind and heart was filled with sorrow and grief, for He was thinking He had lost two important persons in his life. His beloved love-one Goddess Nakki aboard the Deep-Space Shuttle Craft escaping to Blue Planet Earth, He could only hope that it will survive its Galactic Passage along its programmed routes and coordinates, and the threat of Supreme Commander Napoleonious Deep-Space Attack Battle Craft, in his heart is uncertainty.

And then, his childhood dear friend Supreme General Jhesusan, He doesn't have any idea what had happened to him whether He is alive or DEAD, then the more He thinks of what had just happened, the more grief his heart felt because He then suddenly realize that there are a lot of lives that were taken away during that debacle and chaos of fighting during their wedding, IT WAS THE DARKEST HOURS OF HIS LIFE.

As God Anuk was deep in his pondering, Lord Cainos ordered Supreme General Bhudasian and Supreme General Krishnan to arrest God Anuk, and detain him for a while until such time orderly will be restore in the Kingdom with him at the Helm of Command. They will all have to convene in the Chambers of Truth along with other ELDERS and Members of their Secret Society Group to debate and cast verdict on what to do with God Anuk and other enemy or sympathizers of Goddess Nakki and God Anuk, whether to let them live as Diplomatic Prisoner, or perhaps punish them to death and suffer the Eternal Frozen Death in the abyss of Galaxy, FOREVER VANISH IN THE DARKNESS OF UNIVERSE.

Supreme Commander Napoleonious, Head of Unified High Command of Universal Galactic Defense Aero-Police and Space-Force upon receiving the direct orders from Supreme General Krishnan immediately ordered One Squadron of Deep-Space Attack Battle-Craft to intercept the Deep-Space Shuttle Craft before it enters the Black-Hole and traverse the Worm-Hole Universal Passage into another Galaxy, and specifically instructed the Commander In-Charge of pursuit, Commander Kimmy to shoot the

Deep-Space Shuttle Craft at all cost, even if the passenger is Goddess Nakki, the Heir of Planet Nibiru Kingdom's Royal Throne.

Supreme Commander Napoleonious told Commander Kimmy that the escaping Goddess Nakki commits Acts of Treason, and must not ESCAPE, AND THAT THE STANDING ORDER IS "SHOOT TO KILL".

The Deep-Space Shuttle Craft was already at Ultra-Sonic Lightning Speed when its AUTOMATIC SELF-DEFENSE INITIATIVE sounded and alarmed, and in the computer monitors of the cockpit command blinking the words "INTRUDERS, ALERT, ALERT, ALERT, INTRUDERS FAST APPROACHING, ACTIVATING AUTOMATIC SELF DEFENSE INITIATIVE (ASDI) AND INITIATING AUTOMATIC DEFENSE EVADING MANEUVERS (ADEM)"

Twenty Four Deep-Space Attack Battle-Craft were lined-up ahead in Galactic Battle Formation, forming a letter V-Shape battle-maneuver with Commander Kimmy at the lowest-front leading the Squadron.

"Stand-by all Galactic Cosmonauts, maintain DEEP-SPACE BATTLE FORMATION, ACTIVATE LASER-CANNON SPACE-TRAP MINE-FIELDS but wait for my order, just LOCK and LOAD" thus Commander Kimmy ordered HER Deep-Space Attack Battle Craft COSMONAUT PILOTS.

"AYE COMMANDER" replied one by one from the Galactic Cosmonaut Pilots.

Little did they know that at the moment they LOCK AND LOAD their weapons, the Deep-Space Shuttle Craft carrying Goddess Nakki and Centurion Ezriel who were in deep slumber and don't know whats happening, had already automatically track their weaponry system and already making itself automatic calculation of defense and attack maneuvers.

The Deep-Space Shuttle Craft was programmed by God Anuk with Automatic Self-Defense Initiative (ASDI) encompassing Anti-Enemy Radar Detection and Auto-Launch Firing Program for self-defense of any threat detected, with various sort of advance energy weaponry such as laser beams, sound-cannons, electro-magnetic rays, highly charge energy pulse-wave, and the last defense initiative, the time-capsule deep space shuttle's AUTOMATIC ELECTRO-MAGNETIC DEFENSE SHIELD in-case the space shuttle run-out of ammunition or of its energy weaponry, it is the last resort of defense initiative that will protect the Deep Space Shuttle and its passenger to arrive safely in that coordinates of destination programmed in Auto-Pilot Control.

Commander Kimmy felt un-easiness of the situation, knowing she will be the one who will give the final order to the Galactic Cosmonauts Pilots to fire their Deep-Space Attack Battle Craft Laser-Cannons that will surely obliterate the Deep-Space Shuttle Craft. In her heart, she feels anguish for she knows when she give that final order to fire, it will be THE END of Goddess Nakki, and the heavy burden of guilty feeling was crushing her sanity.

Commander Kimmy admired Goddess Nakki a lot and have a very good influence on her, in-fact when she was a young Nibirunian, she always emulate the goodness and beauteous character of Goddess Nakki. She still remembers well when she passed the Deep Space Galactic Cosmonaut Pilot Training Course. It was Goddess Nakki who pinned her Award of Best Deep Space Galactic Cosmonaut Pilot. That day became so memorable to her because how could she forget the beaming and warmest smile from Goddess Nakki pinning her award-badge in her Galactic Aero-Force Suit, and told her, "MAKE GOOD THE MOST OF YOUR LIFE, I AM PROUD OF YOU, YOU HAVE A BEAUTIFUL FUTURE AHEAD, BE A PROUD NIBIRUNIAN WHEN YOU ARE UP THERE DEEP IN SPACE, YOU ARE NOW A COSMONAUT PILOT", it was the happiest and perfect day of her life.

"This is not happening" Commander Kimmy told herself. "How could I betray you my Goddess Nakki? How could they charge you with Act of Treason, You are the epitome of a good Nibirunian, the Royal Heir to the Throne of Planet Nibiru Kingdom. What is the reason they want to kill you? This is a senseless act of killing, oh Goddess Nakki, I admire you so much, whatever you had committed that they are charging you with an Act of Treason and that they want you dead, I am following my MISSION ORDER, PLEASE FORGIVE ME. I AM A COSMONAUT PILOT AND I ABIDE TO MY OATH AND CODE OF CONDUCT. GOODBYE MY GODDESS NAKKI, MAY YOU FIND PEACE ETERNALLY" and with that in her thoughts, Commander Kimmy was about to give the orders of firing their Deep-Space Attack Battle Craft Laser-Cannons when suddenly one of her Cosmonaut Pilot shouted in panic in the communication-radio.

"Commander, Commander Kimmy, the Deep Space Shuttle Craft automatically tracked our weaponry system, it neutralized and jammed our firing activation sequence with "highly charge energy pulse-wave" thus was the voice coming from one of her Cosmonaut Pilot.

Commander Kimmy checked her weaponry system and found out it's true, she didn't noticed the blinking red alarm light in her cockpit weaponry panel because of her deep pondering about Goddess Nakki and her fate.

And then another voice shouted on the communication-radio "The Deep Space Shuttle Craft is coming towards us at ULTRA-SONIC SPEED, it's coming very fast, we should fire now Commander or the Deep Space Shuttle Craft will breach our Galactic Battle Formation"

Commander Kimmy commanded at once "HOLD YOUR GALACTIC BATTLE FORMATION, SHUT ALL WEAPON SYSTEM, I REPEAT SHUT ALL WEAPON SYSTEM NOW"

"BUT COMMANDER, IF WE SHUT OUR WEAPON, THE DEEP SPACE SHUTTLE CRAFT WILL ESCAPE" thus was the replied Commander Kimmy heard from one of her Cosmonaut Pilot.

"DO WHAT I SAY, THAT IS MY ORDER" Commander Kimmy ordered her Galactic Cosmonaut Pilots because She knows and understand that the Deep Space Shuttle Craft have an ASDI program, that anytime it detect incoming threat of any weaponry system, the ASDI (Automatic Self-Defense Initiative) will automatically activate and initiate its own self defense weaponry, and will automatically track and calculate enemy threat weapons including all its capabilities and sustainable damage it may cause.

"Cosmonauts trust me, I am your Commander, do what I say, de-activate all weapons system now" again Commander Kimmy ordered

"Aye Aye Commander" replied all Galactic Cosmonaut Pilots in her communication-radio

As soon as all Deep Space Attack Battle Craft de-activated their weaponry system, the Deep Space Shuttle Craft ASDI analyzed the enemy threat on its computer weaponry program, and calculated ZERO percent threat factor, and de-activated its emission of "highly charge energy pulse-wave" but cautiously retained ASDI as it still analyzed Twenty Four Un-Identified Objects in its Deep Space Anti-Enemy Radar Scanner with de-activated weaponry system.

Commander Kimmy analyzed herself the intention and flight path of the Deep Space Shuttle Craft, where it is heading and its ultimate destination. They were in the vicinity of Constellation Vega where there is a gateway of Inter-Galactic Black Hole time-travel. She suspects that it is where the Deep Space Shuttle Craft is heading, to enter the Black Hole and traverse the Wormholes, the Passage of Time. The destination she can't tell but it is the nearest Galaxy where the Deep Space Shuttle Craft could escape into another Galaxy.

Commander Kimmy had learned in the Deep Space Galactic Aero-Force Academy that the "THE BEST AERO SPACE COMBAT OFFENSE IS DEFENSE INITIATIVE" and that was the tactic she employed during her final Galactic Cosmonaut Pilot Training Course "DEEP SPACE AERO BATTLE TACTIC AND MANEUVER FLIGHT EXAMINATION", that earned her an award "Deep Space Galactic Cosmonaut Pilot TOP GUN" and became top of her Graduating Class.

"Galactic Cosmonaut Pilots Right Wing Squadron, BREAK FORMATION, MANEUVER TO ASTEROID BELT OF CONSTELLATION VEGA, AND STAND-BY FOR AMBUSH, WAIT FOR MY COMMAND OF FIRING" commanded Commander Kimmy to her Right Wing Galactic Cosmonaut Pilots Squadrons composed of Twelve Deep Space Attack Battle Craft.

"Aye Commander" replied all Cosmonaut Pilots on her Right Wing and immediately broke-loose from their Battle Formation and maneuvered their Deep Space Attack Battle Craft in the Asteroid Belt of Constellation Vega.

"Galactic Cosmonaut Pilots Left Wing Squadron, BREAK FORMATION AND FOLLOW ME, MANEUVER BATTLE ATTACK TACTIC BUT DO NOT PROVOKE THE DEEP SPACE SHUTTLE CRAFT, DO NOT ACTIVATE YOUR WEAPON SYSTEM, WAIT FOR MY COMMAND WHEN TO ACTIVATE AND FIRE LASER CANNONS IMMEDIATELY, MANEUVER YOUR BATTLE CRAFT, WE WILL STALK THE DEEP SPACE SHUTTLE CRAFT, FOLLOW AND PURSUE WITH ULTRA-MACH SPEED BUT KEEP DISTANCE OF ONE AERO-MILE, WE WILL SET AN AMBUSH, I THINK I KNOW WHERE IS THE DEEP

SPACE SHUTTLE CRAFT IS HEADING" thus commanded again by Commander Kimmy to her Left Wing Galactic Cosmonaut Pilots.

"Aye Commander Kimmy" we will follow you and stand-by on your command, replied the Left Wing Squadron Cosmonaut Pilots.

Unknown to Commander Kimmy, the Deep Space Shuttle Craft's ASDI (Automatic Self Defense Initiative) was also making its own battle evaluation and computation tracking all the Un-Identified Flying Targets in its Anti-Enemy Detection Radar Scanner.

In its navigation control and weaponry panel computer monitor screen flashes words after words of Automatic Self Defense Initiative Enemy Target Data Analyzation.

GROUP ONE, TWELVE TARGETS
ULTRA-MACH SPEED, LOST CONTACT IN THE AREA OF CONSTELLATION VEGA ASTEROID BELT, POSSIBLE THREAT

GROUP TWO, TWELVE TARGETS, ULTRA-MACH SPEED, DISTANCE ONE AERO-MILE REAR IN BATTLE ATTACK FORMATION.

DATA ANALYZATION RESULT... AMBUSH... ALERT, ALERT, ALERT... ENEMY AMBUSH IN PROGRESS

ACTIVATE ASDI ASAP...

And with-out delay the Deep Space Shuttle Craft re-armed itself and activated its ASDI, prepared for battle confrontation and continued making Data Analyzation of the targets in its computer weaponry program.

"ALERT, ALERT, ALERT...ENEMY CRAFT RE-ARMED, PREPARING FOR BATTLE CONFRONTATION" Commander Kimmy announced in her communication-radio as soon as she saw in her weaponry system computer monitor the warning alert and added at once in panic "ALL SQUADRON GALACTIC COSMONAUT PILOTS, ACTIVATE YOUR WEAPON SYSTEM NOW, PREPARE FOR BATTLE CONFRONTATION, ACTIVATE EVASIVE MANEUVER."

Commander Kimmy reckon that they are already entering the Constellation Vega vicinity, and that in her mind the Deep Space Shuttle Craft was maneuvering to escape, if she fails to stop the Deep Space Shuttle Craft from escaping and fails her Mission Order of Shoot to Kill, for sure her recommendation for Supreme Commander Promotion will not be approve, and worse, Supreme Commander Napoleonious will surely blame her for FAILURE OF HER MISSION and might even cause her a RANK DEMOTION, and worse of all, the loss of Squadron Commandant-ship.

"I MUST ACT AND DECIDE FAST. I MUST NOT FAIL, THIS IS MY VERY FIRST MISSION, I AM VERY SORRY MY GODDESS NAKKI, I HAVE MISSION ORDER TO FOLLOW, AND MY FUTURE CAREER IS AT STAKE" Commander Kimmy told herself, justifying her action.

"Left Wing Galactic Cosmonaut Squadron, STAND-BY FOR FIRING YOUR LASER CANNONS, on my count of ten" ordered Commander Kimmy to all the Left Wing Squadron Galactic Cosmonaut Pilots who were following her on Battle Attack Formation.

"TEN, NINE, EIGHT, SEVEN, SIX, FIVE" Commander Kimmy was counting in her communication-radio, but before even she finish her counting, the Deep Space Shuttle Craft deployed in its path "MINEFIELDS OF CLUSTER SPACE-BOMB."

"BREAK LOOSE, BREAK LOOSE, ACTIVATE EVADING MANEUVER, CLUSTER SPACE-BOMBS AHEAD" shouted Commander Kimmy in her communication-radio, but it was too late, the Deep Space Shuttle Craft had already deployed Minefields of thousands of Cluster Space-Bombs, like a SPIDER-WEB BOMB-TRAP.

Commander Kimmy push EVADING MANEUVER BRAKE BUTTON at once of her Deep Space Attack Battle Craft and maneuvered slowing down so that her Two Escort Back-up Deep Space Attack Battle Craft passed her ahead at Ultra-Mach Speed. It was a perfect trap Commander Kimmy didn't anticipated.

Commander Kimmy watch in horror as her Left Wing Squadron Galactic Cosmonauts Deep Space Attack Battle Craft exploded and obliterated one by one in the TRAP of MINEFIELDS OF CLUSTER SPACE-BOMB deployed by the Deep Space Shuttle Craft. They were blown to pieces like a COLORFUL FIREWORKS in the dark space of Galaxy.

Commander Kimmy had no idea that God Anuk had programmed the Deep Space Shuttle Craft with RULES OF ENGAGEMENT different from their Battle Tactic system. God Anuk sees to it that the Deep Space Shuttle Craft will defend itself at all cost, and with that God Anuk devised Artificial Intelligence (AI) Memory Chip embedded in the Deep Space Shuttle Craft main computer memory driving core to always analyze data well in advance, a ONE STEP AHEAD program so that if the detected enemy target activated, Lock and Load its weaponry and there is imminent threat and danger, the Deep Space Shuttle Craft will automatically deploy its weaponry system (ASDI), SHOOT AND KILL THE ENEMY FIRST, before the enemy could even fire its weapons.

Commander Kimmy was so shocked but remained calmed, "COURAGE UNDER PRESSURE" she keep murmuring to herself, then shouted on her communication radio "Left Wing Squadrons, Radio Check, answer me" and she paused for a while.

"Left Wing Squadrons, damn it, answer me" she repeated again her radio call, and waited for any answer from her Left Wing Squadron Deep Space Attack Battle Crafts, but the SOUND OF SILENCE answering her radio-call was so deafening in her ears, the stillness of deep space darkness and the silhouette of twinkling stars answered her Radio call, she had lost all her Left Wing Squadron Pilots to the CLUSTER SPACE-BOMB MINEFIELDS TRAP.

"Commander Kimmy, are you alright" suddenly she heard a voice calling on her communication radio, "Commander Kimmy, acknowledge my call"

She was delighted at first for she thought it was from one of her Left Wing Squadron Pilot, but when the voice called again, she recognized the voice and it's coming from her Right Wing Squadron Sub-Commander Jezel, by that time she had increased her Deep Space Attack Battle Craft speed to Ultra-Sonic speed upon seeing a loop-hole created by her Left Wing Squadrons Battle Craft explosions from the Cluster Space-Bombs Minefield Trap.

When she passed and escape the Cluster Space-Bombs Minefield Trap, she felt so relieved and elated, she survived and cheated DEATH but in her mind are her fallen comrades, the Left Wing Squadron Pilots who all died in that trap set by the Deep Space Shuttle Craft carrying Goddess Nakki, again she reasoned out justifying what had happened to them as WILL OF DESTINY, for if not for their life and their Deep Space-Attack Battle Craft exploding in the Cluster Space-Bombs Minefields causing a loop-hole and breaching its web-trap, she could have died as well.

“Farewell and Thank You Comrades, I will see you again in another time, in another dimension perhaps, your life will go not in-vain, I promise you all, I will personally avenge all your death, If Goddess Nakki piloting that Deep Space Shuttle Craft even don’t care about your life and didn’t show any mercy, then I too will give Goddess Nakki NO MERCY, She will suffer my revenge for all of you Comrades.” Thus Commander Kimmy promised herself for she thought Goddess Nakki was the one piloting the Deep Space Shuttle Craft, and chased the speeding and escaping Deep Space Shuttle Craft.

“Right Wing Squadron, Stand-by for ambush, Deep Space Shuttle Craft heading your way. Hide your Deep Space Attack Battle Craft in the shadows of the Asteroid Belts and wait for my command to fire your Laser Cannons, we will avenge the death of our Comrade Pilots of Left Wing Squadrons, stay with me, do not fret, I will set myself as a Target-Bait”

“Aye Commander Kimmy, Right Wing Squadrons Deep Space Attack Battle Craft on stand-by for AMBUSH, awaiting your ORDER for firing Laser-Cannons” replied Sub-Commander Jezel

Commander Kimmy set her Deep Space Battle Attack Craft speed to Full Maneuvering Galactic Speed and chased the Deep Space Shuttle Craft exposing herself as Target-Bait, in her mind She’s ready to die for her COMRADES in the Deep Space Galactic Battle. She had decided to sacrifice herself so that she will not lose her FIRST Galactic Mission Order; at least she will die a HERO, and would save her Family’s name and honor, not tarnishing it with FAILURE.

The Deep Space Shuttle Craft continued its Ultra-Mach Speed and readying itself for the Galactic Black Hole Passage that will bring its route into another Galaxy, THE GALAXY OF MILKY WAY WHERE BLUE PLANET EARTH IS.

In its computer panel monitor blinking the WARNING: INTRUDER IN PURSUIT, and tracking the target in its Automatic Galactic Radar Scanner, prepared its Automatic Self-Defense Initiative next weapon, The Electro-Magnetic Energy Blast that will fry all electronic equipments on-board an enemy craft, disabling all that is programmed electronically.

When the Deep Space Battle Craft was traversing the Asteroid Belts of Constellation Vega, it activated its weapon of Electro-Magnetic Energy Blast ahead of its path, for it calculated in its ASDI auto-program enemy detection radar that Enemy Battle Attack Craft were lost contact in the vicinity of Constellation Vega, assessing the situation, probably hiding in the vicinity, and pose as a THREAT.

Commander Kimmy was waiting for the Deep Space Shuttle Craft to maneuver and fight her in Galactic Deep Space Combat, but it seems in her mind as per her calculation and assessment that it has no intent of attacking her, but, if she is right the Deep Space Shuttle Craft is trying to escape into the next Black-Hole, where she knows well as she had learned from the Deep Space Galactic Aero-Force Academy that Black Holes are the wormholes and gateway of time, and that once an space-craft enter into its vortex hole and travel its passages of wormholes into another galaxy, every Galactic Deep Space Pilot must know and understand that there should be NO FIRING OF WEAPONS while inside wormholes or black-holes, otherwise it will explode and all that is within will be VANISHED and LOST in TIME.

Soon Commander Kimmy reckoned that she will lost her pursuit of the Deep Space Shuttle Craft and that her speed is no match, and panicked that she will fail her mission, and again made a hesitant decision ordering the Right Wing Squadrons to intercept the in-coming Deep Space Shuttle Craft carrying Goddess Nakki and Centurion Ezriel TO ATTACK AT ONCE and not let the Deep Space Shuttle Craft escape into the Black Hole.

It was a bold decision and yet a big mistake for Commander Kimmy, for as soon as the Right Wing Squadrons came out from their hiding in the shadows of the Asteroid Belt, immediately their electronic equipments cables and programs fried and all power was lost. It was another blow for Commander Kimmy as again she witnessed some of the Right Wing Squadron crashing and exploding into the asteroids for lack of navigational power and steering. It was a humiliating sight for Commander Kimmy.

"Commander, Commander Kimmy, Give Order Abort, Give Order Abort" shouted one of her surviving pilots who manage to stay behind an asteroid thus the Deep Space Shuttle Craft Electro-Magnetic Energy Blast didn't affected his Deep Space Battle Attack Craft Electronic, it was the voice of Sub-Commander Jezel.

Commander Kimmy tearful and shocked ordered in her trembling voice to ABORT the attack, yet she knows in her heart, she had lost yet some friends in that catastrophic debacle, and some of her Squadrons Best Deep Space Galactic Pilots.

"Surely the GOD OF UNIVERSE is protecting Goddess Nakki" Commander Kimmy murmured herself

"…but I must not give up, I don't want to go home a failure, even if I chased you oh Goddess Nakki at the End of Universe, I will and I will not give up, better to DIE TRYING KILLING YOU IN GALACTIC BATTLE THAN GOING HOME A FAILURE WITH HEAVY GUILT OF SHAME" thus Commander Kimmy promised to herself

"Don't let the Deep Space Battle Attack Craft escape into the Black Hole" ordered Commander Kimmy in her Radio-communication to her surviving Right Wing Squadrons, this time her voice is full of anger and vengeance, she wants to avenge her fallen Comrades.

"REGROUP, REGROUP, REGROUP" commanded again by Commander Kimmy

Meanwhile the Deep Space Shuttle Craft as per its Computerize Navigation Control was already preparing for its Black Hole passage of time in the Constellation of Vega. Data analysis on its ASDI Radar scanner monitor shows that 75% of the enemy were killed and obliterated, six were REGROUPING and chasing on its tail-path. Based on its evasive maneuver calculation, The Deep Space Shuttle Craft will reach the Black Hole in five minutes time, and that the enemies chasing could derail its escape if the enemy fired their weapons and hit the Black Hole thus affecting its Magnetic Gravity Field and could cause explosion that would close its GATE OF GALACTIC PASSAGE OF TIME.

The Deep Space Shuttle Craft analyzing the situation in its programmed navigational control interface with its Automatic-Self Defense Initiative, rationalized it could escape into the Black Hole, and DE-ACTIVATED its ASDI weaponry program.

"Commander Kimmy, the Deep Space Shuttle Craft is escaping now into the Black Hole, what is your order, we are on standby awaiting your order to fire our weapons" shouted by Sub-Commander Jezel to Commander Kimmy after the regrouping of the six remained Deep Space Battle Attack Craft being commanded by Commander Kimmy.

"ALL GALACTIC DEEP SPACE COSMONAUTS PILOTS, THIS IS YOUR COMMANDER KIMMY SPEAKING, ITS BEEN A WILD RIDE FOR ALL OF US EVERSINCE OUR SQUADRON WAS FORMED, AND TODAY ON OUR VERY FIRST MISSION, OUR COMBAT CAPABILITIES WAS BATTLE-TESTED, AND IT IS SAD TO NOTE THAT WE HAD LOST SOME OF OUR DEAR COMRADES AND FRIENDS. WE HAVEN'T LOSE THE BATTLE YET, OUR ENEMY IS ESCAPING INTO THE BLACK HOLE GATEWAY OF PASSAGE OF TIME, ITS DESTINATION I CAN NOT TELL, NOW HEAR ME WELL BECAUSE IT COULD BE OUR LAST TIME TOGETHER, THIS COULD BE MY LAST TIME GIVING THIS ORDER TO ALL OF YOU, OUR FALLEN COMRADES OF LEFT WING SQUADRONS, AND THE SIX MEMBERS OF RIGHT WING SQUADRON DEATH WILL NOT GO IN-VAIN, I WILL PERSONALLY AVENGE THEIR DEATH EVEN IF IT WILL CAUSE MY DEATH AS WELL, I WOULD RATHER DIE COMPLETING THIS MISSION ORDER WE WERE ORDERED TOO, THAN GOING HOME LOSING THE BATTLE. NOW, I AM COMMANDING YOU ALL TO BACK-OUT AND LET ME ALONE CHASE THE DEEP SPACE BATTLE CRAFT INTO THE WORMHOLES OF PASSAGE OF TIME, THE FUTURE CERTAINLY LOOKS UNCERTAIN BUT I WILL ASSURE YOU ALL, I WILL NOT LET GODDESS NAKKI ESCAPE INTO ANOTHER GALAXY, BUT DO NOT FIRE ANY WEAPONS, I REPEAT, DO NOT FIRE ANY WEAPONS BECAUSE IF WE HIT THE BLACK HOLE, IT WILL EXPLODE AND SUCK US ALL IN, BREAK LOOSE FROM THE BATTLE FORMATION AND GO BACK TO BASE, REPORT THE MISSION IS OVER TO THE UNIFIED HIGH COMMAND OF UNIVERSAL GALACTIC DEFENSE. THANK YOU TO ALL OF YOU, BREAK-LOOSE FROM CHASING, I

DON'T WANT YOU ALL DEAD, IT'S ENOUGH OF OUR COMRADES, JUST REMEMBER WHEN TIME COMES, REMEMBER THAT YOU HAD A COMMANDER NAMED COMMANDER KIMMY, AND WE HAD SHARED SO MUCH GOOD MEMORIES, GOODBYE" and with that last words of Commander Kimmy, she put her Deep Space Battle Attack Craft to Full Galactic Maneuvering Ultra-Mach Lightning Speed and chased the Deep Space Shuttle Craft into the Black Hole entrance vortex.

"Right Wing Squadron, this is Sub-Commander Jezel, you heard what our Commander commanded us, I am making my own decision, I WILL NOT GO BACK TO BASE, REPEAT, I WILL NOT GO BACK TO BASE, but I will follow Commander Kimmy, the future looks uncertain, it could be our end, OUR DEATH, but I will not go home a COWARD, I WILL COMPLETE THE MISSION EVEN IN DEATH WITH COMMANDER KIMMY, so if anyone of you decided like me, JUST FOLLOW AND PUT YOUR DEEP SPACE BATTLE ATTACK CRAFT SPEED TO ULTRA-MACH LIGTNING SPEED, NO QUESTION ASK, GOODBYE, ITS BEEN A PLEASURE WORKING WITH ALL OF YOU" and Sub-Commander Jezel blasted its engine following Commander Kimmy into the UNCERTAINTY OF BLACK HOLES WORMHOLES OF PASSAGE OF TIME.

"BEAUTIFUL END"
BY MONAC
(POETIC BREEZE, POETIC FROTH PART 1 – POEM NO. 214)

Now or never until end
Never slip away when
Breathe the everlasting path
Slit the silence there-in

Lay to sleep all yesterday
Yet never leave behind
Along the winding road
Unlimited end abounds

One chance comes around
Lit the path to end
Far ahead a beautiful when
Thing's shines after then

Eternal highway laid upon
Fly to edge way beyond
Everything matters on-hand
Expect the end to come

Journey brought to last
Colors explodes all over that past
Shattered breath fall asleep
A BEAUTIFUL END until then!

EPILOGUE

BOOK 2: "THE BLUE PLANET EARTH"

-THE DEEP SPACE SHUTTLE CRAFT CARRYING GODDESS NAKKI AND CENTURION EZRIEL, WHO BOTH WERE IN DEEP SLUMBER, NOT KNOWING OF THE DANGEROUS AND PERILOUS VOYAGE OF THEIR SPACE-CRAFT HAD ENCOUNTERED, ESCAPED INTO THE GATEWAY OF PASSAGE OF TIME, THE WORMHOLES PASSAGES OF BLACK HOLES INTO ANOTHER GALAXY.

-COMMANDER KIMMY MADE HER LAST BATTLE ORDER AND CHASED THE ESCAPING DEEP SPACE SHUTTLE CRAFT, ALONG WITH SUB-COMMANDER JEZEL AND THE SURVIVING RIGHT WING DEEP SPACE SQUADRON COSMONAUTS INTO THE UNCERTAINTY OF BLACK HOLES. COMMANDER KIMMY THINKING OF HER FUTURE AND VOWING TO AVENGE THE DEATH OF HER COMRADES AGAINST GODDESS NAKKI NEVER SUSPECT IN HER MIND THAT SHE WILL PLAY A VERY IMPORTANT ROLE IN THE 2ND GALACTIC WAR.

GOD ANUK WAS ARRESTED ALONG WITH OTHER SUPPORTERS AND ALLYS OF GODDESS NAKKI, AND WERE IMPRISONED IN THE DUNGEONS OF UNIFIED HIGH COMMAND OF UNIVERSAL GALACTIC DEFENSE INTER-GALAXY PRISONER GARRISON UNDER DIFFERENT COMMANDANT. SUPREME COMMANDER HITLEOROUS WAS PROMOTED TO SUPREME GENERAL BY LORD CAINOS.

SUPREME GENERAL JHESUSAN WAS FOUND WOUNDED IN THE ROYAL PALACE INTELLIGENCE COMMAND OFFICE, AND WAS

GIVEN MEDICAL ATTENTION BUT AFTER HIS RECUPERATION WAS ALSO ARRESTED AND IMPRISONED TO AN UNDISCLOSED GARRISON AWAY FROM HIS CHILDHOOD FRIEND GOD ANUK.

LORD CAINOS DESTABILIZE ALL ENEMY AGAINST HIS LEADERSHIP AND CONTINUED TO EN-ACT ALL THEIR PLANS FOR THEIR IN-COMING ATTACK ON BLUE PLANET EARTH, ORDERING MASS ABDUCTION OF HUMANOID CHILDRENS TO TRANSFORM INTO RUTHLESS ARMY OF DOOM, THE ROBONOIDS.

GODDESS NAKKI'S GREAT ESCAPE FROM PLANET NIBIRU AND ARRIVED AT BLUE PLANET EARTH, WARNED THE BLUE PLANET EARTH'S WORLD LEADERS OF HUMANOID OF IN-COMING GALACTIC WAR.

THE SPY LEGIONS AND THE DEEP-SPACE SPY CRAFT BLACK KNIGHT GATHERED MORE INFORMATIONS AND WERE ALERTED OF THE IN-COMING 2ND GALACTIC WAR, PREPARED AND READIED THEIR OFFENSE CAPABILITIES IN THEIR FORTRESS IN THE SOUTHERN HEMISPHERE OF BLUE PLANET EARTH'S MOON CALLED THE FORT MOON.

THE COMMANDER OF BLUE PLANET EARTH INTERNATIONAL SPACE STATION (ISS) ORBITING IN ITS TERRITORIAL GRAVITATIONAL SPACE WAS CAUGHT SURPRISE WHEN AN UNKNOWN UN-IDENTIFIED FLYING OBJECTS (UFO'S) SUDDENLY CAME OUT ON ONE OF THE BLACK HOLES THEY WERE STUDYING AND MONITORING, CHASING WHAT LOOKS LIKE A FIRE-CANNON BALL OF COMET DASHING FROM NOWHERE, GIVING THEM A SPECTACULAR SIGHT OF GALACTIC BATTLE CONFRONTATION FROM AN ADVANCE CIVILIZATION WAR TECHNOLOGY UNKNOWN TO THEM.

THE BLUE PLANET EARTH HAD BEEN WARNED OF IN-COMING DILLEMA AND CAUGHT UN-EXPECTEDLY. THE WORLD LEADERS OF BLUE PALNET EARTH CONVENE IN THEIR UNITED NATIONS WORLD HEADQUARTERS AND DRAFTED GALACTIC ARTICLES OF WAR IN-PREPARATION FOR THE 2ND GALACTIC WAR WHICH

GODDESS NAKKI DISCLOSED AND WARNED THEM. GODDESS NAKKI GIVE BIRTH TWINS, A SON AND A DAUGHTER.

***THE CHARACTERS AND PLOT BEHIND THE STORIES:

1. THE ELDERS
   = Genaros, Abrahamus, Cainos
2. THE GRAND SACRED GALACTIC WEDDING
   = Between God Anuk and Goddess Nakki
3. THE EARTHLINGS
   = Humanoid Species
4. THE COMMANDERS
   1. Commander Macheavelli = Commander of Spy-Legions
   2. Commander Marlonus = Commander of Spy Sattelite Black Knight
   3. Commander Josselitos = Commander of Galactic Elite Tactical Attack Legionnaires
   4. Commander Llevonne = Commander of Galactic Royal Palace Guard Escorts
5. THE SUPREME COMMANDERS
   1. Supreme Commander Alexandrous = Unified High Command Of Universal Galactic Defense Internal Intelligence
   2. Supreme Commander Ceazarous = Unified High Command Of Universal Galactic Defense Inter-Galaxy Intelligence
   3. Supreme Commander Hannibalkan = Unified High Command Of Universal Galactic Defense Royal Palace Security
   4. Supreme Commander Hitleorous = Unified High Command Of Universal Galactic Defense Inter-Galaxy Prisoner-Garrison
   5. Supreme Commander Napoleonious = Unified High Command Of Universal Galactic Defense Aero-Police and Space-Force
   6. Supreme Commander ShawnTroy = Unified High Command Of Universal Galactic Defense Deep Space Navigational Control
6. THE SUPREME GENERALS OF CENTRAL COMMAND
   1. Supreme General Jhesusan = Unified High Command Of Universal Galactic Defense Tactical Armada
   2. Supreme General Krishnan = Unified High Command Of Universal Galactic Defense Scientific Energy Supply
   3. Supreme General Ahllakdan = Unified High Command Of Universal Galactic Defense Energey Advance Weaponry
   4. Supreme General Bhudasian = Unified High Command Of

Universal Galactic Defense Advance Scientific Research
5. Supreme General Sun Rah = Unified High Command Of Universal Galactic Defense Planet Nibiru Royal Palace Security

7. CODENAME:ENGLUEBOLDERGY2015
= Energy, Gold, Blue, 2015
8. SECRET MESSAGE
=DemiGods Existence on Blue Planet Earth, They are the Rulers and Keepers behind the curtain manipulator of every Nations on Earth, their puppet Leaders are the Presidents of different Earth Nation, forming an alliance of League of Earth Nation's New World Order to fight in-coming Galactic Threat.
9. SPECIAL ORDER
= Invasion of Earth at the right calculated time by Planet Nibiru
10. SECRETS IN BOOK OF TIME?
= Human origin, scientific DNA mixing/experimentation of Nibirus first colonizer to Earth eon of years before to its Living creatures,
= 1st galactic war between the demigods helping humans against the Supreme Gods
= function of pyramids around the world, a powerful weapon of laser beam aimed deep into outer space to fight in-coming Galactic threat, also to serve as Earth's Electro-Magnetic Shield
= one portion of Planet Nibiru fell into earth because of the Pyramids laser beam and became a falling star of fire or meteorite that obliterate life on Earth, but before it touch-down to Blue Planet Earth, the demigods escape into the depth of the oceans and there build their cities, they also help escape some humans into mountain caves
11. COORDINATES DESTINATION
=Blue Planet Earth, Philippines
12. ENEMIES WITHIN?
= The Elders, Secret Society, Demi-Gods
13. THE REAL ENEMY AND ITS LEADER
= The Elders who wants revenge to the Demi-Gods on Earth and the Humanoids for rebelling against their ancestors that sent Planet Nibiru wandering away into Abyss of Universe.
14. ENEMIES AGENDA AND PLAN?

= Masquerading on peace-accord, but will hunt down the DemiGods living on Earth to kill them all, then the annihilations of all human race for the control of Earths minerals for their needs (Gold, Silver, Mercury, Hydrogen/Deuterium, etc)

14. PEACE ACCORD COMPROMISE?
= Earth's league of nation, (UN/NWO), demigods ruling earth, homecoming of Nibiru, fear, joy, excitement of seeing ancestors but fear of revenge
15. GODDESS NAKKI UNIVERSAL PLANS?
= Universal Galactic Peace and Inter-Planetary Co-Existence
16. GALACTIC WAR?
= 1st war - galactic war on Earth, in-coming 2nd war, war of Blue Planet Earth and Planet Nibiru
17. TAKE-OVER, COUP D'ETAT?
= During wedding after Goddess Nakki announcement of universal plan, the enemy, ELDERS and some LEGIONS reveal their true identity and monstrous appearance and plans of revenge, annihilation and destruction of Earth
18. CHILDREN OF GOD?
= Goddess Nakki's twin daughter and son who were born and raise on Blue Planet Earth, Philippine island of Leyte, (arrival of deep space shuttle come in SUPER TYPHOON)
19. PLANET EARTH AGENDA?
= Annihilate, revenge of the elders to the humans and demigods, and total control of blue planet
20. LIFE IN BLUE PLANET?
=experimented by the Planet Nibiru's 1st colonizer of Blue Planet Earth to make slaves for the purpose of mining Blue Planet Earth minerals, some of the results of the experimentation are Centaurs, Cyclops, Nephilims, Sphinx, Mermaids, Big Foot, then perfected the Humanoids by copulation with the APES
21. THE DEMI-GODS?
=Supreme Commander Lucifer, Commander Draculatis, Commnader Temptress, Commander Ezriel
22. THE SUPER HUMANS?
= Titans, Medusa, Hercules, Achilles, Apollo, Zeus, Poseidon,
23. THE HIGH-BREED HUMANS

= Superman, Batman, X-Men, Ironman, Thor, Greenman, Spiderman, Hulkman, Wonderwoman

24. THE FIRST GALACTIC WAR?
    = War between the cast-away and humans against the Nibirus who first came to Earth eon of years ago recorded in the Book of Time
25. FIRST CONTACT
    = Nibirunians came to Blue Planet Earth Eon of Years ago and experimented life until they perfected the Species called Humanoids
26. MYSTERIES OF PYRAMIDS –
    = Energy, Gold, Mercury, Hydrogen, Laser beams
    = Earth's Electro-Magnetic Defense Shield if activated together around the world, and could be a laser-cannons that was fired against the Supreme Gods Planet Deep-Space Craft Nibiru.
    = Developed by Supreme Commander Lucifer and other DemiGods with the help of the Humanoids they teached, used during 1st Galactic War against the Nibirunians, then during 2nd Galactic War, will be activated again with the suggestions of the DemiGods to the Humans to defeat again the Nibirunians, against The Elders who wants revenge and avenge their Forefathers lost during 1st Galactic War
27. THE REBEL DEMIGODS/CAST-AWAYS –
    = Supreme Commander Lucifer and his Loyal Legionnaires who came to Earth with a mission, but later on rebelled against Planet Nibiru's Supreme God
    = They teached Humans of great knowledge to help them build the Pyramids all over the world for the purpose of making it into a weapon and defeat the Supreme Gods Legionnaires and it's advance and powerful civilization during 1st Galactic War that sent the Nibirunians vanished into Universal Galaxy
28. THE 1ST ATTACK AT 2ND GALACTIC WAR?
    = After the Coup D' Etat of The Elders and the rogue Legionnaires of Planet Nibiru during God Anuk and Goddess Nakki's wedding ceremony, they proceeded at full speed to Blue Planet Earth, ordering the Spy-Legions

and the Spy –Craft Black Knight to begin attacking BluE Planet Earth which ignited the 2nd Galactic War, the Earth Nations joined forces under the command of USA Forces but were no match to the war technology of the Nibirunians at first, then came Goddess Nakki and her children and help the Earth Nations. The DemiGods resurfaced disguising their good intent of helping the Blue Planet Earth to defeat the Nibirunians because the Elders wants total revenge and annihilation of all Humanoids.

29. CHILDREN OF GOD DEFENDING EARTH SIDE BY SIDE WITH EARTHLINGS
= The children of God Anuk and Goddess Nakki, Ariannea and Sheenyea who were born and raise on Blue Planet Earth after Goddess Nakki escape from Planet Nibiru as planned by God Anuk. They have special Powers and together along with the humans and their mother Goddess Nakki, fight the Evil intent of the Nibirunians under the Elders Command. Sheenyea joines NASA Joint World Space-Force Command, and Ariannea joined the United Nations World Defense Army Joint Command.
30. THE DEMI-GODS COME TO RESCUE AND HELP HUMANOIDS?
= Supreme Commander Lucifer along with his Legions of Demi-Gods resurfaced and came out from their dwellings deep in the oceans, lakes, mountain caves and even from volcanic deeps to help the Humanoids along with Goddess Nakki and her children, Ariannea and Sheenyea fight the Nibirunians during 2nd Galactic War, for Supreme Commander Lucifer sees again an opportunity to complete his dream of becoming God of Gods. Supreme Commander Lucifer conceal his agenda on pretext on helping the Humanoids, but in his mind dances the thoughts of finishing what He didn't finished during the 1st Galactic War, the complete defeat and humiliation of Planet Nibiru ruling Gods. In the final battle, Supreme Commander Lucifer and God Anuk fight each other for final battle of Good and Evil Supremacy..
31. PLANET NIBIRU

= is not actually a Planet but an asteroid of enormous size bigger than Blue Planet Earth, which was transformed by the pioneers of Nibirunian Civilization into an advance colonies of different species from different Galaxies. They developed an advance technology deep-space propulsion system fueled by Deuterium, a Hydrogen Energy, that can travel into Galactic Universe with Ultra-Sonic Light-Year Speed. It traverse a deep-space navigational route that passes distant Planets of different Galaxies, firstly by attacking then colonizing the unsuspecting Planet, then mining and taking the colonized Planet's Natural Resources of energies and minerals for Planet Nibirus civilizations survival. They also absorb brilliant and outstanding civilization of different Galaxies and intermingle with their existing society to create hybred living forms adapting to their civilizations perfection of Nanotechnology and Singularity, to create that PERFECT LIVING ORGANISM CALLED NIBIRUNIANS.

32. UNIGALITIZINES
    = UNIVERSAL GALACTIC CITIZINE, THE CITIZINES OF PLANET NIBIRU

HEROES, HEROINES AND CHARACTERS IN THIS FICTION STORY...

SERPENTUM, NIBIRU PLANET THRONE SOVEREIGN CROWN

God Anuk, Son of the Star Sirius, Blood of the Constellation Orion

Goddess Nakki, Daughter of Universe, Blood of Milky Way

PLANET NIBIRU'S THRONE SCEPTER

PLANET NIBIRU'S GALACTIC DEEP SPACE ATTACK BATTLE-CRAFT

PLANET NIBIRU ROYAL ESCORT LEGIONNAIRE'S ARMOUR CROSS-SHIELD

PLANET NIBIRU ARMY LEGIONNAIRE'S ARMOUR CROSS-SHIELD

PLANET NIBIRU ARMY LEGIONNAIRE'S LASER BOW

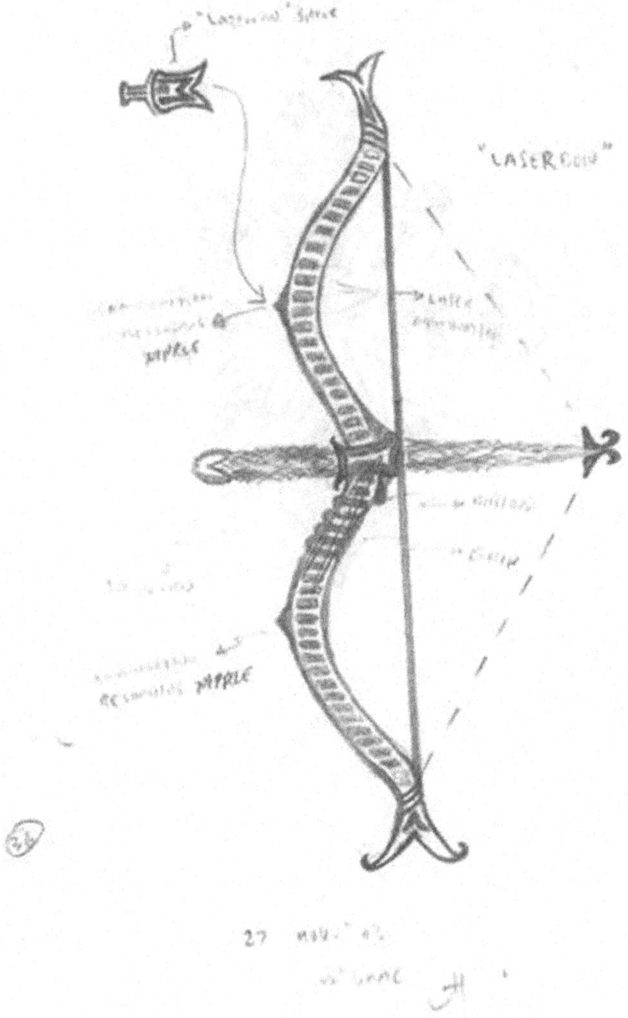

PLANET NIBIRU SUPREME GENERAL JHESUSAN

PLANET NIBIRU'S SUPREME COMMANDER LUCIFER

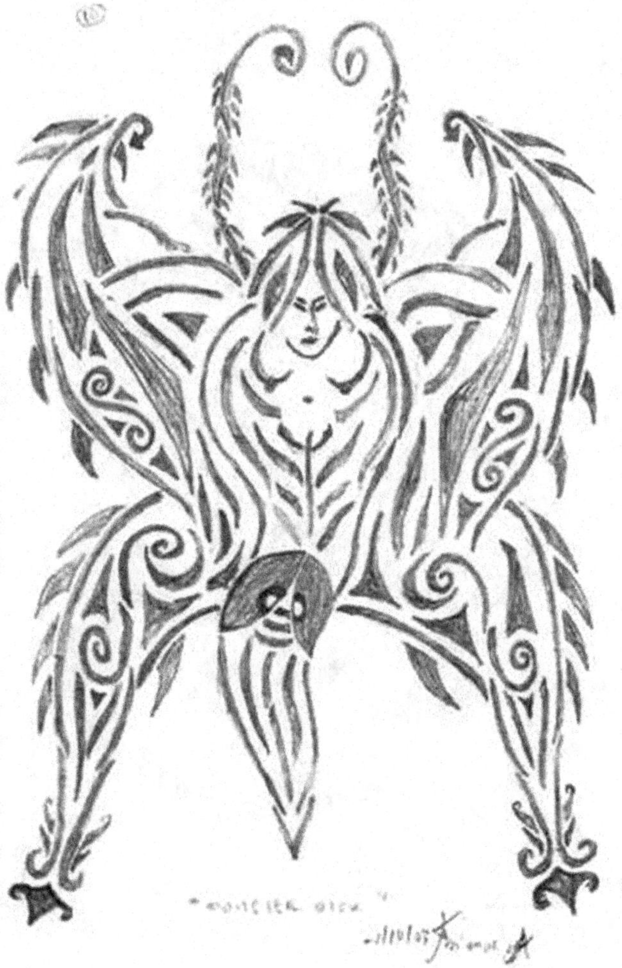

PLANET NIBIRU' COMMANDER DRACULATIS

(32)

PLANET NIBIRU ROYAL GALACTIC DEEP SPACE CRAFT VIMANA

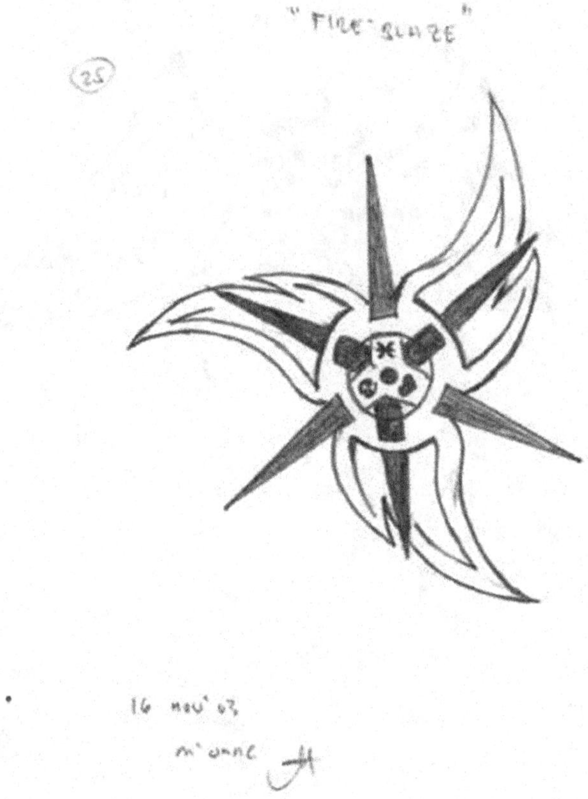

PLANET NIBIRU GALACTIC ARMY SPACE-FORCE BATTLE ATTACK SPACE-CRAFT

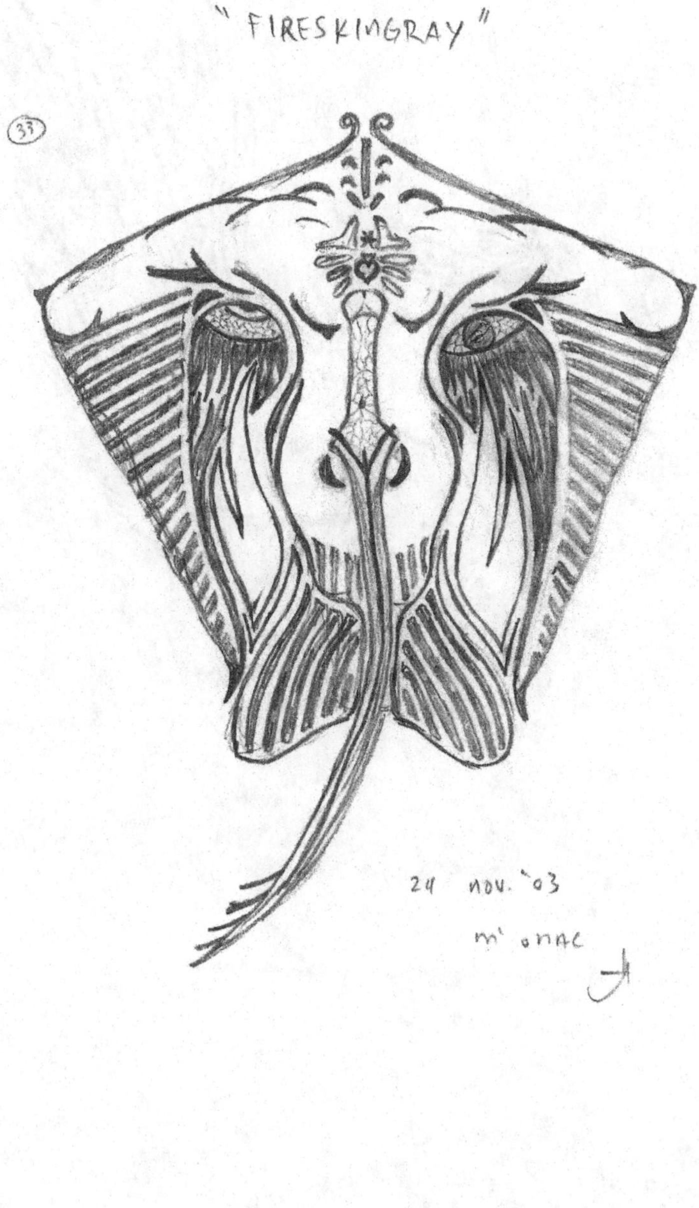

PLANET NIBIRU'S DREATHGON

PLANET NIBIRU'S EGGVOLUTION

PLANET NIBIRU'S EGGVOLUTION

PLANET NIBIRU ADULT FEMALE NIBIRUNIAN

PLANET NIBIRU'S ARMY LEGIONNAIRE'S WEAPON-1 SLITTER

PLANET NIBIRU'S ARMY LEGIONNAIRE'S WEAPON-2 SKINNER

PLANET NIBIRU'S ARMY LEGIONNAIRE'S ARMOUR MAGNETIC SHIELD

PLANET NIBIRU'S QUEEN EVANUS, WIFE OF LORD GOD ADANIS

PLANET NIBIRU ROYAL PALACE ESCORT LEGIONNAIRE'S LOGO

PLANET NIBIRU GODDESS NAKKI'S ESCAPE DEEP SPACE SHUTTLE CRAFT

PLANET NIBIRU ARMY LEGIONNAIRE'S WEAPON LASER-CANNON

BLUE PLANET EARTH'S HUMANOIDS NAMED "MAGANDALENA"

PLANET NIBIRU ARMY LEGIONNAIRE'S WEAPON-3 FIREBLADE

PLANET NIBIRU ARMY LEGIONNAIRE'S WEAPON-4 FIRECROSS

PLANET NIBIRU'S DEEP-SPACE COSMONAUT COMMANDER KIMMY

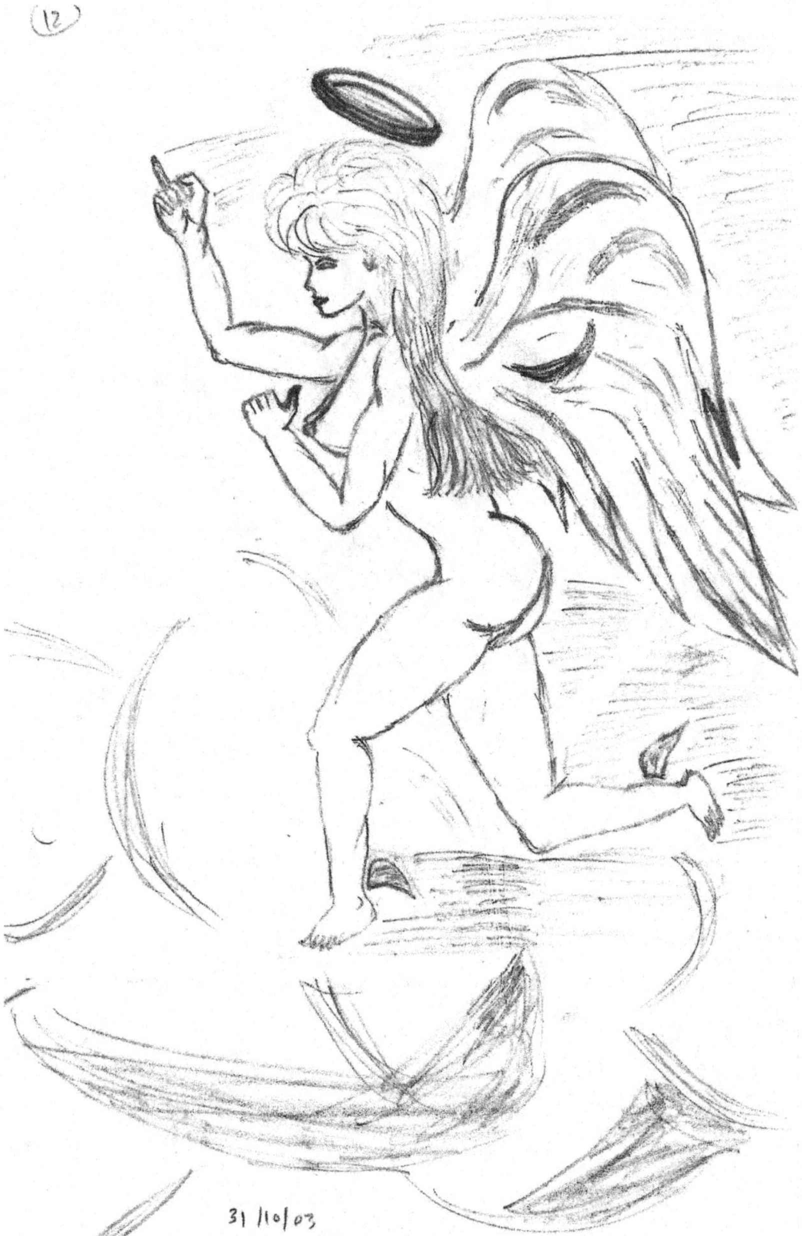

PLANET NIBIRU'S ELDERS LORD CAINOS

"DEMI-GOD, COMMANDER TEMPTRESS"

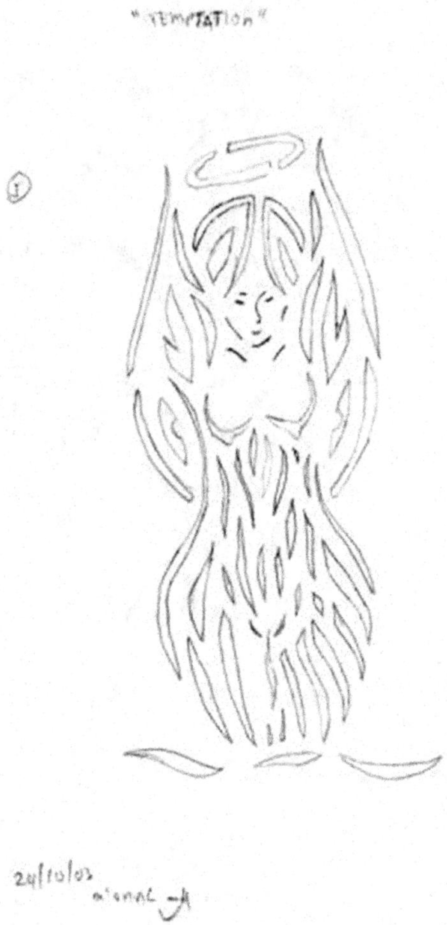

"DEMI-GOD, COMMANDER OCTOPUSSY"

GODDESS NAKKI'S BLUE PLANET EARTH FIGURE

THE TWINS, ARIANNEA AND SHEENYEA

THE TWIN SISTER, ARIANNEA'S EARTH FIGURE, DAUGHTER OF GOD ANUK AND GODDESS NAKKI

THE TWIN BROTHER, SHEENYEA'S EARTH FIGURE, SON OF GOD ANUK AND GODDESS NAKKI

THE FUTURE LOOKS UNCERTAIN, UNTAMED.
EARTHLINGS, BE WARNED.

CAPTAIN MARLON G. CANO
MOBILE, ALABAMA, USA / 04 SEPT. 2014